This is a work of fiction. Names, characters, places, and incidents either are the product of the author's imagination or are used fictitiously. Any resemblance to actual persons, living or dead, events, or locales is entirely coincidental.

Copyright © 2023 by Ayala Emmett

All rights reserved. No part of this book may be reproduced or used in any manner without written permission of the copyright owner except for the use of quotations in a book review.

First paperback edition July 2023

Book design by **Orli Langerman**
Photo by Karen Walker

ISBN 979-8-218-23259-7

https://www.facebook.com/thejewishpluralist/?fref=ts

AFTER the DISAPPEARANCE

AYALA EMMETT

CHAPTER ONE

The letter arrived the day before her daughter's birthday. It was a hot day and Rena had turned on the sprinklers in her garden. Several hours later she looked out and saw roses bent down by water and large puddles everywhere. She ran out, turned off the sprinklers, and noticed the envelopes jutting out of the mailbox.

When Rena pulled out the mail, she saw an envelope with the parliamentary emblem. It said KNESSET in bold letters. Her name and address were typed. The letter did not seem alarming and suggested no urgency. Her mind was on her sewing. She wanted to finish Zohara's birthday dress before her daughter came back from school. She thought the mail could wait.

Ordinarily, Rena was not casual about letters or careless about watering her garden. She looked apologetically at her beloved fruit trees, her plum, guava, loquat, and pomegranate. To her flowers she said, "Sorry. I forgot about you." On the northern side of the yard, Rena grew roses, dahlias, zinnias, calla lilies, and honeysuckle and jasmine for fragrance.

Shortly after Rena and Benny bought the house in Shomriya, Malka, her mother-in-law, had offered to plant a vegetable garden for her. Rena wanted flowers.

She had flowers in every room of their small house. In the bedroom she often had roses, which Benny liked. She brought flowers to her friends in Tel Aviv.

Rena could still recall vividly and painfully how, when Benny had first invited her to meet his parents, she had brought roses. White and yellow and red, wrapped in wet towels to sustain them on the hour-long bus ride. Malka had thanked her but had to look long and hard for a container. She finally found a large pickle jar. It still held the smell of dill and garlic and the spices, siding with Malka, refused to yield to the fragrance of the roses. Rena knew how wrong her gift had been.

She fell in love with flowers when she learned how to garden in kibbutz Oz. She came to Palestine in 1936 with Iris, who was her closest friend. They had grown up in a small town near Krakow and were seventeen years old when they came over. Rena and Iris lied to their parents. They told them that they were going to Palestine just for the summer. Once there, they went to kibbutz Oz. They never returned to Poland.

Going back to her house and holding the unopened mail Rena thought, as she often did, of the frantic letters her family had written at the time, imploring her to come back from the wilderness. Zion was not a place to live in, it was a yearning, a place in the heart: "Come back home," they wrote.

On thin crinkled paper, her parents pleaded their case in Yiddish. "*Tayere kind*, dear child," her father wrote, "your mother cries every night." Her mother wrote, "*Tayere kind*, your father misses you every day."

Rena had kept all their letters. Smudged and stained, her parents' tears and her own now indistinguishable. Letters in neat piles marked by dates, bundled and tied, like her daughter's hair, with colorful ribbons.

Her parents' last letters were about the uncertainties for Jews in Poland. "*Tayere kind*, your father says that God wanted you to go to Palestine. Now we will all follow you." Rena sent the necessary documents. It was too late. In 1941, silence replaced anxious correspondence. No more letters from Poland. Then the news. Her parents and two sisters murdered. Rena's sorrow was now firmly moored in what she had come to see as her failed duty. She no longer re-read the letters.

Yet in her Hebrew calendar she still penciled in significant milestones. On the birthdays of her parents and her sisters she took out the bundled letters and touched them to her lips, kissing them lightly in the way her mother had taught her to kiss the prayer book. She could still take a deep breath and fill it with the scent of her mother's prayer book, a fusion of musty old pages, cinnamon, and black pepper. Her mother had started each morning and ended each evening at the kitchen table, reciting the appropriate prayers with her daughters.

Rena had abandoned the prayer book on her first day in kibbutz Oz. Back then, she thought of herself as liberated. At the time, she could not tell the difference between defiance and freedom.

No one called her *tayere kind* anymore. No one in Shomriya who grew up on Yiddish wanted to hear it again. Hebrew was a language they had all feverishly embraced. After the war, when refugees from the Holocaust and immigrants from Arab countries arrived, they were greeted by signs reading, "Hebrew people – Speak Hebrew."

The pioneers were like the prophet Jonah. The one who ran away from God the way they had run away from the diaspora. They wanted a state without the musty ghetto. Yet while Rena spoke of her parents in Hebrew, she still loved them in Yiddish. She mourned them in Yiddish.

With the mail in her hand Rena stepped into the sunny porch and thought of the ring her mother had given her to keep her safe on the journey to Palestine. She would give the ring to her daughter tomorrow. She had been saving the ring for Zohara's graduation to a new school. But Zohara was going through a hard time now, and Rena hoped that her mother's ring that had reassured her would now do the same for her daughter.

When Rena saw her mother-in-law walk toward the house, she put the mail on the shelf where she kept her art supplies. On days she did not go to her studio in Tel Aviv, the spacious enclosed front porch was her favorite spot to work. Surrounded by large windows on three sides, the porch was full of light and changing hues as the sun made its way from east to west.

Placing the unopened letters with her paints and brushes was just a convenience. It was certainly not meant to hide the mail.

Malka knocked on the screen door and entered without waiting. "Rena, I don't want to disturb you. I know that you want to finish Zohara's dress. I need to talk to you."

Rena was irritated, but she could tell that her mother-in-law was upset. "Hi, Malka. Come in. Do you want a cup of coffee?

Malka shook her head. She did not sit down, but stood leaning against the wall. Rena looked at her mother-in-law in her faded khaki outfit. She was still considered an attractive woman by the local gossips, who were not always kind.

Rena had seen photographs of the striking twenty-year-old Malka, a girl from Odessa who had come to Palestine in 1915, five feet nine, slim with long limbs, a long neck, thick brown hair. She had strong, prominent cheekbones, beautiful large, light brown eyes, and skin that tanned easily. Now, at sixty, she still had the posture of a dancer. And the lines in her tanned face gave her what people in town called personality.

"Is it about over-watering my garden?"

"I wouldn't interrupt you to talk about gardening skills," Malka said.

"Well, what is it about?"

Malka took out a crumpled handkerchief and wiped her sweaty face.

"Would you like some water?"

"No, no. Thanks. I just came to tell you that I'm worried about the article Benny is writing on the rights of Arab workers." She raised her right hand to stop Rena's response. "I'm sure that he avoids telling me because he knows that I don't approve."

Rena went over to Malka. She stretched out her hand as though to touch her, but stopped short of doing so.

"I'm worried," Malka repeated. "The two of you keep insisting on more rights for Arab workers. Benny should not publish this article."

Rena raised her voice.

"When is it the right time to talk about justice for Arab workers? Isn't our party the workers party? Benny is still working on the article." Rena could not stop. "Benny is a good journalist, and the newspaper has a very competent editor. If it's too inflammatory, Mike won't publish it."

"Mike?" Malka moved and leaned against the door. "I wouldn't count on him. This will come down to Benny's decision. You and Benny are thinking about Arab rights. But are you two thinking about Zohara?"

"I don't understand…"

"What it will do to her, when her parents are threatened?"

Rena looked directly at Malka. In Poland, Rena's eyes used to turn, depending on the color of her clothes, from blue to green. But in Palestine her eyes had taken on a cobalt blue as a permanent color. She felt emboldened by the change. When confronted, it gave her courage to look directly rather than avert her eyes as she had been brought up to do.

"Benny is writing an article and suddenly we are careless parents?"

Malka was not averse to use her height to intimidate even her daughter-in-law. Or at least it felt intimidating to Rena, because unlike Malka she was not tall, nor did she look tough. When she had first come to Palestine many people had told her that her "type," as they referred to fair-skinned people, could not withstand the merciless sun.

Her eyes had not seen snow for years and her skin had forgotten about it. Her arms and legs had toughened and adapted to the year-round sun.

Rena took a deep breath. "People know Benny's views. Who has ever threatened him?"

Malka was suddenly not her usual tall self. She seemed to shrink, the same way she had when she heard that her husband Yair had been killed, as though her spine was collapsing.

"Yes, they claim they love Benny. He is a war hero. And the son of a war hero." Malka adjusted her sun hat. "So far nothing has happened. But he hasn't published the article. The threats will come."

Rena, who might have felt compassion for Malka's diminished stature, was angry. Anger kept her counting the differences between them, beyond their political disagreements. They did not have the same views on homes or gardens. Malka's house was functional and frugally furnished. Rena's house was full of things that had no practical purpose. They were meant to please the eye. Her art, her friends' art, and things she picked up at the flea market; an old sewing machine and an old gramophone turned into stands for statues and plants.

Suddenly it was not just a matter of differences between them, but about Malka's shortcomings. Rena knew that she was not being fair, but all she could do at that moment was to hold their differences against her mother-in-law.

Hot spots appeared on Rena's face. They intensified and spread to her throat and ears. "I hope that you're wrong, Malka. But if there are threats, Benny and I will deal with that."

Malka made a knot in the crumpled handkerchief and looked as though she might cry. Instead, she left, letting the screen door slam behind her.

Rena went into the kitchen and drank some lemonade. When her hands felt steady, she finished her daughter's dress. She forgot about her mail.

CHAPTER TWO

On the morning of her birthday Zohara woke up feeling that her life was suddenly hanging, like a loose tooth, between childhood and adolescence. No longer looking forward to her father bringing her favorite candy when he came home from work. Not nearly ready, as her friend Shoshi was, to wear a bra. Not even close. And that other thing had not happened yet. It had happened to Shoshi and to all her close friends. And here she was on her thirteenth birthday and her body, a painful disappointment.

On all her previous birthdays, Zohara had looked forward to the day. This year was different, though her parents did what they had always done. On the ceiling, between door and sink, her mother had hung, as usual, a bright Happy

Birthday banner. Her father had made her favorite breakfast, an omelet, surrounded by large fresh strawberries and steamy sweet milk with a touch of coffee in a large mug. On special occasions her parents let her have coffee and she really liked the taste.

On the morning of her thirteenth birthday, she drank her coffee with a silent but powerful prayer. "Please, God, make me grow up quickly. It's really important to me. This is not just about drinking coffee. I know that I don't have to spell out my reasons to you." She did not consider it extravagant to ask God to make her feel part of a grown-up world that seemed far more secure than her own.

Zohara loved the small kitchen, the table that her father had made and her mother had painted. She hoped that the kitchen, like God, would be helpful. For as long as she could remember, the kitchen had been a reliable place with a familiar rhythm. Everybody in her family had a special relationship with the kitchen at different times of the day. In late afternoons, the kitchen belonged to her. The chair by the window was one of her favorite reading places. When she came home from school, she covered the table with her homework and her books. Often Shoshi or one of her other friends would come over and they would do their homework right there at the kitchen table.

Zohara would take out tall glasses for lemonade. From the shelf over the sink she would take down a square tin box. She would open the lid and the smell of cookies, trapped inside all day long, would come out in a happy powdery hum, "thank you, thank you," free at last. Zohara and her friends would inhale with gusto. Tiny crumbs would settle quietly in their notebooks and would remind them the next day that there was life outside of school. Zohara used to feel part of things even on days when she came home by herself. Her grandmother would come over from across the street to ask her to help on the farm. In a few months this part of her life would be over.

Zohara looked forward to the early evening when her mother would return from her studio and fill the kitchen with her voice, the radio, and the spicy smells of her cooking. Whether she helped her mother prepare dinner, or just sat there watching her mother's hands chopping and cutting, Zohara would talk about her day. Lately, in the kitchen, Zohara had confided in her mother that her body had somehow forgotten that she was going to be thirteen. Didn't her body know how to count? She was not reassured by her mother's promise that her body had not forgotten. It was just taking its biological time.

Early mornings the kitchen belonged to her father. He was usually the first to get up. He liked to whistle when he was by himself. His whistling, like his taste in music, was eclectic and like his singing was terribly off tune. He didn't seem to care. The smell of Turkish coffee and omelets would wander slowly from the kitchen to her room. Zohara knew it was morning before she opened her eyes.

When she finished her coffee, her father said, "Your thirteenth birthday is special. It is your last one in elementary school. Next year you'll be in the best school in the country. And we can take the same bus in the morning." He looked at her. "...Of course, you'll want to go with your friends."

Not feeling thirteen, Zohara said, "I won't know most of the kids in this new school. They will all be rich spoiled city kids." What she really wanted to say was that she would still look way too young.

A light morning breeze came through the open windows and gently passed through the Happy Birthday banner. It brought in the sweet fragrances of the flower garden, which seemed careful not to overpower the smell of her father's coffee. Her parents hugged and kissed her. She wanted to cry.

Her mother brought out the dress she had made for Zohara from a fancy evening gown that had arrived in a package from her brother's American family. The relatives meant well. After Israel's War of Independence, the American relatives had begun sending clothes, shoes, hats, gloves, and handbags. Almost everything was color-coordinated. When Zohara and her mother opened the parcels, they would laugh. "What beautiful things, but who would wear them here?"

Zohara, like all the kids, knew that the country's first prime minister, even at formal state events, wore khaki pants and a shirt open at the collar. No tie. For people in Shomriya this small man with a crown of white hair set the fashion, not Paris or Milan. For Zohara, whose main ideas of the United States came from the Hebrew editions of *Huckleberry Finn* and *Uncle Tom's Cabin*, the expensive urban clothes were a puzzle.

"Do they really have to match everything in America, or is it just your brother's family?"

Her mother, who did not say much about her brother Joe, told Zohara, "I think that they follow the style. When you go to America you'll also dress differently."

"Why would I want to go to America?"

Zohara, who loved to read about other people's adventures, was frightened by the idea of going away. "Uncle Joe and Aunt Susan look like movie stars."

"Well, they live in Chicago, which is a large city, bigger than Tel Aviv. They just don't know how life is here. They want to send us the best, share with us."

Zohara wanted her mother to talk about her brother Joe. She missed not having any aunts or uncles around. There was only Iris, who was like an aunt, but not a blood relative. "Did you like your brother when you were growing up?"

"He was my older brother and I looked up to him."

No matter how many questions Zohara asked, it was clear that her mother did not want to say much about her brother Joe, alive in America. Zohara knew that her mother had also had parents and two sisters, but she rarely spoke about them, either. It was not just her mother. In Shomriya, including at her school, there was silence around everything that had to do with the Holocaust. The only exception was the special day every year when the whole country commemorated the death of six million Jews.

A week before Zohara's birthday, her mother had had a show in a gallery in Tel Aviv. Zohara went with her father to the opening of the exhibit, which her mother had titled *Gifts from America*.

Art, like books, was something to listen to. Zohara waited for the paintings to sing. Her father understood. She liked that her father understood things other people didn't. The two of them stood silently in front of the seven paintings. The collage pieces sat on a very large structure on which her mother had drawn a map of the United States. On six of the frames her mother had arranged her photographs of Shomriya, the small modest houses surrounded by orange groves and strawberry fields. Between and around the photographs, she had glued handbags folded like envelopes. She had painted American stamps on the handbags. The seventh collage consisted of a huge question mark made of American coins, pennies, and dimes, discovered in the pockets of coats.

At the opening, people told Zohara, "Your mother is a great artist," and talked to her like a grown-up. Her grandmother came over and said, "This is genuine Israeli art."

After the opening of her mother's show, Zohara read the reviews. An art critic wrote in *Haaretz*, "Rena Sasson's art is daring, bold, and political. She questions the wisdom of our economic dependency on the Americans."

A rival critic claimed, "At a time when the public needs solidarity, Sasson's art places her outside the national consensus, one of a small group of leftists who undermine our country's unity."

As Zohara read aloud the second review, her voice raced with anger. She had heard the word "leftists" about her parents before. It was not stated as a political opinion, but as though her parents were in the wrong. But she did not mention this to her parents. Her mother put an arm around her and kissed the top of her head. "Whether they praise it or denounce it makes no difference. Art matters, not the critics." In her heart Zohara gave the critic an F.

Now her mother was holding up the dress with a big smile that went from her lips to her eyes. She had turned a white evening gown from Chicago into a beautiful girl's dress with pleats, a round collar, and short puffy sleeves. On the collar her mother had stitched a delicate red and pink design copied from a Yemenite dress.

This was a dress that her friend Shoshi would call 'stunning.' Yet even this new Israeli version of east and west seemed too elegant to Zohara. She hugged her mother with the dress almost crushed between them. Her mother knew how unsure she had felt lately and had wanted to make her a dress in which everything was round and full.

When Zohara was dressed for the party, her mother hugged her and said, "You look beautiful." Her father added, "And so grown-up." She saw herself in the mirror and felt much better. She did look more grown-up. Maybe God was going to grant her wish. Perhaps this would be the year her body would realize what it was supposed to do.

Zohara had her birthday party in the late afternoon in their flower garden. Her friend Shoshi had come home from school with her for the party. On a large wooden table, her parents had placed food, juices, and a birthday cake. It was a warm spring day and a slight breeze made the white tablecloth flap and spread the sweet scent of honeysuckle and roses. Zohara took a deep breath.

Her mother handed her a small box. "When I left home, my mother gave me her ring. I want you to have it, Zohara." Zohara hugged her tearful mother. There was so much she wanted to know. Why had her mother come to Palestine, and why had the others stayed behind? She opened the box. "Thank you, Mom. This is so much more than beautiful." A tangible link to her grandmother. She put the ring on her left hand and when she touched it the red stone felt alive and hot.

From her father she got the Hebrew edition of *Gulliver's Travels*. On the cover, a giant man was stretched out on the ground, immobile, hands and legs and hair being tied down by hundreds of six-inch humans. While Zohara laughed and hugged her father in delight, her grandmother pursed her lips. "Jonathan Swift, an Irish writer. What next?"

She looked at her father and saw him smiling warmly at his mother. "This is a book for all ages, for young and old." He put an arm around his mother and said to Zohara, "This will probably be the last book you let me read to you." Zohara looked at her grandmother and saw fear in her eyes. Yet in a flash it was gone. Her grandmother looked back at her with her usual firmness. Zohara wondered if being thirteen meant feeling constantly confused.

Iris, her mother's closest friend, gave her an antique gold bracelet. "In this white dress, you look like your name, Zohara, radiant and bright."

As Iris spoke, Zohara looked at Shoshi and hoped that she would not mind. She and Shoshi had been often taken for sisters when people first met them. They both had dark hair, olive skin, and large brown eyes. Zohara was surprised because she did not see a strong resemblance.

In Shomriya it was Shoshi who was considered strikingly flamboyant. Her curly long hair and dark eyes always seemed to be on fire. Adults called her beautiful, and Shoshi acted and walked with the confidence of a dancer.

Being less used to attracting attention to her looks, Zohara enjoyed Iris's praise. It was her birthday. The white dress gave her a momentary glow, a temporary relief from what was happening in her heart.

Shoshi gave her a diary with a smooth olivewood cover and a small shiny key to open and lock the writer's words. The card read, "To my best friend Zohara. So many blank pages and I know that you'll fill them all with your thoughts, hopes, and secrets." Zohara traced the dark and light shades of the wood. "This is beautiful. I am going to write in it tonight. But I don't have any secrets." As soon as she spoke, Zohara wished she could take back her words. She had a big secret. She loved Daniel, Shoshi's older brother. She had never told Shoshi how she felt. When she visited their house, she pretended not to notice him.

Her father said reassuringly, "Everyone has secrets. All kinds of secrets. A diary is a very good place to talk about them."

"Dad, do you have secrets?"

Benny looked at her with serious attention. "Of course. We have a right to keep them to ourselves and to share a few when we feel like it. Your mother is very fortunate. She can tell important ones in her art."

But Zohara had not forgotten the art critic who called her mother a leftist. No one could call Shoshi's mother a leftist. Actually, none of her friends' mothers could ever be described that way. In Shomriya it was not exactly a compliment. The only people who were proud to be leftists and intellectuals were her parents' friends from Tel Aviv or from the kibbutz.

Her mother came over and stood next to them. She stroked Zohara's hair and retied a very loose white bow. Zohara smiled, and Iris took a picture of the three of them.

After the birthday party, before she went to sleep, Zohara picked up her diary. Zohara's room was small, a bed, a dresser, a slim desk tucked under the window, a bookcase on each side of the desk, and a chair. It was also a good place to listen, especially at night. When Zohara sat down, she could hear the frogs coming to life in the garden, the neighborhood dogs barking, and her grandmother's donkey, Vashti, joining the nightly chorus. Vashti seemed to enjoy being part of the sounds even in old age, when her bray sounded feeble. Zohara cupped her hands to her mouth and called out into the night, "Good night, Vashti."

Zohara listened to her parents' voices from the other room and to the sound of Bach playing softly on their record player. Bach's music was dependable; the same notes came back again and again, beautiful and reassuring. The familiar sounds wound themselves around her heart like the scarf her mother would wrap around Zohara's throat when it hurt.

Zohara took out the tiny key and opened her new journal. Looking at the white pages without lines, she began to write. "Today was my thirteenth birthday. I had hoped that by now my body would be more grown-up. Dad said that I already look grown-up. Mom said I looked beautiful, and Iris said so too. I do like my name, but I don't know if I like it when people talk about it meaning splendor. I hope that Iris and Dad are right, about me looking more grown-up, and boys, and all that. But I pray that Daniel will like me.

"Shoshi is my best friend, but sometimes I envy her because looking at her you know right away that while she is only a year older than me, she definitely looks fourteen. Her body is not confused. The boys in school are all in love with her.

"In three months, we'll all graduate and on my next birthday I will be in high school. Shoshi and most of my friends are going to different schools.

Shoshi is going to School of the Arts, and I'll miss her.

"Everyone that I love was here today except Daniel. I wish I could start reading *Gulliver's Travels*, but I'm too tired. I know that I'm going to like the book because I can tell that Lemuel Gulliver goes places and has great adventures. A note to God: I think that my grandmother could use your help. I know that she doesn't believe in you, but that wouldn't matter to you. P.S. I could use some help, too. Mom says that the reason for my not having breasts yet and no menstruation is genetic. She had to wait until she was almost fourteen. And she is sure that it will soon happen to me. Never mind genetics, I count on you. Thank you, God, in advance."

CHAPTER THREE

Zohara's mother had gone to her first town council meeting as a new elected member. Zohara felt happy. It meant that her mother was not just a 'leftist,' but that the people in town trusted her. Zohara was looking forward to having dinner at her grandmother's. As soon as her grandmother opened the door her father said, "I have something to tell you, Mom."

"You sound serious, Benny. Can you just wait until we sit down?"

"Of course. Let me help you bring things from the kitchen."

Her father opened the kitchen door and a nice smell invaded Malka's dining room. That felt good because Zohara knew that her grandmother had cooked only because they were coming for dinner.

Malka was scornful of all things domestic. She had never tried to cultivate what she called culinary skills. Dinner, she often said, was a time to rest the body and stimulate the mind. Food was incidental. Conversation was everything.

On all occasions, ordinary and ceremonious, her grandmother served meatballs, mashed potatoes, and a salad with vegetables from her garden. Her dishes were not sought after, and she never baked. But for dessert her grandmother always made sure that Zohara had her favorites, assorted Elite, the best chocolate in Israel, fresh strawberries from Malka's field, and cream that she whipped with a hand mixer and a generous amount of sugar.

Sure enough, the dessert was right there. Her grandmother always put everything, including dessert, on the table. She told Zohara that she did not like to get up between courses. For a hostess to leave the table, she said, was ill mannered. It interrupted the flow of a good discussion.

While they served themselves, Zohara was quiet. Being an only child, she was used to serious adult conversation. Even before he spoke she could tell that what her father had to say was going to be somber. She saw him looking at his mother. Malka put her hand on top of his, patting it slightly, as she would when she reassured Zohara. Their plates filled, the only sounds in the room were forks hitting china. Zohara took mashed potatoes first and spread them around with her fork. She put a meatball in the middle and pressed it down slowly and began to eat. The meatballs were juicy, full of pine nuts and garlic. "Delicious," she told her grandmother. For a moment she felt content and thanked God. Silently, because her grandmother did not believe in God.

Vashti let out a friendly bray. Some of the dogs joined her. Yael, one of the neighborhood mothers, shouted for her kids to come in. "I'm counting. One, two..." It was getting dark outside.

Her grandmother looked at her plate and seemed satisfied that she had eaten as much as she wanted. "I'm ready, Benny."

Her father drank some water and put the glass down. "I know that I should have talked to you earlier about my article on Arab workers' rights," he said, "but now is as good a time as any."

Malka put her fork down. "Something happened?"

"Just before I left the office today," her father said, "Zev Shai called. He would like a chance to talk to me about my article before I publish it."

"Caution sounds good…"

Her father asked Zohara if she wanted some water. She put out her glass and he almost missed it. He was going to upset his mother.

"I hope that Zev and the party would have the courage to support all our workers, Jewish and Arab," he said. "It's our moral duty."

Her grandmother's hands were shaking as she replied that she was against opening the Workers'

Union to Arab workers. "My generation came to this land with the hope of creating Hebrew workers."

Does her father realize how distressed his mother is?

"You and your generation achieved your dream," her father said. "Look around you, this whole country is Hebrew workers."

Zohara did not lose her appetite, but she stopped eating. Her grandmother looked at Benny.

"You, my son, are about to go public on a very divisive issue. This is not the right time."

Zohara saw her father put his hand on his mother's. He kept talking.

"When the Founders signed Israel's Declaration of Independence, they wrote that the state, and I quote, 'will maintain complete equality of social and political rights for all its citizens, without distinction of creed, race, or sex.' They signed it. Are we not bound by it?"

Her grandmother's voice was shaking now, just like the hand that she had retrieved. "Benny, I am not talking about the Declaration. Golda Meir and Rachel Kagan are friends of mine. Rachel has been fighting for women's rights and supports our struggle for equality."

"There were only two women signers, Grandma?" Zohara hoped to stop the conversation about Arab workers.

Malka sat up straight and looked at her. "Out of thirty-seven signers of the Declaration they included only two women. Political representation of women is what we need to fight for. Your mother as the first woman on the town council is where we fight. And win."

When her father nodded in agreement, her grandmother had more to say. "Right now, to call on the *Histadrut* to drop the word 'Hebrew' from its name would be seen as blasphemy."

Her father collected their dishes and took them to the kitchen. Her grandmother piled sweets on Zohara's dessert plate.

Zohara could not understand her father's stubbornness. She understood about being treated well, and she knew that there used to be an Arab village on the eastern side of Shomriya. Hardly anyone in Shomriya ever mentioned the village. And she was still very young when the Arabs had left. She barely remembered them. Silently she agreed with her grandmother: Her father was the only person in Shomriya who talked about Arab rights.

Strawberries did not stop her father talking. "Our party's decision last year to accept Arabs as equal members honored its name; it must take a stand and ask the *Histadrut* to be inclusive."

Zohara had heard her grandmother say, on several occasions, 'You just don't know when some lunatic fanatic will decide to become a hero.' Why had she thought that she wanted to grow up quickly and catch up with Shoshi? Zohara regretted her birthday.

When they got home, her mother was not yet back from her meeting. Zohara said into the silence of the house, "Dad, can something awful happen when you publish your article? Grandma is really worried."

"I know. I am her only child. It makes her very protective of me. Are you afraid?"

"A little." That was hardly the whole truth.

Her father tried to be helpful. "Don't be afraid. I won't do anything dangerous. Just remember, Jews don't kill Jews over politics. But if you're afraid and you want to talk to me, we'll talk before I publish the article. I promise. Would you like to read it when I'm done?"

Why would she want to even see that article? "I don't know. Can we read some more of *Gulliver's Travels*?"

Zohara picked up a Persian pillow from her favorite chair, sat down, pulled her legs up, and hugged the pillow. Her father turned on all the lights and put on a Damari record. She was one of Zohara's favorite singers.

"Do you want me to make you some hot chocolate?"

"Not really. Let's just read."

"Would you like to read, or would you like me to read?"

"You read."

Her father settled on the sofa and looked for the place they had left off the night before. Damari's "A Camels' Caravan" played softly in the room. Zohara closed her eyes and listened to her father read in the voice that he had adopted for Lemuel Gulliver. Her parents, who sometimes read aloud to each other, also still read to her. She loved not only to read books but also to hear them.

Zohara enjoyed the sound of words, as did her father. When her father became Gulliver, his incredible adventures took Zohara far from

Shomriya. In the Irishman's good company, she almost forgot about her body and her grandmother's fear.

***

The next morning, while Benny made breakfast, Rena told her family about her first meeting as a town council member. Rena wanted to be part of Shomriya, not just its artist, but an elected official who could bring new ideas to public attention. She told Zohara and Benny that she had enjoyed it even though anger had flared over renovating the school. "Jacob shouted that the old school was just fine. When the vote was in favor of renovations, he got so upset that we thought he would hit the mayor. People rushed over to hold him. Jacob kept yelling, 'You're all going to regret it.'"

While Rena washed the last of the breakfast dishes, Benny said, "It seems that I won't have much time for my Buber research tonight. Zev Shai has invited me for dinner and to talk about my position on Arab workers."

Rena put down the last plate slowly and carefully, but her words rushed out. "How did Zev know that you're going to be in Jerusalem?"

Benny, drying the dishes, looked at her. "I am not sure. There goes my evening. Zev probably thinks he is honoring me by having me to dinner at the Knesset. But I will make a case for the rights of all workers."

Rena did not respond to his smile. She was now wiping a perfectly clean counter. She finally wrung the water out of the sponge, giving it such a tight squeeze that her hand hurt. She tried to speak as calmly as she could. "No. Zev wants to show off his new status as a member of the Knesset. Ever since I met him in kibbutz Oz, I've never liked him. I know that he claims to support the workers and the oppressed. He is not who he pretends to be."

Benny put the towel down. "Don't you think that people can change? Family is not destiny."

Rena wondered what she could say now with Zohara right there. Zohara did not have to know about Zev.

Rena chose her words carefully. "It's not because he comes from a bourgeois family. Zev is all ambition and no morals. How he has managed to persuade our United Workers' Party otherwise is beyond me…"

A hummingbird flew straight into the glass window. Poor thing. It lost its balance, regained it, and flew off unhurt.

"Is there something you know about Zev that I don't?"

In a low voice, Rena answered, "Rumors floated in Oz about something that happened to a woman he dated." She looked at Zohara, who was sitting at the kitchen table absorbed in her book. "You are going to have dinner with him and I'm sure that you'll figure out what he is up to."

"I will be back tomorrow night."

Rena nodded.

If Zohara was aware that her parents were having a serious talk or that Rena had not finished what she had to say, she gave no indication. She closed her book and seemed intent on making sure that she had gathered up all her homework. She was ready for the short walk to the edge of their street with her father.

Rena stood outside the iron gate of their house on Herzl Street and watched her family walk to the main road. The blue sky was so pure that it cast a glow on everything, the asphalt road, the strawberry fields, Zohara's red satchel, and Benny's battered army knapsack.

At the end of the road, Benny gave Zohara a kiss on the top of her head. She turned right on Ben Yehuda and Benny waved and turned left to go to the bus stop. Rena looked at her family and wanted to feel the usual joy. Instead, she felt uneasy.

CHAPTER FOUR

Benny walked toward the bus stop on Ben Yehuda Street, four kilometers, straight as a rod, running from west to east. It was Shomriya's first street, and the pioneers had liked the idea of a long road. Over the years Shomriya had settled itself on both sides of it. Slowly, new little streets had sprouted on each side of Ben Yehuda. To go from one street to the next parallel one, people created footpaths that over the years had hardened into unofficial public trails.

From the sky, Shomriya looked like a giant millipede resting on its belly. Locals fondly described the shape of Shomriya as "unique," "a place with character."

Benny had grown up in Shomriya. In 1955 it was still rural and proud of its sweet strawberries and beautiful oranges. Most Shomriyans were looking forward to more paved roads, streetlights, and shops with luxury items; imported goods, toasters, steam irons, and General Electric were new in places like Shomriya. Benny had just passed the shop with red neon signs when he saw Jacob.

"This is what is going to ruin us." Jacob pointed his finger at the store's display window, almost jabbing the glass.

"Good morning, Jacob."

"I know you, Benny. Don't try to distract me. We are losing the land to gadgets."

Jacob was one of the early Shomriya pioneers. The pioneers loved the land intensely, sensually. Enamored with the land, they wrote poems and dedicated songs to "Mother Earth." The joke in Shomriya was that Jacob would start his day by kissing the earth. Jacob began working shortly before dawn. In the dark, it was hard to tell the difference between kneeling to weed and kneeling to pray. For the town folk, facts never stood in the way of good gossip.

Recently, Benny had spotted cracks in what used to be a consensus on farming as a way of life. More Shomriyans reduced the size of their farms, tended much smaller citrus groves and strawberry fields, kept only a cow or two, and had two dozen chickens in their backyard. Others gave up farming altogether and went back to their earlier professions or took up new ones and, like Benny, commuted daily to Tel Aviv.

Jacob was still standing there with his finger glued to the store's display window. Perhaps he hoped that if he kept it there long enough the store would disappear. "I'm on my way to help your mother and you're running off to the big city."

Benny admired his mother for keeping most of her strawberry fields. She would often look at her stained hands and say, "I intend to work in these fields until the end of my life. I hope to grow old and to die with this good red juice covering my hands." If she wished that her son would take up farming, she kept it to herself.

What stood between them now was not the issue of farming, or modernization. How could she be so passionate about women's rights and so indifferent to the rights of Arab workers?

Something must have shown on his face because Jacob looked at him and seemed to soften. "Go. Go. Write some articles about the rights of workers. We need journalists like you. Real socialists."

"You know me, Jacob. I fight simultaneously on two fronts. For the right of Jews to a state and the right of Israel's Arab citizens to equality within the state." He did not need to make political statements to Jacob, but he wanted to say more than he had said last night to his mother, to clarify, justify, win her over to his side.

Jacob squeezed Benny's shoulder. "I know. You do what you have to do. I'll go help Malka. I'm late." He turned around and before Benny could say anything he was walking away toward Herzl Street.

Benny was not sure whether Jacob shared his political views. He was aware that people rarely criticized his position, at least not publicly. Rena said this was because he had been a commander in the Israeli army. She was right that his military credentials shielded him, to some extent, from criticism. But would it stretch far enough for Shomriyans to accept his struggle for equality for Arab workers? He was writing about Buber's early position on Arab rights, but Buber now wrote about Jewish mysticism and was no longer politically engaged.

Benny did not want to miss the bus and picked up his pace. At thirty-six, Benny was like his father, a lean, athletic man with dark eyes and firm chin. Summer, spring, and fall, Benny wore short-sleeve shirts open at the collar, short khakis, a pair of sandals. On cold days he wore a sweater, a jacket, and long khaki pants.

Since he was planning to go to Jerusalem, he had taken his knapsack for the overnight stay. He walked toward the newspaper kiosk. Raffi the owner greeted him with his usual joke. "You're a journalist. You write the news. Why do you need to buy a newspaper?"

Handing him his change, Raffi said, "You always want to read what the competition says. Am I right?"

Benny put the paper in the briefcase he had inherited from his father. It was worn by age and the weather but was still elegant and professional looking. Benny did not consider himself vain, but he liked balance, he liked the fact that the briefcase gave him some formality that was otherwise absent in his rather informal appearance.

Despite the open windows it was already warm on the crowded bus. He moved to the back of the bus and sat down next to Dov, who was one of Shomriya's male gossipers. Benny put the knapsack under the seat and Dov leaned over, touched it, and whispered, "A Jerusalem outing, I see. The usual Buber stuff? Secret documents?"

CHAPTER FIVE

When Benny got to his office, he saw Shifra standing at the door crumpling a piece of paper. "I was just going to leave you a note to call Zev."

Shifra was older than Benny, in her early forties, a short, thin woman with large hazel eyes in a small face. She was a member of kibbutz Oz and spent the week in Tel Aviv. Benny occasionally had lunch with her in a small Yemenite restaurant not far from the office. Shifra loved its spicy food. Ordering her favorite lamb and rice with pine nuts, she would lament the fact that kibbutz food was so bland.

Going back to the kibbutz every weekend gave her a special perspective as an economics writer. As with all who worked outside the kibbutz, her salary went to the kibbutz. The kibbutz provided her with living expenses. She told Benny that the arrangement kept her humble. Taking her turn to serve food in the dining hall, like every other member, kept her in touch with her friends at Oz. It put her working days in Tel Aviv in perspective.

In the crowded Yemenite restaurant Shifra would often lower her voice and whisper to Benny, "It's so restful to come back to work. But don't ever tell anyone."

Shifra was standing outside his office.

"Did Zev say why he called?"

"Not to me. I was surprised because he usually has his secretary deliver messages. He is even more high and mighty since he was elected to the Knesset."

Benny thought that Shifra, like Rena, sounded angry at Zev. Before he had a chance to ask her about it, Mike, the chief editor, interrupted. "You going to meet with Zev today?"

"I don't know. He just asked me to call him back. I wouldn't mind if he canceled. I want to work on my Buber book."

"If he cancels, let me know. Buber, I'm afraid, will have to wait. I have something interesting for you. Some story about a serious security leak, someone high up may be spying for the Soviets. It'll be a huge scandal if it's true."

"Spying for the Soviets? I want to hear about it. But I need to talk to you for a minute."

Benny's phone rang. He stepped into his office. It was Zev.

"Benny, I only have a minute. An important vote coming up on the floor. Glad I caught you."

"Well, if you want to cancel it's okay. We'll reschedule. Mike has some work for me. A rumor going around about a spy for the Soviets. Know anything about it?"

There was utter silence on the other side. "Zev? Zev? Are you still there? Do you want to cancel?"

"Benny. I'm being paged. I can't talk right now. No, I don't want to cancel. Why would I want to cancel? I must run now. I'll talk to you later. In Jerusalem."

Mike came in. "What's up? Did he cancel?"

"No, he didn't. He said he had to cast an important vote. He'll talk to me when I get to Jerusalem."

"So, he still wants to meet..."

"Mike, what are the rumors about him?"

Mike, big-framed and overweight, heaved himself into the only other chair in Benny's small office. As usual, he complimented Benny on his neat desk. "I don't know how you do it." Uncluttered, Benny's desk had only a black typewriter, a mug holding pencils and pens, a pad, and a black phone.

The books on the shelves were neatly organized by author. Martin Buber's books were all first editions. Benny's book, which he had hoped to work on in Jerusalem, would explore the intersection of Buber's political ideas about a binational state and the dialogue between God and humans.

Benny sat down. "Mike, what happened at Oz?"

Mike folded his hands and looked down. "Zev had a relationship with a young woman. People said that she was in love with him, and that he just used her. She was found dead. The police said it looked like suicide. But they suspected murder."

"Zev was the suspect?"

Mike sighed, hoisted himself a bit, his chair creaking. "He was. He denied it. Most people believed him. A few didn't."

Benny leaned forward. "This is very serious. I'm surprised I didn't hear about it before." He was hurt that Rena had never mentioned any of it. Why had she kept it from him? She hardly talked about her family who were murdered in the Holocaust. But the Zev story was different. He looked at Mike.

"Well, people didn't talk about it. You know how kibbutz people are. They keep everything inside and under a tight lid. It's now that he has become a member of the Knesset that rumors have begun to surface again."

Benny shook his head. "A bit late, I'm afraid. The right thing would have been to confront it before putting him on the party's nomination list."

The teacart appeared, Miriam pushing it easily along the corridor. Miriam, a cheerful woman in her fifties with frizzy reddish hair, a love for baking and a talent for poetry, stood at the door. "Benny. I was going to read you my new poem, but I can see that you're busy. In the meantime, can I get you anything? Real tea? Good coffee? The best sandwich in Tel Aviv? Delicious pastry? I recommend my apricot cake."

"Benny needs something really strong."

"Oh. That we don't have here, except opinions, of course. But I can see that you don't need that right now. You look pale. A cup of tea would help."

Without waiting for an answer, she put on Benny's desk two cups of hot water and two tea bags, several slices of lemon, and fresh fragrant mint leaves in a small dish. Miriam often told Benny about the calming powers of mint. She looked around. "I always tell you, Benny. You have the tidiest office in the whole building. I bet the cleaning woman loves it. What's to clean?"

"You never say anything half as nice about my office," Mike said.

Miriam laughed. "Well, Mike, what can I say? You have the largest office. You're the boss."

Benny, distracted, tried to respond to Miriam. "When I come back from Jerusalem, I want to hear your new poem. You should quit the food business. Your poetry is too good."

"Don't worry, Benny. I'll still be here when you come back. Working for a living and dreaming of my poems in print. I can already see it, a slim volume, a beautiful dust jacket, with my name modestly visible. In the acknowledgments I'll thank you for encouraging me to write. In the meantime, good luck with Buber."

When she pushed the cart down the hall, Mike stood up slowly, closed the door, and sat down again.

"Look, Benny. No one thought that Artzi would die suddenly, and that Zev would replace him. It was a political fluke."

"Mike, he shouldn't have been on the list of candidates until the rumors could be checked out."

Benny did not try to hide his anger and Mike was aware of it. "The police did their best at the time. They couldn't find any evidence. No new investigation today, fifteen years later, would turn up any new evidence. We must give the guy the benefit of the doubt. He was an outsider, the son of a capitalist family. Arrogant. He claimed he was scapegoated by some members of the kibbutz."

Mike was defending Zev. Benny wondered what that was all about. "I'm not sure that I can talk to Zev before I clarify for myself what's going on."

When he wanted to get his way, Mike was known to use his excess weight to his advantage. Benny was not surprised when Mike began to breathe heavily and put his hand on his heart.

"Benny, Benny, Benny…You are a political reporter… not a criminal investigator. Digging into Zev's life is not your job. This isn't one of your military operations in which you're in charge."

Mike's last remark took Benny by surprise. "That was uncalled for. I don't know where this is coming from." He looked at Mike, who was wheezing audibly.

Was it something in their conversation about Zev that had triggered bitterness?

Mike took his hand off his chest, leaned forward, and touched Benny's arm. "Just kidding. But seriously, Benny, leave Zev's history alone."

"Mike, I need to think about it. I'll try to call our neighbor, Yael, and see if she can go and get Rena. I wish our request for a phone would go through."

Mike, eager to focus on something other than Zev, said, "Well, you didn't want me to use my connections to get you a phone, you wanted to go through the formal application procedure. That means waiting."

Without meaning to, Benny raised his voice. "I know. I appreciate your offer."

As Benny reached for his phone, Mike said, "Whatever you decide to do, just let me know before you take any action. But I would suggest dropping it. It's an old story. Remember. Here you're a journalist, not a commander. In the meantime, I will ask Gabi to start working on the spy story. If it turns into something serious, I'll ask you to get involved."

Benny looked straight at Mike. "I know that you're in charge here, Mike."

"You army officers. Whether you know or not, you always bring your rank to civilian life."

Mike left, and Benny sat still, letting Mike's acid accusation fill the air. Benny wished he could talk to his father about it. He felt how much he missed his father. It had been seven years since Yair was killed and Benny still wished they could go on one of their long hikes. His father had often taken him, even when he was very young, on what Yair called "getting to know the land" hikes.

Benny imagined the two of them somewhere, in the Negev desert, or in the Galilee, late at night, getting ready to roll out their blankets. They would choose a good spot, use their flashlights to check the ground, make sure the camera was in a safe place. They would spread the blankets, put their knapsacks under their heads, and listen to sounds of jackals, owls, and insects. Under the stars they would talk about the day's hike, the view, the plants, reptiles, birds, and animals they had seen and admired. Benny would mention Mike's comment about the army. He could easily imagine his father saying, "It's hard for a man in this country not to be in combat and not to be called for reserve duty."

"Do we bring a sense of power and entitlement to our work?"

"Well, you should watch for it, son. Ask yourself if this is what you're doing."

In his mind, Benny could hear how his father would just leave it at that. Yair would let him sort out his thoughts and his relationship with Mike. He knew he needed to get to work. He drank the tea Miriam had left. It was cold now, but the mint gave it a pleasant tangy taste.

He thought about what he had just learned about Zev; not only Rena but Shifra too had never mentioned it. Zev's past in kibbutz Oz emerged as one of those secrets that even the gossipers avoided. Benny went out of his office to look for Shifra, but she had gone out on an assignment. He left a note on her desk saying, "I need to talk to you."

Benny heard the usual noise in the newsroom. He liked it. Rivers of news, good and bad, exciting and ordinary, tragic and uplifting, from around the country and the world. It was their job to sort, sift, and decide. Which news would inform the readers, touch their hearts? Open their minds? On that morning Benny asked himself whether his article on Arab workers would provoke more anger than sympathy.

Benny went back to his office and didn't go out for lunch. He tried several times to call Yael Ramot, the neighbor whose phone they all used. There were very few homes with phones in Shomriya, and most people who had a phone were willing to accommodate those without. Yael was not at home, however, and Benny could not talk to Rena as he had hoped. He looked once again at Shifra's desk. She was still out.

Benny made several calls and took notes. Miriam came in quietly, took the empty cup, and left him some more tea. She put down a piece of apricot cake and a fork. He cradled the phone under his chin and wrote on his pad, "Thank you."

He stayed longer than he had intended. In one of the calls, he inadvertently stumbled on the rumor that someone in the Knesset was spying for the Soviets. As soon as he hung up the phone, he saw Yigal Adir, the newspaper's accountant, standing at the door. Before Benny could say anything, Yigal turned around and left. Just as well. He was already late and whatever Yigal had on his mind would have to wait. Benny had very little to do with the financial side of the paper, and the spy story was now on his mind; it was much more than a rumor. Mike would want to know about it and let Gabi follow the lead. Benny was not about to talk to Gabi directly. Mike would take offence and remind Benny that the paper had a chain of command. He looked for Mike, but his office was empty, he was still out. Benny wrote him a detailed message.

At two in the afternoon Benny collected his notes, put them in his briefcase, and got ready to leave the office to take the bus to Jerusalem. On his way out he went to Mike's office and almost collided with Miriam. She was just clearing away some empty teacups. Benny said, "I have something that Mike would find very interesting." At that moment Yigal was again standing at the door, but as soon as Miriam and Benny looked at him, he mumbled something about looking for Mike and left. Miriam said, "Yigal gives me the creeps." Benny had to agree. He had noticed Yigal's prowling, but he didn't pay much attention to him. Right then he did not want to think about Yigal. Benny wanted to get to Jerusalem before the library at Hebrew University closed. Abigail, the librarian, had called to say that the Buber document Benny was looking for was there and she had made a copy for him. The spy story was

Mike's to deal with. Benny put an envelope on Mike's desk. It read CONFIDENTIAL.

CHAPTER SIX

Rena watched Benny walking to the bus stop. Since she had heard of his plan to meet Zev for dinner, Rena wished she had said something to him when Zev had become a member of the Knesset. She should have shared with Benny the rumors in kibbutz Oz about Rachel's death. She turned around to face her porch. She had planned to start working on charcoal sketches for her new project. Instead, she just stood there looking at the rock and cactus garden.

She and Benny had collected these beautiful rocks on the beaches of the Mediterranean and brought them to Shomriya. She looked at the prickly pear cactus, *Tzabar,* which she had planted. In April the cactus had beautiful yellow flowers, and a hardworking bee was already busy flying into one of them. Rena watched the bee buzzing nervously in and out and finally, covered in yellow dust, taking off. In early summer these flowers would turn into sweet red fruit covered by tiny, deceptively soft thorns, and kids carrying cups or bowls would come by and ask if they could have some.

Tzabar was the term the pioneers had given their children born in Israel. They proudly claimed that their brash and outspoken children, like the *Tzabar* fruit, were prickly on the outside but oh, so very sweet inside.

Tzabar did not apply to her. She was not born on the land. Rena walked toward the porch, mindlessly pulling out weeds on the way.

Inside the porch Rena felt as though she had forgotten something she was trying to remember. But what that was, she could not figure out. Shaking her head, she looked around and noticed that the sun in the east was casting a particularly strong reddish light on the porch. It shone intensely on the long wooden table pushed under the northern windows, next to a small bookcase. She walked over to the table, looked at the grainy cedar pattern, and touched the smooth, warm surface.

She was not breathing very well. She needed more air. Rena turned around and opened all the windows on the eastern side.

A cool morning breeze with a hint of fresh cow manure settled itself momentarily on the porch. Rena saw Jacob turning manure in Malka's field. She thought about his outburst at the town council the night before and wished she could have been more supportive of him. She had great affection for Jacob, but he was on the wrong side of the school issue. As though reading her mind, Jacob turned around and waved to her. She waved back. She wanted to call out to him but instead looked at the porch, searching for the right spot to work.

Rena wanted to pay attention to her project, but she was restless. She went around straightening the familiar porch furniture. She pushed the wooden bench against the wall. She puffed the pillows on the chairs and the armchair and dusted the 1930s art deco standing lamp with its large, colorful silk shade. She finally went over to the art corner that occupied the southern side. She pulled her easel into the middle of the porch facing the garden.

She was about to walk over to the yellow shelves where she kept a small array of paints, brushes, charcoal sticks, pencils, drawing paper, and her pads. She remembered that she had bought new charcoal pencils, and that they were still in her bag inside the house. When she came out again, there was Malka on her porch. She looked at Rena's easel. "Do you need anything for dinner?"

This was not an unusual question. Malka would often bring produce from her garden, corn, peas, tomatoes, potatoes, cucumbers, eggplants, peppers, strawberries, whatever was in season and ripe. Over the years Rena's relationship with Malka had grown into one of mutual respect, sprinkled with moments of disagreement and an occasional outburst.

Rena had not forgotten Malka's question from the other day: "Are you two thinking about Zohara?" Malka's question about dinner was not meant to take back her concern. Yet Malka would occasionally use farming produce as a peace gesture. Rena did not return Malka's generosity. She tersely reminded Malka that Benny would be in Jerusalem, she was teaching an evening art class, and Zohara was invited for dinner at Shoshi's. Regretting her harshness, she added, "Some strawberries would be nice. We could have them as a late dessert." When Malka left, Rena wanted to say something comforting to her, but the hurt, like a tongue depressor, silenced her.

She looked out at the cactus and rock garden. As she stood there, she could hear Malka say, "A waste, such a waste. Cacti belong in the desert, or in Arab villages."

A small turtle walked slowly under the prickly pear that she had brought from what used to be a small Arab village, Abu Nabil, bordering Shomriya. The turtle, oblivious to the origins of this cactus, decided to rest right there. In 1948 the whole village population, under considerable pressure from Shomriya's leaders, had taken their belongings, gotten onto several trucks, and gone away. No one, including Rena and Benny, asked the leadership to reconsider and invite the Arab villagers to stay. Shortly after the war, bulldozers came and demolished the empty buildings. They were considered a health hazard.

Some months later Rena went to the site of the former village and brought back the prickly pear and put it in their rock garden. She told Benny that she had gone by what used to be Saleem's house and seen the cactus plants. She was ashamed. "Perhaps if we had tried to convince the town council that the people of Abu Nabil could stay, would be no threat to us, they would be here today," she told Benny. She brought the cactus to their garden. "One day, when Saleem comes back, I will be able to give him something from his village. I have a feeling that we will meet again."

Benny didn't think the decision whether the Arab village stayed or not was up to Shomriya. It had been made higher up, by the national leadership. But this did not make Rena feel any better. She should have spoken up.

Benny's article on Arab workers' rights, of those Arabs who had remained in Israel, was an attempt to rectify their previous silence on the injustice done to the people of Abu Nabil. Even after having won the war, Benny's article on this divisive issue was important, and Malka should have known it. She and Benny needed Malka's support.

As the sun made its way around the porch, the day felt warmer. Rena went to the kitchen and got a glass of lemonade. She put on Mozart's Symphony No. 41 and waited for the Jupiter music to begin. She started sketching slowly and without thinking, just trusting her hands do their work.

At noon Iris appeared unexpectedly. "I hope this isn't a bad time."

"I'm so glad you came," Rena said.

Iris, like Malka, was tall and regal, but not as slim. She sat down on the bench and sighed. "I need to talk to you. Can you come have lunch at Mendel's?"

"Yes. That would be great."

"You mean it?"

Iris looked surprised because Rena usually did not like to be interrupted when she worked. Today she was grateful for it. She liked going to Mendel's Café, which like all other important places in town was right at the center of Ben Yehuda Street. Rena wanted to be among people and away from her house and easel.

Mendel's Café was what she needed. It was situated at the heart of Shomriya's hub of literature, aesthetics, and gossip, flanked by Leah's beauty salon on one side and Bialik's bookstore on the other. "My two guardian angels," Mendel Gefen, the café founder, would joke. He was a self-declared atheist and did not believe in the supernatural.

Rena said, "I'll see if Leah can give me a haircut after lunch."

Leah's beauty salon was Shomriya's concession to modern feminine aesthetic needs. It was the major source for all dubious news, false facts, and malicious gossip. Loyalty in Shomriya was everything. While she could have her hair done in Tel Aviv, Rena went to Leah's for a haircut. For women the salon offered perms and weekly styling. Once a week, women would come to Leah. She would set their hair in pink curlers, put them under loud dryers, and use special combs to create professional bouffants.

One or the other would say to Rena, "You're so lucky to have curly thick hair. You don't know how lucky you are." Invariably someone would admonish her, "You could tease your hair a little bit, give it more volume." Or, in the intimacy of the hair salon, someone would offer cosmetic advice about how to conceal her freckles.

The women would tell her about going to bed wearing hairnets. Each morning they combed their hair ever so lightly, trying their best not to disturb the hairdo. After six days women could not wait for Leah's girl to shampoo it and for Leah to give their hair a new weekly shine. They walked out pleased, smiling, and feeling more beautiful than when they walked in.

Iris laughed. "You want a haircut today? You are lucky. I just saw our mayor's wife coming out of there. You will be spared making small talk with her." It was rumored in Shomriya that Dinah the mayor's wife would sneak, through the back door, in the middle of the week for an extra shampoo and styling. But Leah's lips were sealed on what most women considered the height of extravagance. Malka, as she often said, never set her foot in Leah's place. She had a pair of scissors in her kitchen for the infrequent trimming of her long hair.

Rena suddenly revived. "If Leah will give me an instant appointment, I'll treat myself and buy a book as well."

"Make use of all that Shomriya can offer. Don't ignore our bookstore." Iris was laughing loudly. She took a pillow and put it behind her back and sighed with pleasure. "This is a great porch."

"How do you think Bialik would feel about the town making use of his reputation?"

"Bialik? What do you mean?"

"Well, our small town's bookstore uses the name of our great poet. I mean here we are in this farming town, and we have appropriated him. Even I do it."

"How exactly are you doing it?"

"The title for my new project comes from Bialik's poem about the pure daughters of Lilith weaving one and the same garment for high priests and for swineherds."

A silence filled the porch. Iris got up, took off her sunglasses and looked at the easel. A turtle sitting under a cactus plant, the turtle's neck stretched out. Its eyes hooded and mysterious. "A turtle and a prickly pear are *The Same Garment*?"

Rena confessed, "I don't know yet what it means."

"I don't see the connection to your painting."

Rena did not mind. She had yet to fully understand how the poem was connected to the cactus that came from Saleem's village and the accidental turtle. But she didn't worry about it. She often began her projects with a title, and she trusted her intuition that the rest would fall into place.

Bialik had come to Shomriya once. Mr. Zeller, the local photographer, was there to commemorate the event. He was the only professional photographer in town. He always made everyone look much better than in real life. In the large photograph that graced the bookstore, Bialik, who had already been quite sick at the time, had a rosy, healthy smile. The townspeople loved it.

When the town heard the news that Bialik had died they came to the bookstore, looked at the photograph, and shook their heads in tender disbelief. "He looks so alive," they whispered.

Iris went back to sit on the bench but did not change the topic. "And after his death we held on to his wife. You really loved her, Rena."

Rena felt an unexpected wave of sadness at the thought of this short, plump woman with a soft, round face. She always treated people in a friendly yet shy and self-effacing manner. For several years, until her death, Bialik's widow would come to Shomriya every summer. She would first greet Shlomo Barzilai, who owned the bookstore.

Escorted by Shlomo she would then slowly climb the three steps to Leah's beauty parlor. Leah herself would give her the best of the salon. Her hair shining, her nails freshly painted, smiling kindly, Mrs. Bialik would finally sit down at Mendel's to sample his pastry.

When Rena wiped her eyes with the back of her smudged hand, Iris asked, "Are you okay?"

"I don't know."

"Do you remember how quickly word would get around that Mrs. Bialik was in town?"

Rena nodded.

In Mrs. Bialik's presence, they all felt that Hebrew poetry, their farming, and kindness mingled together to produce a sweet sense of wellbeing. Her visits made many aspiring poets sigh with yearning and hope.

Rena felt tired and sat down. "I miss her. My painting 'Mrs. Bialik Comes to Town' is one of my favorites. She reminded me of my mother, even though they looked so different. I loved them both."

Iris remained silent. She was not going to talk about their families.

"I was very surprised when the elders chose my painting over all others in the contest. They hung it in Town Hall."

Iris smiled. "And now you have been elected to the town council."

"That was unexpected."

"Why? You belong on the council and the painting is beautiful. Smiling adults and beaming children standing around Mrs. Bialik and her big white bag in Mendel's Café. Everyone looks kind, generous, and caring."

"There were a few good paintings in the competition."

"You are an artist with a keen eye. When Shomriyans have doubts about who they are, your painting makes them feel proud of themselves."

Rena was silent. She was not so sure the town was grateful.

Iris broke her silence. "Let's go to Mendel's."

Mendel's Café was Iris's second home. Iris had been engaged to Raphael, Mendel's son, who had been killed in the 1948 war. His untimely death devastated Mendel and broke Iris's heart. Cooking had become Mendel's obsession. Iris had stayed single. She and Mendel supported each other in their grief. Rena could see how over the years Iris's close relationship with Mendel kept them both connected to Raphael.

As she prepared to put away her easel and charcoals, Rena heard Malka across the street, calling to Jacob to come in and have lunch. "Leave the eggs alone, Jacob. They're not going anywhere. They'll be there when you come back." She saw Jacob obediently wash his hands in the outdoor sink.

She turned to Iris. "What's new with Mendel?"

"What's new with Mendel? The usual. Saul wants him to sell the café because of his heart condition. But to sell the café would kill Mendel for sure. Mendel needs the place to stay alive. Saul wants to talk to me. He thinks I encourage Mendel to stay on, and that I am to blame for his refusal to sell. But he thinks highly of you. I need you to be there."

Rena wiped her stained hands on a rag. "Yes. Let's go. I just have to go inside and clean up a bit." In the kitchen, washing her hands, Rena considered Mendel. She had often thought that Mendel, without knowing it, neglected not only his own life, but also that of Saul, his surviving son, and his grandchildren. It was obvious he cared about them, but he was probably unaware of what he had denied Saul and his family.

Iris, a therapist, should have known better. She had a blind spot where Mendel was concerned because she too could not get on with her life. In the last two years Iris had made attempts to go out on dates. But it seemed that no man could compete with the memory of the young, brave, and dead Raphael.

Rena returned to the porch ready to go. She was wearing a large hat. Iris put on her fashionable sunglasses.

"Let's go. I'm getting hungry just thinking of Mendel's lunch."

Mendel's Café had about ten tables outside, under the shade of jacaranda trees. Mendel's food, dairy for breakfast and dinner and meat for lunch, the main meal of the day, did not vary with the seasons. He offered the same menu, winter and summer. His hot lunch was fine, but his breakfast and dinner menu was a feast. Fresh bread, puffy soft omelets, yogurt, salads, cheeses, fruit, and a choice of pastry. All year-round, people came for the beverages as well. Hot tea that Mendel served from a giant samovar he had brought from Russia, thick Turkish coffee that he had learned to make in Palestine, and sweet sodas. He used only local fruit, oranges, grapefruit, guava, pomegranate, strawberries, and plums, all his own secret soda recipes.

Rena and Iris found a table close to the Bialik bookstore. Shlomo saw them and came out. "Good to see the two of you. How are you, Rena? Quite a ruckus yesterday at the town council meeting. Sorry I couldn't make it. I heard that Jacob was quite a sight. Malka should have a word with him. He's really losing it."

Mendel came out with two sodas. "Leave them alone, Shlomo. And don't start on poor Jacob. He was always a stubborn mule, but he is a good man." Mendel put the drinks down and kissed Iris and Rena on their cheeks. "How are you, Rena, and how is our Benny? And the Buber book? Shlomo. When Benny's book will be published, we'll have another Bialik event here. Our very own famous writer."

Shlomo pointed to the store's display window. "Right there, Rena, in the middle, next to Bialik we'll put Benny's book. I just talked to him about it a few days ago. He came in to get *Gulliver's Travels* for Zohara's birthday. I bet Malka had a fit over a book by a foreign writer. I warned him. But he said Zohara would love it."

Rena smiled. "You were right, Malka didn't approve, and Zohara loved it. Last night she went to sleep with the book in her hand."

Shlomo was beaming. "Now there is another budding writer. This girl will follow in her father's footsteps. But I'd better let you two eat before Mendel tells me that I'm interfering with his business."

When Shlomo left, Iris reached into her handbag. "Before I forget, I have the photographs from Zohara's birthday. I framed the one with the three of you for Zohara."

Rena held the photo. Family happiness, like a breath blown against a glass window on a cold winter day, could have just melted away, turned into an ephemeral memory or sweetness forgotten. Instead, Iris's camera had given it substance, and a life of its own. Iris had turned their contentment into a black and white photograph.

"Zohara will love it. Thank you, Iris. You are a good photographer."

Iris had tears in her eyes. Rena offered her a napkin. "Iris?"

"Oh, don't mind me. Tell me what's going on with you."

"I will. But are you okay?"

"Yes. I don't always know what my tears are about. I do want to hear what's going on with you. I could see when I came in today that you were really upset."

"Zev Shai."

"What about him?"

"Benny told me that he was going to meet Zev Shai. Zev, he thinks, wants to persuade him not to publish his article on the rights of Arab workers."

Iris put a straw in her plum soda and stirred the dark bottom. "How did he manage to become a member of the Knesset? Why is Benny even talking to him?"

"The meeting was Zev's idea. He wanted to let Benny know where he stood on the issue of the rights of Arab workers. But Benny doesn't know about Zev. He wasn't at Oz."

Iris sounded surprised. "How come you haven't told Benny?"

Rena took a long sip. The cool soda felt good. She kept her hand wrapped around the tall glass. There was charcoal around her nails.

"I don't know, Iris. Please don't say anything. I will tell Benny about it when he comes back."

Iris said nothing.

"The kibbutz and its insistence on secrecy is to blame for the fact that so few people know about Zev. Poor Rachel." Rena could feel a surge of the old anger, frustration, and shame. Iris just sat there.

"I should have told Benny as soon as I heard two weeks ago that Zev had become a member of the Knesset. Why didn't I do more for Rachel at the time?"

Iris spoke quietly, almost in a whisper. "You can't blame yourself. I didn't do anything either. There was little that we could do. We had absolutely no evidence of wrongdoing. Nothing. It was just a gut feeling, and you can't go around spreading rumors based on hunches."

"I did not do the right thing."

"Let me remind you that you tried at the time. You told the police what you suspected. They obviously were unimpressed. And then Zev managed to become a major political player."

Rena saw Saul walking over. From a distance he looked friendly. But he was angry at Iris. She could tell by the way he waved, a gesture more like a dismissal than a greeting. He went into the café.

Iris stated the obvious. "He doesn't want to talk to me."

CHAPTER SEVEN

It was definitely not a good morning. A bus drove by, leaving behind a sickening smell of gasoline and a cloud of dark smoke. Zohara had been walking very slowly. She sighed and picked up her pace. She didn't like to be late for school. Everything had been so much easier when she was young.

Zohara wondered about that man Zev. It was clear her mother did not like him. Her parents' not talking about something in front of her did not happen often. Usually, her parents treated her more like a grown-up. She was proud of the way they talked to her.

People in Shomriya called her, behind her back, of course, a serious girl. No. The truth was that some said she was much *too* serious.

She had once overheard their neighbor Yael say to someone at the grocery store, "Zohara Sasson, thoughtful? Smart? Too much so if you ask me."

Zohara had kept her eyes on the bread shelf. No one had asked Yael for her opinion. That didn't stop her. In a smug, all-knowing voice she had said, "It's all her parents' doing. And her grandmother… They all talk to her as though she was an equal. I guess it's all these socialist ideas. They should treat her more like a child. She would be much better off. Less serious."

When had Zohara begun to feel uncertain about everything? Was it when she noticed that Shoshi's body was changing? When she began to doubt that her own body would ever change? When she realized that there were things she could not talk about with her parents or even with her best friend?

"Zohara. Wait for me!"

Zohara turned around to see Ronnie running up to her. Ronnie, red-haired and freckled, with a pair of short but strong legs, had always been a fast runner. She was not even breathless when she said, "I just saw your father at the bus stop."

"Hi, Ronnie."

Ronnie, as usual, spoke as fast as she ran, and with the same enthusiasm and energy. "I envy your father. I wish I could go away. I can't stand it anymore. Four more months before we're going to be free from this school."

"It will be different next year, Ronnie."

Ronnie sighed. "Four more years of school in Tel Aviv. Still, we'll have to come back here every night."

"I wouldn't like to stay in Tel Aviv. I like my room."

"This place is just so confining, Zohara! My sister Lily is planning to study biology as soon she's out of the army. I'm so jealous of her. I can't wait to go to the army. I'm so fed up with school. But you love it, Zohara. You're so good at it."

Zohara didn't say that at the moment she wasn't in the mood for going anywhere and didn't feel she was good at anything. Instead, she said, "Some classes, but not biology."

A horse and wagon full of manure passed them on the road. The wagon hit a bump and lost some cargo. Zohara and Ronnie inspected their legs and laughed with relief. Safe.

"Can you come over after school?" Ronnie asked.

"Not today. I'm going to Shoshi's."

Ronnie spoke with as much sarcasm as she could muster. "No dance classes for our princess?"

Not all of her friends liked Shoshi. Fourteen years old and Shoshi was already known as a talented dancer. She performed for all major celebrations in Shomriya. For the last three years there had been no school event or Independence Day celebration when Shoshi had not been invited to show off her talents.

Zohara was looking forward to going to Shoshi's house for dinner. She liked Shoshi's father. He was known in Shomriya as Mr. Abarbanel. On the phone, and when he first met people, Shoshi's father always introduced himself formally by his last name. Some people in town talked about him as distant, or even haughty. Zohara liked his formality. She said none of this to Ronnie. "I can come over on Friday," she offered.

Ronnie said, "Okay," but went on, "You must like to go to Shoshi's. She is practically family to you."

Zohara did not argue. The Abarbanels were like family. Yair Sasson, her grandfather, and Sammy Abarbanel had grown up together in a tightly-knit Sephardi community in the Old City in Jerusalem. Her grandfather was fifteen years older than Sammy and had been like an older brother to him. Both families were descended from Spanish Jews who had been exiled from Spain in the 15th century. Shoshi had an intense interest in her family's Spanish roots.

The last period for the eighth grade on that day was Jewish history, which Zohara loved. Some twenty minutes into the class Shoshi raised her hand. "Why is this period in Jewish history called 'The Expulsion from Spain'?"

"Okay, Shoshi. What would you call it?" Yehuda Manor, the new, young teacher, asked.

Shoshi pulled on a strand of her thick hair and looked defiantly at Yehuda. "I don't know. It's just that we use polite words to talk about cruelty. You just told us that thousands of Jews were killed when they refused to convert and become Catholics. They were forced to leave Spain, a country to which they had made all these contributions in science, medicine, philosophy, and commerce."

Yehuda Manor said calmly, "Go on."

"So for hundreds of years, Jews are Spanish and then one day, boom, finished, it's all over?" Shoshi pounded her hand on her desk. "They were told that they were the enemy. Not because they betrayed the king or something like that. Just because they were Jews, and not Catholics. And these royals told them, 'Convert, get out, or die.' Not very attractive options."

The whole class was suddenly paying attention. Finally, some real excitement after a long, uneventful day. Girls stopped passing notes. Boys stopped looking for erasers to throw at tired, unprotected backs. Was Shoshi going to make a fool of herself?

For a split second Shoshi seemed as though she was about to stop. But she took a deep breath and went on. "So, to me the word 'expulsion,' in our very own text, is just too bland. It doesn't include the deaths, torture, forced conversion. We make it sound almost nice, like expelled from school, or something." A girl giggled briefly in the back. No one joined.

Shoshi looked very angry. Kids looked from Shoshi to the teacher. They all knew her. But Yehuda Manor had just recently joined the faculty, when their old history teacher fell off a ladder and broke some bones.

Zohara's heart went out to Shoshi. Some of the girls looked gleeful, hoping that Shoshi would now be humiliated, or at least reprimanded. But unlike his predecessor, Yehuda did not seem to take Shoshi's outburst as a challenge to his authority.

"Shoshi. You seem to really care about the issue, and you have a good point. If you can come up with a better term to capture that period to replace the term 'expulsion' in our textbook, we'll write to the author, Professor Jacob Katz at the Hebrew University, and suggest something more appropriate."

After their last class, Zohara and Shoshi walked out together. "Why were you so mad at the teacher?"

"Zohara. You just don't get it."

"What?"

"That we, Sephardi Jews, are not seen as important as Ashkenazi Jews. What makes eastern European Jews think that they are better than us? Can you explain it to me? Ashkenazi Jews think we are inferior." Shoshi's hair seemed to fly in all directions.

Zohara was about to say, 'But this whole town admires you, you are the local star, and all the boys are in love with you.' But what came out instead was, "Inferior?"

"What do you think they mean when they say that Jews from Yemen or Morocco or Syria are 'primitive'?"

Zohara put her thumbs under her satchel straps, held on to them, and began to walk very fast. She felt a pounding in her head.

Shoshi was just as fast. She wasn't done. "Professor Katz who wrote our history book comes from Eastern Europe, from Hungary. I checked it out. He is Ashkenazi. So, he isn't shocked by what happened to Sephardi Jews in the fifteenth century. Why is it, Zohara, that you can't see it?"

What Zohara wanted to say was, 'What do you know about seeing? Do you see an undeveloped body in the mirror when you look at your body?"

She was planning to tell Shoshi about it. But right now she felt that their friendship, like a punctured balloon, was losing air. A divide she could not put into words invaded their walk. "Shoshi, I don't want us to fight. Can we just forget about it?"

Zohara had not expected to cry. But there it was, a flood of uninvited tears. No wonder her body was immature.

Shoshi seemed surprised and upset. "Zohara, I'm sorry. I forgot that Malka and your mom are Ashkenazi. Honestly. I love your mom; I think she's great. I think of you as one of us because of your grandfather, may he rest in peace." She took Zohara's hand and held it. "You. You look, you know, more Sephardi. Oh, I don't know what I'm saying. Let's just forget about it. Let's go to Mendel's and get a soda. My treat. And if you really want to, we can peek and see if Shlomo has some new books you're interested in." She let go of Zohara's hand. She pulled her hair into a rubber band. "I'm just so dumb."

Zohara was ashamed of crying. She blew her nose discreetly. Shoshi, she realized, misunderstood her crying. She simply could not tell Shoshi how miserable she felt.

Shoshi was kicking a stone, moving it along like a ball.

Zohara said, "No. No bookstore today. I have enough to read, and besides I just started *Gulliver's Travels*."

Zohara could smell the asphalt. It was hot and she was sweaty. "Let's go to Mendel's. A soda sounds great."

The café was quite empty and the large jacaranda trees offered plenty of shade. As soon as they sat down, Mendel came over. "Well, lovely ladies, what can I get for you?" Zohara wanted a simple grapefruit soda. Shoshi ordered the same.

Mendel raised his hand to chase away the bold sparrows picking food from the tables. A cloud of birds rose and with a loud and chaotic chirp settled on the jacaranda branches, waiting patiently for Mendel to go back inside. Mendel wiped the table with a clean rag. He said to Zohara, "Your mother was here for lunch with Iris. How is Malka doing without your help today?"

"Grandma will be fine. Jacob probably came by and helped her out."

After school, Zohara often went over to her grandmother's place. She liked farm work almost as much as she liked reading books or going to Shoshi's house. She knew that her grandmother could hire all the help she needed. But she didn't. She would tell Zohara, "We need to redeem the land with our own hands. Every time you start working, just dig your hands slowly in the ground and feel the soil breathing through your fingers."

Malka would stretch out her voice and inhale as she said the word *breathing*.

Mendel came back and placed two tall glasses and two straws on the table. He asked Shoshi, "How is the Abarbanel family doing? I'm going to give you some pastry for your mother." He went back into the café and returned with a large bag. "Mrs. Abarbanel's specials."

On the way home Shoshi said to Zohara in mock conspiracy, "Mendel is in love with my mom." She gave Zohara a light elbow push. "Don't look so shocked, I'm not serious."

"I know you were kidding." Zohara was hurt. Did Shoshi consider her too young to understand adult stuff? If she were wearing a bra, would Shoshi still treat her the same way? As they entered the Abarbanels' house she saw Pnina. Zohara forgot how upset she was.

"Look who's here! Zohara. Let me look at you. You seem to grow up so fast, and of course you just celebrated your thirteenth birthday."

Zohara thought that Pnina Abarbanel, with her black hair, smoldering black eyes, and dark eyebrows, was beautiful. She was always impeccably dressed even at home. On that day, she wore a lovely beige dress and a string of corals.

Pnina wanted to know if she could offer them a snack. Shoshi handed her Mendel's cookies, and the girls went to Shoshi's room at the other end of the house. Zohara felt calmed by the Abarbanels' house. It was, by Shomriya standards, large and elegant, full of beautiful Oriental carpets, antique furniture, and colorful pillows. As they passed through the living room Zohara bent down and very lightly touched a silk runner on the coffee table.

When Mr. Abarbanel came home, Zohara and Shoshi went into the dining room. It was a large room with a dark, glossy table. Mr. Abarbanel always sat at the head of the table and his wife sat at the other end. Pnina turned to her son. "Daniel, please get a chair for Zohara."

Daniel placed Zohara's chair next to his. Zohara hoped that no one noticed how pleased she was.

She liked the Abarbanel boys, the identical twins, Jonathan and Micah, Yehuda who at age eight was shy, and Benjamin, the youngest, who had explained to Zohara how electricity worked. And she loved Daniel.

Zohara had not forgotten what Shoshi had said earlier about Ashkenazi contempt for Sephardi Jews. Mr. Abarbanel, like her grandfather, was a seventh-generation offspring of a Jerusalem Sephardi family, the pillar of the Jewish community in Palestine until the 1920s. That counted for something. And what about the fact that Zohara's grandfather and Sammy Abarbanel had joined the Zionist pioneers who came from Eastern Europe? Did they not all work in the pre-state years to make Palestine a homeland for

Jews? Why hadn't she thought of that earlier? She could have pointed it out to Shoshi.

Shoshi was wrong. No one in Shomriya thought of them as inferior. Sammy was a successful businessman, importing agricultural machinery and farm equipment. It was rumored that Sammy Abarbanel had enlisted the help of his relatives, scattered all over the globe, from Alexandria to Paris and as far as the Americas, to buy arms for the *Haganah.*

Pnina offered seconds of her yogurt soup and passed around the bread. When Daniel passed the breadbasket, his fingers touched Zohara's hand ever so lightly. Zohara felt a tingling, like the pleasant shiver that comes from the first cool evening breeze after a warm day.

"Mr. Abarbanel. What was my grandfather like when he was young?"

"Your grandfather had a reputation in our community as a promising scholar. His family hoped that their only son would go to France and study in a Yeshiva and come back to be a rabbi in Jerusalem."

"My grandfather? A rabbi? But he didn't become one…"

The twins wanted some juice. Daniel reached to pour for them. Speaking, as usual, in the plural, they protested, "We can do it."

Mr. Abarbanel settled it. "Let Daniel do it now. Next time you do it yourselves."

Mr. Abarbanel turned to Zohara. "Obviously the Sasson family was disappointed when Yair said that he would not study to be a rabbi but instead would fight for Jews to have a state."

Shoshi collected the soup bowls and took them to the kitchen. Zohara got up to help her put them away and bring in the salad and a tray of cheese.

When they sat down again, Shoshi surprised her. "Dad. Tell us more about Zohara's grandfather."

Mr. Abarbanel first helped Benjamin make a cheese and olive sandwich. Benjamin loved olives with everything. When he had enough olives on his cheese he put on another piece of bread. Mr. Abarbanel cut it in half and spoke. "Zohara's grandfather liked to quote from Holy Scripture. He quoted Ecclesiastes and said that for everything there was a season. The time had come for a Jewish national liberation movement."

Mr. Abarbanel looked around. "He told us that to convince his parents, he quoted from the prayer book, from the Amidah Prayer." Now Mr. Abarbanel took on his deep, beautiful, chanting synagogue voice. "Sound the great shofar to announce our freedom. Lift a banner to gather our exiles and reunite our people scattered in the four corners of the earth."

Zohara tried to reconcile the grandfather who recited sacred texts with the one who had married Malka and become a secular Jew. She liked to go to synagogue. Had it something to do with her grandfathers? One had been a rabbi in Poland, the other had been designated to be one and refused.

Her parents, like most Shomriyans, were secularists. They believed that being Jewish had a national, not a religious, significance. Zohara's grandmother, who called herself an atheist, said that Zionism was a liberation movement responding to European anti-Semitism. It was going to give Jews a secular home in Zion – without oppressive religious practices. Malka had often told Zohara, "Until the Zionist movement, we were a nation without a home. Now we are a nation in our own state. Those who still want to hold on to antiquated religious practices are welcome to it. Not me."

Pnina turned to Zohara. "Would you like to come to synagogue with us to hear Daniel? He reads Torah so beautifully."

Zohara, sitting in the middle between these two opposing views, needed to make a choice. But before she could say anything Pnina suggested, "Why don't you talk to your parents and see what they say."

Benjamin and the twins excused themselves. It was Yehuda's turn to clear the table.

Mr. Abarbanel asked Zohara, "Did your father go to Jerusalem to work on the Buber book?"

Before Zohara was aware of it, she blurted out, "He was going to meet this Knesset man, Zev Shai. So he won't have much time for the book "

"Your father is following his late father in writing the Buber book."

Mr. Abarbanel filled his glass with water and took a sip. "Martin Buber was Yair's hero on the issue of a bi-national state. I didn't agree with your grandfather. Most of us didn't agree with Buber. Your grandfather accepted the majority decision to have a separate Jewish state. I respected him for it."

In the hush that settled in the room the doorbell rang. Jonathan ushered Rena in. Mr. Abarbanel rose to greet her. "Good to see you, Rena. We were just talking about your father-in-law. How are you? I hear that your show in Tel Aviv was a great success."

Her mother looked pleased. "I certainly enjoyed doing the show."

Shoshi gave Rena her place and went to fetch an extra chair. Pnina gave Rena a plate and urged her to eat.

"You look so pale, Rena."

When everyone, including Zohara, laughed, Pnina joined them and said, "I don't mean fair, I mean pale. You look a bit tired, dear. You work too hard." Then, to everyone's surprise, Pnina said that if Rena's art class was at a more convenient time, she might take it.

Rena flashed a big smile. "Are you sure? Next time I could schedule the class earlier. I'd love to have you in my class."

"I never had art when I went to school."

The twins and Benjamin came back for dessert. Benjamin gave Rena a kiss. "I want to sit next to Rena." Shoshi moved over.

Pnina told her, "Your show was wonderful."

Shoshi added, "The whole town was there."

Everyone laughed because whatever disagreements people in Shomriya had, they always saw themselves as loyal and united. They believed that when push came to shove, Shomriyans staunchly defended their own. If Rena had a show in Tel Aviv, Shomriyans would show city people that Shomriya produced art.

Shoshi recounted how official Shomriyans had showed outsiders Rena's painting in City Hall and told them how the artist had arrived at seventeen, a girl with soft hands from Krakow, to work in the orchards in Shomriya.

They laughed at the town, at themselves. They loved their town. For a moment Zohara felt happy.

The twins, white powdery sugar around their mouths, said, "We came to your show. Can we to come to your art class?"

"In the summer I offer a class for kids. I'd love to have you."

When Zohara and her mother were standing at the door Mr. Abarbanel joined them and said to Zohara, "I am so glad you came to dinner. You gave me an opportunity to talk about Yair. I miss him. Give my warm regards to Malka." He turned quietly to Rena, and almost in a whisper, said, "When Benny comes back, please ask him to get in touch with me."

CHAPTER EIGHT

"Mom, who is this man Zev that Dad is meeting tonight?" They had just stepped out of the Abarbanel house. Zohara had not planned to bring up his name, but there it was. She could see that her mother was startled.

Rena took Zohara's hand, squeezed it, and kept holding it. "He is the new member of the Knesset for our party. You know that Boaz Artzi died suddenly three weeks ago."

"He came to our house a few times."

"He had a heart attack and died unexpectedly."

"How sad."

"Zev was next on the party's list."

"So Zev is not as smart as Artzi?"

"Zev is smart. No question about that..."

Zohara's worries were not over. "Mom, are you also afraid that Dad is in some kind of danger?"

Rena stopped, faced Zohara, and took her other hand. "No, of course not. Why would anyone want to hurt your father?"

For the second time that day, Zohara cried. Only this time, with her mother right there, she let herself go. She sobbed. Rena walked with her to a nearby empty bench. Zohara was glad that the street, not yet dark, was empty. She would not have to be humiliated, reduced to the most childish position.

Zohara and her mother sat there for a while. It was a pleasant twilight hour, bringing with it a cool breeze. Rena took off Zohara's satchel and spread her sweater over Zohara's shoulders. She hugged her tightly. Zohara stayed under her mother's arm and managed to blow her nose. "Grandma is afraid. She said so last night. She didn't exactly say it. But I could tell."

Rena wiped Zohara's tears with her hand, kissed her cheek, and said softly, "We need to talk with you about Dad's article. Tomorrow night when he comes home, we'll talk."

Zohara did not want to talk about that article. She did not want to bring it up or know anything about it. She wanted to go home, say goodnight to Malka and Vashti, sit in her favorite place, and read *Gulliver's Travels*. Reading her mind, her mom said, "Let's go home and read a chapter in your book."

It was a clear evening, not a cloud in the sky. When it got dark, the streetlights came on. They cast a pale pure glow that made Shomriya look peaceful.

Zohara and her mother greeted the people who were now coming out for an evening walk. A few wanted to talk to Rena about the town meeting. Zohara was grateful that they had not been out earlier when she was crying.

When they got home, Zohara crossed the street to see her grandmother.

Malka was pleased to see her. She took her hand and held it.

"I missed you. No matter how good Jacob is, no one is as good with Vashti as you."

"I'll take her out tomorrow."

"Oh, she'll like it. So how is Mr. Abarbanel?"

"He sends his regards."

Her grandmother was coughing. Zohara was not sure whether Malka liked Mr. Abarbanel. She wondered if Malka could be jealous because he had all these stories about Yair before he met Malka. But that night, because of Shoshi's earlier outburst, Zohara had a new idea. Did Malka think that the Abarbanels did not like her because she was not Sephardi? Or because she fought for women's equality, built roads, worked in construction, and liked being a farmer?

Malka took some chocolate out of a round tin box. "I saved it for you."

Zohara thought of how her grandparents had left the kibbutz because of Malka. She and Yair had left kibbutz Kalaniyot because her grandmother complained of sex discrimination. She had told Zohara that Yair's friends blamed her for their leaving.

In Zohara's mind, her grandparents settling in Shomriya meant that her grandfather loved Malka. When she said this to her father, he laughed. "You are absolutely right. My father would have followed her to the end of the world. Luckily, they both wanted to farm in Shomriya."

The dogs started barking and Vashti brayed, a message to Zohara. It was quiet in the kitchen.

"Grandma. Why did you come to Shomriya?"

Malka offered her another chocolate and said, "You know the story."

"I know. But tell me again."

She put an elbow on the table and her face in her hand. She could feel the ring of her other grandmother.

"After your father was born, the kibbutz did not allow me to return to work in the fields. It decided that as a woman it was now my duty to work in the communal children's house, or the kitchen, or do other domestic chores. 'It is a mother's duty.' These were the words they used. I could not see what my love for my son had to do with farming."

Malka tucked her hair behind her ears, showing her strong cheekbones. "Their true prejudice was loud and clear; a woman's place is in the home. Just like the bourgeois. The truth was out: where women's rights were concerned, the socialists were no better than the capitalists."

"What did Grandpa say?"

"Your grandfather said I had a right to go back to agricultural work. But the majority rejected my request."

Malka told Zohara that she had hoped to shame the kibbutz. At every meeting, she reminded them that times were changing for women. She read from international feminist manifestoes; she told them that women in Germany and in the United States had gained the right to vote. But she failed. The vote in the kibbutz was against her.

"I cried a lot. I wanted to stay, but on my terms. So, we left and bought this land in Shomriya."

"And my dad went to school here?"

"I worked in the fields and when he came back from school your father was at my side."

She looked at Zohara. "Now I'm a happy woman again. I have a granddaughter who loves the land."

Zohara could see the purpose of weeding and imagined that the plants were grateful. "We have the best conversations when I work with you."

Her grandmother got up, filled the kettle, turned the gas on. "Would you like some hot chocolate?"

"Not tonight. I'm going to say goodnight to Vashti and go home. Grandma, did the Sasson family feel sad when Grandpa didn't want to be a rabbi?"

Malka turned the gas off. She wiped her hands on a striped towel that hung on a small white hook.

"I think that they were disappointed. We can talk about it some more when you are not so tired."

"Okay…"

Malka looked sad. Zohara went over and hugged her. Real tight. Right into Malka's shoulder she whispered, "Do you miss Grandpa?"

Malka whispered back into Zohara's hair, "Yes. I miss him very much."

Zohara and her grandmother walked to Vashti's stall. The donkey looked old, waiting patiently; her ears moved as she picked up the visitors' approach. Zohara hugged her neck. "I love you, Vashti. Don't die yet." Vashti responded with a raspy but brave bray, rousing the neighborhood dogs. "You see, you still have a lot of life in you, Vashti. You got the dogs excited."

Her grandmother walked Zohara back to her house and kissed her goodnight.

Zohara washed her face and hands, brushed her teeth, and put on her nightgown. She looked in the mirror. Even in this lovely nightgown with pink lace around the collar, she did not look alluring or fascinating. What she saw was only her own childish, skinny face. Zohara sighed. She went to her room, got *Gulliver's Travels,* and went out to the living room. She gave the book to her mother who was already settled on the sofa.

Zohara took the red afghan, covered herself, and curled in her chair to listen to her mother read. She did not have her father's deep voice. But her mother had a talent for acting and she captured Lemuel's feelings. "The last of these voyages not proving very fortunate, I grew weary of the sea, and intended to stay at home with my wife and family." On these last words Zohara felt her eyes closing. She, like Gulliver, was exhausted.

Rena suggested that she go to bed. Her mother pulled the blankets around her and kissed her goodnight as she had done when Zohara was a little girl. It was probably because of her crying earlier. The moment of feeling grown-up on her birthday had evaporated. On the way out of the room her mother said, "Oh, I forgot. Iris left a framed photograph from your birthday." Zohara asked her mother to put the picture on her desk so that it faced her as she fell asleep. Her parents looked happy.

***

Rena had a pile of books on the nightstand. She picked up Maurice Nadeau's *The History of Surrealism*. Instead of opening the book, though, she listened to the radio: Brahms's Piano Concerto Number Two.

She hoped that listening to the music would help her fall asleep. Instead, she felt restless. She had thought that Zev was out of her life when she left Oz. Seventeen years, and she had not forgotten a thing. Poor Rachel.

Rena went to the kitchen, poured milk into a pan, and warmed it. She added honey and drank the milk slowly. She wished they had a phone so that she could call Benny in Jerusalem.

There were very few telephones in Shomriya. The Abarbanels had one, and so did their neighbors who lived a few houses down the street. If anyone wanted to reach one of the neighbors, they could call Yael and Yitzhak Ramot.

It was understood that people would not abuse the phone privilege and that calls would be made judiciously for urgent messages, good or bad news, a birth, a death, an accident.

She missed Benny and wanted to hear his voice. She fell asleep with the radio playing and the lights on.

"Rena." She heard an urgent voice and a persistent knock on the door. She looked at the clock. It was ten minutes past midnight.

CHAPTER NINE

"Rena. It's Mike." She was very frightened. Why would Mike, who lived in Tel Aviv, come to Shomriya in the middle of night? She went to the door against her will, like a sleepwalker. Under the dim outside light she saw Mike and Sarah, his wife.

Rena turned on the porch light. They stood there looking anxious. She felt her heart careening out of control. "I know it's after midnight. There's no reason to think the worst, but I thought I'd better come and tell you. Benny hasn't checked into the hotel in Jerusalem. He didn't show up for his meeting with Zev." Mike had rehearsed these words all the way from Tel Aviv.

Sarah put an arm around Rena. "There's no reason to panic, we don't know what happened. But Mike and I thought..."

Before Sarah could finish, Mike said, "The police have been contacted and they're already working on it."

Like the heavy hail that threatened her garden in early spring, their voices swirled around her. Rena refused to catch a single word. She just wanted her guests to be a dream from which she would wake up. She would open her eyes, be in her bed, and Mike and Sarah would disappear. Instead, Malka appeared from across the street. Oh, Malka. Don't come. Please don't come.

Malka walked toward her, ghostlike in a long white cotton nightgown, her white hair flying around her face. Mike shifted his weight from side to side. He began to breathe audibly through his nose. To Malka he said, "It's not as bad as it looks, but you should sit down."

Malka paid no attention to him. She walked up to Rena. "What happened?"

Rena just fell into her arms and began to sob. Shaking, she pressed herself against Malka's body.

Hide me. Cover me. Shelter me. Malka kept her arms around her.

Mike spoke again. "We don't know where Benny is right now. The police are looking. There must be some explanation."

Malka and Rena walked together to the bench. Rena put a fist in her mouth. She felt a scream inside her. Malka looked at Mike, her lips trembling but her voice steady. "Tell me what you really know, Mike. I want to know what happened to my son."

Sarah asked, "What can I do? Rena, can I do something?"

Rena managed to speak in a hoarse whisper. "Sarah, do you know where Iris lives? Could you go get her?" Sarah nodded, and Mike handed her the car keys.

Mike pulled a chair and sat very close to the two women, his knees almost touching Malka's. He tried to sound reasonable and calm. "Benny left the office at two in the afternoon to go to

Jerusalem. We're pretty sure that he got on the bus. The police will check it. He didn't show up at the hotel, or at the Knesset for his dinner with Zev Shai."

Rena let Malka do all the talking. "The police. Who notified the police?"

Mike looked at the floor. "Zev did. He used his position to get the police going right away, or they would have considered it a missing person case for the time being. Which it probably is..."

This was no bad dream. Rena needed to protect herself against the onslaught of empty words that would come again and again. Unwelcome waves of useless talk.

Malka spoke in anger now. "Don't be a fool, Mike. Missing person. Benny was never missing from life. From the time my son was a little boy he was always present, reliable, and exactly where he should have been. He would have left a message for Zev or for the hotel. Something happened to my son. The sooner we know the facts, the better."

Mike sat on her porch and rocked back and forth.

"Malka, here are the facts. Benny came to the office this morning. We talked for a few minutes. I had a new assignment for him, but he was going to meet with Zev. I left the office around noon. I had a lunch appointment. When I came back to the office, Benny was gone. At ten, Zev called my house, worried. Benny hadn't shown up at the Knesset. He'd waited until eight thirty. He called Hotel Tikva and was told that Benny had not registered. He asked the clerk to call him if Benny showed up."

"My son would have called, left a message..."

"You want the facts. An hour later, when Zev had heard nothing, he called the police. Then he called me. He said he would have called you, Rena, but you don't have a phone. He said to tell you that if you need anything, anything at all, don't hesitate to call him. He thought that it was too early to jump to conclusions. He'll be in touch with the police. "

Mike was trying to get comfortable in a too small chair. He got up and sat in a larger chair.

As soon as Mike mentioned Zev, Rena became attentive. She sat up straight. She gathered, one by one, all of Mike's words, storing them carefully in her mind. She must from now on listen carefully.

Malka steadied her voice. "Mike, I know that you are my children's friend. I am asking you to use your influence and get a police officer to come and give us an account of what he knows...we need answers."

"I promise you, Malka, I will do my best."

The silence on Herzl Street was interrupted by Sarah's approaching car.

Iris came in, and without looking at Mike went over to the bench. Rena got up and the two hugged, Iris patting her back. Iris was crying. Sarah sat in a chair next to Mike and took his hand. Malka now sat very straight and looked at her.

"Sarah, I want you to hear what I am about to tell Mike. I'll raise heaven and earth. I'll use all my connections to get to the truth of what happened to my son."

Mike put a hand on his heart. "Malka, I know that this is very difficult. But we don't know yet what happened. You seem to assume the worst. But it's been only a few hours. Benny is just missing."

"Were you ever 'missing'? What kind of nonsense is this? A man leaves his office in Tel Aviv at two in the afternoon and doesn't show up at his hotel in Jerusalem or for an appointment at six. Benny wouldn't cancel an appointment without letting anyone know. It is already the next day. Something terrible has happened to my son."

With all her heart Rena wanted to believe there was a reasonable explanation, but knowing Benny as she did, she knew that Malka was right. There was no reasonable explanation. She had known it from the moment she saw Mike on her porch.

"Mike, I think that you and Sarah should go home and get some sleep. We're grateful for your help."

Sarah reassured her. "We can stay as long as you need us."

Rena went over and touched Sarah lightly on the arm. "I know, Sarah. I know. But right now, there is nothing to do but wait for more information." She looked at Mike. "What I need from you, Mike, is that if you have any news, anything, call the Ramot house. This is an emergency. They won't mind. Please don't let anyone go into Benny's office. Promise me that you'll go from here straight to the office and lock the door." She did not avert her eyes.

Mike sighed, looked at the floor, and said in an aggrieved voice, "What if the police want to search?"

"The police will do what they need to do. Just please give me your word that you will lock Benny's office. When I can get to Tel Aviv, we will go into his office together."

Sarah patted his knee and he looked at Rena. "I'll do whatever I can."

Sarah stood up and almost pulled Mike out of his chair. "I am not a journalist. But if you want me to come with you to Benny's office, Rena, I'll be glad to."

Rena was surprised. Sarah usually deferred to Mike. "Yes, Sarah, I'd like it very much for you to come with me. I'll let you know. You should go home." Even in her agony, Rena felt Sarah's friendship.

She walked Mike and Sarah to the gate and watched as Mike heaved himself into the driver's seat and Sarah walked around to the passenger side. Rena waited for the car to leave.

***

Sarah could see Mike's hands tightly gripping the steering wheel.

"These women, they're closing ranks. I love Benny. He's one of my closest friends. They treat me as the enemy, just because I am his boss. They act as though I could have prevented it."

"Well, could you?"

Shifting gears in anger the car lurched as Mike shouted, "What?"

"I am asking. Could you have prevented it?"

"Sarah, what the hell are you talking about? We don't even know what happened."

Sarah felt a pounding in her head.

"Please, Mike, don't say it again. Malka was right. This is a small country. People don't just disappear. No one reported traffic accidents. The police already checked the hospitals. What likely explanation could there be?"

"Am I imagining it, or have you just aligned yourself with those women on the porch?"

Sarah, who had rarely contradicted Mike in their ten-year marriage, moved away from him and sat so close to the door that she seemed as though she was ready to jump out.

"You heard me, Mike. I offered to go with Rena to Benny's office and I plan to keep my promise."

"For God's sake, Sarah. You're not a journalist."

Sarah closed her eyes, but she could clearly see Rena's agony.

"I don't think that a journalist is what Rena needs when she goes into her husband's office. She needs a friend."

"We don't know what happened. And I refuse to act as though we do."

Sarah looked into the darkness and spoke straight into the chill that had settled between them. "Malka was right. Something terrible has happened to Benny."

CHAPTER TEN

Rena walked from the gate to face a porch where Benny's disappearance had established itself as an inescapable fact.

For the first time in their relationship, Rena had turned to Malka for support. And then Malka had referred to her and Benny as "my children." Not since that last letter from her parents had anyone claimed her as their child. In that moment of unbearable pain, Malka's words were an unexpected gift. Rena's heart was pounding, but her mind was clear.

She took Malka's hand. A farmer's hand that was surprisingly soft. How was it possible that in all the years she had known Malka, she had never held her hand? Well, that was not true. She did hold her hand when Yair was killed seven years ago.

"What should I say to Zohara?"

Malka was crying quietly, wiping her eyes with trembling hands.

Rena tried to clear her throat.

"I wish I had some magic. Magic to make her father's disappearance go away. What I can do is tell her, as gently as possible, the truth." Rena almost choked on the word *truth*. She stopped. It was very quiet on the porch.

In the soft light of the lamp, she saw Malka's ashen face and braced herself for the words that were already rolling in her mouth. "I have to tell Zohara that we don't know where her father is. I will tell her that the police will come to our house." She needed to breathe. A deep slow breath. "I'll wake her early, and talk to her so that she doesn't have to stumble into it..."

Rena willed herself not to let the pain rise in her body. Let it stay, for now, a knot pressing against her ribs.

"You are shivering." Iris went into the house and came back with a sweater. She put it on Rena's shoulders. It was one of Benny's. For a moment Rena felt hopeful.

While Shomriya was still sleeping, Rena wrote down everything they had heard earlier from Mike. It was a calm night, and the silence helped her concentrate. When she had finished, Rena went soundlessly into the house and brought out some blankets and pillows. The beginning of a vigil.

Bundled up, they waited for night to turn into morning.

Malka sat up straight in her chair. Rena took her hand again. It felt so cold that Rena rubbed it lightly to warm it. Malka looked at her. "You know that I didn't agree with Benny about publishing his article. But right now, it doesn't matter. It doesn't matter at all. I'm proud of my son and everything that he stands for." She stopped, took a deep breath, and in a stronger voice started again. "Mike knows something he isn't telling us."

The sun came up. It was the same sun that always lit up the front porch. It had suddenly become a space of dread and apprehension. Life from now on would be both familiar and irrevocably changed. Rena folded her blanket, picked up her pillow, and went to talk to her daughter.

***

Watching Rena go into the house, Iris turned to Malka. "I'm going to pray for Benny." Malka sat motionless, her hands resting on the blanket that covered her legs, her eyes shut. Iris knew better than to offer Malka false words of hope. She told her, "I haven't set foot in a synagogue since I left Poland. Shortly before I left, my father gave me a piece of paper on which he wrote the prayer for a safe journey. He told me to say it on the train and on the ship going to Palestine."

Malka just looked at her.

"I still have it. A yellow piece of paper with my father's beautiful writing. Every letter luminous, like a diamond. I have looked at it so many times, I know the prayer by heart."

Iris sat straight and moved her lips in prayer. Malka whispered, "Can I hear you pray?"

Iris nodded. "I'm going to make it specific to Benny. Because my father told me that even though God knows who we are, or who we pray for, it's important to mention specific names." She started in a traditional chant, "God, may your protecting love be with Benny Sasson, son of Malka and Yair, as he sets on his journey. Guard him from the perils of the way and bring him to his destination in peace. Help him to fulfill his mission without mishap, and may he return to his home in life, in joy, and in peace. Amen."

Crying quietly, Malka reached over and squeezed Iris's hand. "You really memorized it."

"It's the last thing my father gave me. It was the last time I saw him alive."

"The last time." Malka kept repeating the phrase. "The last time I saw my son I spoke in anger." A light breeze from the north window moved the sorrow in the air.

CHAPTER ELEVEN

Sleeping, Zohara looked even younger than her age. A vulnerable thirteen years old. If Rena only could turn the clock back, make Benny's disappearance go away. "Zohara, sweetheart, I need to wake you up." She sat down on her daughter's bed.

"Mom. What time is it?"

"Come here, I want to hug you. I need to talk to you."

Zohara asked again, "What time is it? It looks so early."

"It's five thirty. I'm waking you up because I need to tell you something." This was harder than she had thought. A big lump settled in her throat. It threatened her vocal cords. The words refused to come out.

Zohara sat up and looked at her mother. "Mom. Mom! What is it? What happened?"

Rena wished she didn't have to speak words Zohara would remember. She put her arms around her daughter, pulled her closer, and said as gently as she could, "It's about Dad."

"What? What happened to Dad?"

"He didn't arrive at his hotel in Jerusalem yesterday and we're worried."

Zohara started crying, holding on to Rena. "Why, Mom? Why? Where is he? What happened?"

"We don't know, sweetheart. We don't know yet. The police are looking for him."

Zohara raised her voice. "How could it happen? How could he not be in the hotel? Oh, Mom, Mom. I want him to come home."

Rena kissed her daughter's head. "I know you do."

Zohara kept crying. "Mom, please tell me that he'll come back."

"I hope so. I really hope so."

She let her daughter cry and press against her. Rena rocked her in her arms and told her how much her father loved her.

"Mom, can we go look for him?"

"The police are already doing it and they may be here soon to tell us what they know. Why don't you get dressed so that you'll be ready. Just a pair of shorts and a shirt is fine. Here, I'll get them for you."

Zohara looked not just thin, but fragile. Rena's heart broke for her daughter.

Vashti's bray came through the window and Zohara asked, "Does Grandma know?"

"Yes. She is here on the porch."

Zohara tore through the house and ran to Malka. "Why did it happen? Why?"

Malka hugged her granddaughter, holding her tight. "I don't know why it happened. Did Mom tell you that the police are looking for him?"

Zohara just nodded and cried. Iris came over and they stood there, two tall women and a girl who had already grasped the gravity of the situation.

While Malka got Zohara to sit next to her on the bench, Rena tried to focus on practical matters. They needed to eat something before the police arrived. It would be a long day and they would need their strength. Her hands were shaking as she turned on the faucet to fill the kettle. She had to try several times before she managed to light a match to turn on the gas.

She took out four cups, milk, bread, jam, and the strawberries that Malka had left the night before. She looked at her flower garden. Benny loved the fragrance of roses.

She steadied herself and with both hands held on to the table that Benny had made. She rearranged her face when she heard them come in.

She gave Zohara hot milk and a bit of coffee in it, a slice of bread and butter, some strawberries.

Malka looked at her granddaughter, who hadn't touched a thing. "Zohara, dear, I need you to go check on Vashti and give her some breakfast. The chickens also need some food and water. So please, have something to eat, and go take care of things for me."

"I can help," Iris offered. "I've never done it before, so you can show me what to do. Just in case I have to help out."

Zohara took a few sips of the sweet, diluted coffee, had three strawberries, and stood, her face frightened and tear-stained. Iris took her hand as they walked out.

Rena sat there with Malka. They were breathing each other's grief. Rena didn't turn on the radio, and in the silence of the early morning she heard a car stop at the front gate. She heard the dread in her voice. "It's the police." But when she went to the door, she saw Sammy, Pnina, and Shoshi get out of the car.

Shoshi ran and almost crushed Rena. Rena felt herself holding on to Shoshi's affection. She turned to Pnina who came through the gate looking, as usual, impeccable. She put her hand lightly on Rena's face. "My dear Rena." This was the second time that someone had claimed her. She cried.

Sammy was dressed to go to his office in Tel Aviv. Like his wife, he dressed more formally than anyone in Shomriya. Malka stepped onto the porch, still in her long white nightgown, one of Rena's shawls around her shoulders, her white hair now combed and braided. Sammy took the woman who was Yair's widow briefly in his arms. "Why, Sammy? Why?"

Sammy looked concerned and sad, but he was not the kind of man to offer useless reassurance. "I don't know yet why. But I promise you, Malka, that I will do everything I can to find out. I love

Benny. I'll be here for him and for you. You can count on it."

"Sammy, how did you find out?"

"Nathan Tovim from Hotel Tikva called. As soon as he hung up, a friend in the police called. Pnina thought that we should bring Shoshi to be with Zohara. One day out of school won't hurt her."

The Abarbanels, each in their own way, would be there for her family. There was Pnina sitting on the bench next to Malka, looking as though she was on her way to visit one of her sisters in Jerusalem, her eyes filled with sadness.

"When I woke Shoshi she got ready in two minutes. I have never seen her get up so quickly. She can stay here, and if the girls want to come over to our house, you can let them. I'll be there. I'll keep an eye on Zohara. How is she doing?"

"She is very upset. She is at Malka's, feeding Vashti."

Shoshi was off and out the gate. She remembered to close it behind.

Malka asked Sammy what his friend in the police had to say. Rena took out her notebook.

Sammy looked shrewdly at Rena. "Yes, of course. What an excellent idea."

Sammy sat down, put one leg over the other, cleared his throat, and spoke slowly. According to the friend, Zev Shai had called the police station in Jerusalem around ten last night. He had said he was concerned. A journalist, Benny Sasson, had been expected for dinner at the Knesset at six thirty. At six thirty Shai had gone to the Knesset restaurant. He saw another member of the Knesset from his party, Eli Porat, eating by himself, and asked him if he wanted to join their conversation. Porat, who knew the journalist, agreed, and the two talked while waiting for Benny.

Sammy paused. He wanted to know if he wasn't speaking too fast for Rena to write.

Rena told him that she was catching every word.

At seven thirty, when Benny still hadn't shown up, Shai decided to order something to eat. At eight, Porat left. Shai waited some more, then called Hotel Tikva and was told that Benny hadn't registered. He spoke to the clerk and asked him to call him if Benny showed up. At around ten thirty, concerned, he called the police. He had checked with the editor of *Kol Hapoel* who told him that Benny had left the office at two in the afternoon. He asked the police to try and locate bus drivers who had left Tel Aviv at that time and see if anyone had seen Benny getting on a bus. It just so happened that he, Shai, had a newspaper photograph of Benny. If the police would send someone around, he'd give them the picture. At first the police were reluctant to start a search so soon. Shai insisted that Benny's not showing up was alarming. He was very concerned, he said, and he was personally asking them to start a search right away.

Every time Rena heard Zev's name her heart pounded with anger. She waited for Malka to speak. "Sammy, what do you think? Tell me the truth."

Sammy shifted his legs and put his hands on his knees. "I want to tell you that our friend Nathan Tovim from Hotel Tikva called as well. It doesn't look good. I wish I could tell you not to worry, but I'm very concerned. I have my own connections at the police department. I know that two investigators are already on their way from Jerusalem and should be here soon. If you want me to stay, I'd like to hear what they know. When I get to my office, I'll make some phone calls."

Rena saw a police car turn onto Herzl Street. The little street had seen more cars in the last few hours than it would normally see in days.

Rena asked Sammy to stay. She closed the notebook and put it back on the table. She went to the gate. The policemen introduced themselves as Lieutenant Gad Avni and Sergeant Ari Tal.

Sergeant Tal said, "Rena Sasson and I have met before. Hi, Rena." He didn't say that he knew her quite well. Rena took her cue from him. "Hello, sergeant."

She invited them to sit on the porch, introduced Malka, and said that the Abarbanels were family and were staying. No one spelled out how exactly they were related. When the lieutenant turned to Sammy, he said, "I didn't catch your first name."

"My name is Mr. Abarbanel."

"I like to be on a first-name basis. It makes things easier."

"Yes, I can understand how it would be helpful in your profession."

Then Malka spoke. "Lieutenant, tell me everything you know. When did you first hear of it?"

The lieutenant was guarded. He seemed to think carefully about what he wanted to tell them. Pnina looked at him benignly. "Go on, lieutenant. Please. It was so good of you to come. We are ready, you can tell us everything from the beginning."

Under most circumstances, Sammy would be in charge. Would ask questions. But he just sat there like a benevolent uncle. The lieutenant straightened his shoulders and smoothed out his uniform. "I got a call last night from a member of the Knesset, Zev Shai. A brilliant politician, a future star in the Knesset, if I might add. He told me that he had just called the station to report that a journalist who was going to meet him for dinner didn't show up. Mr. Shai made it very clear to me that the journalist was the soul of punctuality."

Rena followed as closely as she could everything he said. She took notes in her head.

The lieutenant made a dramatic pause. In a light tone, Pnina said, "Please go on." He cleared his throat and spoke again. "Mr. Shai had waited, then called the hotel. He was very concerned because he had verified that Benny had left Tel Aviv. He called me personally because he wanted to make sure that the police start the search right away. He asked me to use my influence and not wait. You're all very lucky to have such an influential friend."

Pnina, still smiling, said, "Thank you, lieutenant, this is very helpful. We're all grateful."

The lieutenant looked only at the woman who was talking to him. Pnina graciously waited for him to go on.

"Well, I promised Mr. Shai to do whatever I could and called the station. My sergeant here was on duty. He is one of my best men. A search was under way. I called Mr. Shai to reassure him. He insisted that I come here in person to convey to you that the police are doing their very best."

Rena wanted to scream, "What did you find out?" But before she or Malka could speak, Pnina turned to Gad and in a gentle voice said, "With your permission, let me ask your sergeant here a question." Without waiting for an answer and still looking directly at the lieutenant but speaking to

Ari, she said, "Could you be so kind to tell us what happened at the station?"

The lieutenant said, "I'm not sure how much at liberty we are to disclose information..."

Pnina leaned a bit forward. "I know that I'm ignorant of police matters. Forgive me if I don't express myself correctly. We are a very anxious family here. Sergeant Ari was there when the call came in and when the search started. So could you please help us?"

A crow settled in the rock garden and let out loud cries. Rena took a deep breath. Pnina could have been one hell of a lawyer.

Ari looked at the lieutenant, who nodded and gestured with his hand, go ahead. But his eyes, Rena thought, warned the sergeant.

Ari looked around, met Rena's eyes, and said, "Mr. Shai told me about the scheduled visit. He hoped that Benny would show up because he hadn't called to cancel. Mr. Shai made a call to Hotel Tikva, then called Mike Lev, the editor of *Kol*

Hapoel. Mr. Shai finally called us. Mike Lev agreed that he should call the police right away because according to him, too, it was unlike Benny not to show up."

Ari looked at his superior, who motioned him to continue. "Mr. Shai suggested checking whether Benny had actually left Tel Aviv. He happened to have a newspaper photo of Benny. I said that I would come right away. I went over to the Knesset building. When I gave the guard my name, I was told that Member of Knesset Shai had gone home, but that he had left something for me. The guard handed me an envelope with a newspaper article and Benny's picture, a black and white photo; not very clear, but good enough. We got the names of several bus drivers. One of them remembered that Benny had been on his bus. He saw him get off at the central station in Jerusalem."

Sergeant Ari said quietly, "There was no doubt about it because the driver knew Benny. He was in Benny's army unit."

There was a chilling silence on the porch. Rena let out a cry. She felt as she had when she was in labor. Her legs were shaking uncontrollably. She put both her hands on her knees to keep them from bouncing.

Ari continued. "When we verified that he had gotten off the bus at the central station, we searched the neighborhood. We combed the area between the central station and Hotel Tikva, and a squad is still looking. We hope to find someone who saw Benny when he left the station. So far, nothing."

Sammy spoke in a commanding voice. "Lieutenant, is there anything else you know that sheds light on what happened?"

The lieutenant seemed to grow taller as he looked around, his eyes full of authority, speaking man to man. "Well, I am not at liberty to disclose leads, but..."

"Oh no. I'm not talking police leads. Just any idea, a clue, as to who would want to harm someone like Benny Sasson? A man who is widely loved and respected. Any idea, from your rich experience, which would give you a clue as to who would want to hurt Benny? Did Mr. Shai, who, as you said, is a brilliant man, say anything?"

The lieutenant seemed to like the fact that his special relationship with a member of the Knesset had not gone unnoticed. "Mr. Shai was baffled too. He mentioned that, well, yes, Benny was liked by some people."

"What some people?"

"The M.K. pointed out that Benny was very pro-Arab and was going to publish an article on their rights. Mr. Shai thought I needed to know it so that I could enlarge the scope of the investigation."

Sammy asked, very matter of factly, "Enlarge the scope of the investigation in what direction?"

The lieutenant was caught up in his own story. "Mr. Shai thought that not only the Jewish right who oppose Benny's ideas could be involved but also, more likely, that it could be some Arab group in Israel who objects to any attempts by Jewish leftists for a rapprochement." He seemed to enjoy giving the last word an affected French pronunciation.

Rena, agitated, was ready to say something scathing. Ari's eyes warned her. Instead of speaking, she brought her legs up onto her chair and sat hugging her shaking knees.

Sammy sounded reasonable. "Let me just clarify it for myself. Mr. Shai thought that Benny's not showing up could be the result of someone wanting to harm him because of his pro-Arab position. So, it could either be Jews on the extreme right or it could be someone in the Arab community who opposes, how did you describe it, 'rapprochement' with Jews?"

"Yes, exactly Mr. Shai's word. That's about the gist of it."

Malka sat there with her hand still on her mouth. Pnina had lost her smile.

"Thanks, lieutenant. We appreciate your coming. I'm going to give you and the good sergeant here my card. If you hear anything, anything at all, please call me immediately."

Rena could no longer help herself. "You really don't know where my husband is, or what happened to him. Do you? You have no clue at all."

The lieutenant had an injured look on his face. "Rena, if you don't mind my saying so, this is a difficult time and you're distraught. It's understandable. Mr. Shai warned me that you could get very emotional. I understand that he knows you from kibbutz Oz. But you have to believe me that we're doing everything we can to get to the bottom of it."

Before Rena could speak, Pnina walked over to her and whispered, "Don't say another word."

Sammy took the lieutenant by the arm, as though he were his dinner guest, and walked him to the gate. Ari said almost inaudibly to Rena, "I'll be in touch." And in a louder voice, "As the lieutenant said, as soon as we know more, we'll be in touch."

"An upstart, arrogant lieutenant." Rena had never heard Sammy call people names before. His anger supported her perception of the lieutenant.

For a moment, Rena laid aside her apprehension about Benny to admire Pnina. "Pnina, this Jerusalem family of yours raised one shrewd woman."

Malka apparently was also impressed. "Well, Pnina, you sure handled that lieutenant very well. I would have antagonized him in a second, but you ran circles around him."

Pnina looked around. "We're family. That's what family is for."

To Rena, kinship terms like family were suddenly precious and painful. She wanted to hear them and could hardly bear it. She went inside and got some lemonade and glasses and offered Pnina and Malka a drink. She looked at the rock garden and there under the prickly pear was the same turtle she had seen the day before. It was hard to believe it was only yesterday that she had started her drawing. It felt like another lifetime.

Rena took the pad and wrote down all that she had heard. She felt that having what people said in writing was necessary... If Zev was involved, she had no doubt about his skill in obscuring and altering the facts, in lying and deceiving and getting away with it. She'd seen him do it in Oz, fifteen years before, as a young outsider in a kibbutz. What could he do now when he was powerful and had parliamentary immunity?

Malka and Pnina were talking quietly. She sat listening to the women's voices and looked at her drawing still on the easel. It looked helpless, suspended, unfinished.

CHAPTER TWELVE

Standing in her grandmother's barn, Zohara saw the police car stop across the street. Two police officers got out. Iris, who was standing on the other side of the barn, came over.

"Do you want to go back to the house?"

Zohara shook her head. She did not want to hear anything they had to say. She was glad to be right there with Iris in Vashti's stall surrounded by the familiar smells of hay, grain, and donkey manure.

Zohara did not mind cleaning up after Vashti. She scooped the dung into a special bucket. The donkey made a contribution to fertilizing Malka's garden. Zohara usually complimented Vashti, but right then her heart was not in it. She went out and put the dung in a compost barrel at the edge of the garden. When she returned to the barn, she saw that the police car was still there. 'Just find my father,' she begged silently.

She had just finished cleaning the stall when Shoshi burst in.

Shoshi came over and hugged her tightly. "I'm going to stay with you today."

Zohara had just composed herself enough to do her chores. With Shoshi there, she started crying again. "I want my father to come home, Shoshi. That's all I'm asking. That's not too much, is it?"

Shoshi would not let go of her. She now grabbed Zohara's hand and held it so tight it almost hurt. "No, of course not. I'm so sorry about what I said yesterday. Making you feel like your family is not really Sephardi. I just have a big mouth, Zohara. I love your dad."

Zohara went over to put grain in Vashti's trough. Unlike yesterday, she did not care if Shoshi or anyone else saw her crying. She just wanted to stay there feeding Vashti, with Iris next to her and

Shoshi talking about her father. It made him feel real and present.

Vashti brayed. The old donkey was hungry. Zohara took the shiny copper bucket off a hook and walked over to the feedbags in the corner. As she opened the flaps of a burlap sack, a small cloud of powdery grain and a pungent smell slowly rose. Zohara went to the trough and poured grain for Vashti's breakfast. With her hand she piled it in front of the donkey. Vashti licked her hand, sniffed, grunted, and started to eat with obvious enthusiasm.

Zohara said in a near whisper, "My dad says that food is the only thing Vashti can still enjoy. I tell him that she also likes to bray and that she loves it when I brush her."

She cleared her throat. "Iris, when you feed her, you shouldn't give Vashti too much, she'll eat it all. She doesn't know what's good for her. She doesn't like to exercise anymore. Sometimes she looks at me, begging, and I want to give her more.

But she's already overweight. So, I give her just one bucket."

Iris seemed to absorb the information. "I'll do things exactly the way you do. I won't let Vashti talk me into giving her more than she needs."

For some reason Iris's words calmed Zohara. They watched the donkey lick the bottom of the trough.

Shoshi looked at Vashti and carefully patted her neck. "Does she still like fruit? Does Iris know that this crazy donkey loves fruit? She'll even eat guava. Won't she, Zohara?"

Zohara wiped her face with the back of her hand and stood there inhaling the barn. "Vashti has a sweet tooth."

Shoshi wanted to know what next.

"I'm going to take her out and walk her for a while."

Iris looked at one of the beams where the bridle was hanging. "Do you want me to get it down for you?"

Zohara shook her head, no. "We no longer use the bridle. It hurts her mouth."

Out of the stall and in the yard, Vashti looked gray and frail. She seemed a bit dazed by the sun. For a moment she looked as though she was planning to return to the barn, her eyes pleading old age. 'Vashti, you must be here for me,' Zohara begged silently. She thought of the photograph showing a younger, more vigorous Vashti. Zohara was a toddler sitting in the saddle. Her father was standing next to Vashti, smiling. On the back of the black and white photo her father's clear handwriting read, 'Zohara's first solo ride on her second birthday. April 1, 1944.'

Zohara cried again. Iris took out a clean handkerchief, wet it at the outside sink, and brought it to Zohara. She placed it on her swollen and puffy eyes. The wet cold handkerchief felt good.

When her father taught her how to ride a bike, Vashti came over and pushed the bike. Not as hard as she could but hard enough to get Zohara off balance. Her father said that Vashti was jealous. She saw the bike as competition.

Shoshi went over and stood close to Vashti's ears. "Like the biblical Queen Vashti who refused to obey the king, you too have a mind of your own. Good for you." Vashti seemed to like that. She raised her head a bit and had a spark in her dim eyes.

Iris told them that she hated taking care of chickens, disliked the noise and the smell, but wanted Zohara to show her around anyway.

They took baskets for collecting eggs and went into the chicken coop. Shoshi said, "Zohara! How can you stand it? Iris is right. It stinks in here."

To Zohara it was farm smell. But Shoshi's being there was a huge sacrifice. In all the years they had known each other, Shoshi had not come near the chicken coop. Zohara wanted Shoshi to know that she understood how she felt. "Just be careful with the eggs. This is not the place to scramble them. Pick them up one by one, carefully. Like this."

Shoshi laughed. It was hard to believe that she, Zohara, was teaching Shoshi something. The same Shoshi who always seemed to know everything.

Shoshi looked around. "They make so much noise. How many chickens does Malka have?"

"Around three hundred. Only she knows exactly how many. But she doesn't like to use numbers."

"Why?"

"I don't know. She just keeps certain things to herself."

Shoshi seemed to be paying attention to the way she placed the eggs in the basket, but she kept talking. "So, each chicken has her own space? It looks like a cage to me. All they do is eat, drink, and lay eggs. I wouldn't like to be a chicken. I think someone needs to invent a special air purifier for farms."

A few minutes later Shoshi called excitedly, "Zohara, Iris, I just saw this chicken drop an egg.

It's still warm, and so beautiful and perfect. It looks like porcelain. Come see."

Zohara was pleased. "See? This is farming too."

Shoshi stood there in genuine amazement. "I can't believe it. This is so beautiful; it's almost like dancing. I know what I'm going to do. I'm going to compose a dance called 'A Fresh Egg.' What do you think?" She looked at Zohara. "Oh, there I go again. Dramatizing. I don't know how you can stand to be my friend. My brain is no larger than a chicken's."

But Zohara didn't mind her friend's outburst. She really didn't. Shoshi cared about her. She liked Shoshi to be herself. But she did not know how to say this to her friend.

"No, you don't have a small brain. You're very smart. And your dancing is great."

When they had collected the eggs, the three of them brought the baskets carefully to the shed between the house and the barn. They put the eggs on a long wooden table. Zohara pulled out a bench and gave everybody a clean rag. It was peaceful in the shed. She could hear the muffled sounds of cars on the main road, the chirping of the sparrows in the lemon trees, and the rhythm of the sprinklers in the strawberry fields.

Zohara showed them how to clean any dirt that might be on the eggs. She pointed out the special scale with a container shaped like an eggcup. "The eggs need to go into separate cartons, marked extra-large, large, medium, and small. If you're not sure where to put an egg, use the scale."

Shoshi began by weighing every egg. Zohara had to smile. "You'll never finish sorting the eggs."

Shoshi looked at her and said, "You don't use the scale at all. How come?"

"It's doing it over and over — like dancing. I've done it so many times that I can tell by just looking at it. When I'm not sure, I weigh the egg."

They talked mostly about the eggs. Iris, holding a rag in one hand and an egg in the other, said, "I like cleaning them. I'll just do that and leave the sorting to you two."

When they had finished, they stacked the egg cartons neatly on the table and washed their hands in the outdoor sink.

"You have a smudge on your forehead." Zohara gave Shoshi a clean rag. Shoshi tried to remove the smudge. "Is it gone?"

"Just above your left eye. You got it."

Shoshi asked, "What happens to the eggs now?"

"Jacob will come later and take the eggs for shipping. The cracked ones we put in Malka's refrigerator. Mendel will pick them up later and use them in the café."

Shoshi wiped her hands. Zohara picked a few leaves from the lemon tree. Crushing them, she gave some to Shoshi and Iris. "This is natural farm fragrance. Rub the leaves between your palms and you'll have a nice lemon scent."

Shoshi rubbed the leaves, then put her hands to her face and inhaled. "Heavenly." She looked at Zohara the way she looked only at adults she admired.

In the middle of her anguish about her father, Zohara felt something good happening. The distance she had felt yesterday between herself and her friend was almost gone. She told Shoshi, "Don't forget the beautiful, perfect, warm egg. I saved it for you. It's not going to some store in Tel Aviv, to be gobbled up by some rich city kid." Zohara gave Shoshi a little box with yellow straw; in the middle sat a gleaming egg. "Your inspiration for the dance 'A Fresh Egg,'" she said.

Shoshi took the box and held it very carefully. "Thank you. This is just the best thing. I won't break it or scramble it. Maybe your mom can show me how to paint it and preserve it. Not today, I know. But when...there I go again, talking too much."

Shoshi looked at the egg nestling in the box and smiled. "You know something, I won't miss school at all, especially not Biology. Wait until I tell the teacher everything that I've learned here today. He will be amazed."

Iris shaded her eyes with her hand and looked around. "Are we done with morning chores?" When Zohara nodded yes, Iris said, "Shoshi is right. You do know how to run this farm. You're also an excellent teacher. Thanks for showing me the ropes. I have to go to work this morning. Are you going back to your house?"

Zohara looked at her and shook her head, no. If she went back, she would have to see her father's absence. Malka's farm, ignorant of her father's disappearance, was what she wanted.

"I'm going to do some weeding. I like to see clean rows of tomato plants." She turned to Shoshi who stood there, still holding the box, "You'll see, Shoshi, that when you crush tomato leaves, they, too, have a great scent."

"Oh good. Weeding. Some nice work outdoors, not with the smelly donkey or the stinking chickens. I haven't done much weeding in my life. It's not exactly my kind of thing. But I am a quick learner. What do you think?"

Shoshi took Zohara's hand just the way they used to when they were little, and they walked over to the tool shed to get the spades. Zohara turned her head and looked across the street. The police car was gone.

CHAPTER THIRTEEN

Iris arrived at the porch as Rena was finishing her notes. Rena put the pad away and asked how Zohara was doing.

"Zohara and Shoshi have decided to do some weeding in the vegetable garden. I hope it's all right. I'm sure they know more about it than I do."

Pnina, sitting in a comfortable armchair holding a cup of tea, looked a bit concerned. "I don't think that Shoshi knows much about gardening. I'm not sure that she won't pull out some plants."

Malka, who was usually fanatically fussy about her garden, was far from worried. "Today the girls need my good soil. It's very soothing. When they put their hands in the earth and pull the weeds, they will feel the life of the earth and it'll do them good."

Iris turned to Rena. "I have a patient at nine this morning and two after her. But I'll come back at lunch. My first afternoon patient is at two."

Rena knew that life must go on. "Thanks, Iris."

Out the window she could see a slow truck making noise on Ben Yehuda Street. A small car was trying to pass it, using the horn to no avail.

Iris was holding a glass of water. "We have been through so much together. You and Benny were there for me when Raphael was killed. I couldn't have come out of it without you. I wanted to die myself…"

Rena touched her arm.

"First I lost my whole family, and then Raphael. I did not want to live. In the end I did because you came and brought me to this porch." She waved her glass in a half circle motion around the porch.

"You brought out a mattress for me to sleep on right here." She pointed with the glass to where the bench was standing. "You had your own sorrow. Yair had been killed just a few months earlier, but you helped me. You took care of me. You too, Malka. You came every morning to sit with me before you started working. I'll never forget it."

Iris began to cry and the other women joined her. A large group of sparrows came down to look for seeds and brought the rock garden to life.

Rena walked Iris out. When she opened the screen door, the sparrows flew off. Rena and Iris walked to the gate in silence. Rena thought about how just the day before, she had stood at the gate and watched her family walk away down the street. She closed her eyes and vividly saw again Zohara's red satchel, in step with Benny's backpack. Yesterday Benny had been walking to the bus stop and she wanted to turn the clock back..

A breeze wrapped itself gently around her sorrow, infusing it with the usual mix of fragrance from the garden and a strong scent of roses.

Encouraged by the weather, the roses had suddenly decided to give their April best.

CHAPTER FOURTEEN

Sergeant Ari knew that there had been no news of Benny in the last twenty-four hours. No more information than Rena had already had in the early morning hours of Wednesday. The police had no new facts. Nothing beyond Benny's getting off the bus at the central station in Jerusalem. It seemed as though Benny had stepped off the bus and vanished.

Lieutenant Gad hinted at some political motivation. "Just a theory, mind you, but quite plausible." To support it the lieutenant stated the obvious: that the trail went cold from the moment Benny stepped off the bus.

Ari thought about the bus station. It was too small and crowded for the traffic it saw. In that tight, crowded space, no one noticed anything unusual. Benny could have just stepped into the busy street. Nathan Tovim at Hotel Tikva told Ari that Benny usually walked to the hotel. He would register, put his things in his room, and go about his business.

Sergeant Ari decided to do some legwork. He found out from Mr. Tovim that Benny would often go straight from the hotel to the nearby Hebrew University library. But what if Benny had changed his pattern and gone to the library first? Ari could not believe his good luck. At the front desk he met Abigail, a senior librarian; she said right away that she knew Benny quite well. He did not quite expect it. He had a photograph, but he did not have to use it.

In the hushed voice of libraries Abigail said, "Yes, I know Benny Sasson. He often stops at my desk to see if some material he has ordered is here."

They remained standing at the front desk. It was quite a busy place with people, young and old, checking out books, asking for assistance, or putting in requests for reading material. An irritated young voice complained rather loudly that he needed a book for an exam.

Ari wanted to know how well Abigail knew Benny.

She knew who Benny was. They talked sometimes. She also knew that he came from a well-established Jerusalem Sephardi family. She emphasized his family roots in Jerusalem.

Sergeant Ari was watching her very closely. The librarian spoke in a matter-of-fact voice and looked the sergeant straight in the eye. "A week ago, Benny called to find out if I have a copy of the resolution that Martin Buber put for a vote before the Zionist Congress in Carlsbad in September 1921."

She stopped, looked around, thought for a moment, and then went on. "The resolution called for coexistence between Jews and Arabs in Palestine. Benny mentioned that he wanted to use a quote from the document in an article he was writing about the rights of Arab workers."

She knew quite a lot about Benny's research, Ari thought. It could be because she was a good librarian; it could be that she sympathized with Benny's views. Or perhaps it was just the opposite: she knew about his research because she did not agree with his position.

She had found the document Benny wanted and expected him to pick it up on Monday, but he had not shown up. She was still holding it for him. The sergeant asked if there was really such a quote in the resolution.

"Yes," she said with great confidence. "Buber's document said that 'a deep and lasting solidarity will manifest itself between us and the working Arab people.'" She invited Ari to come to her desk. She walked the same way she spoke, sure of herself, firm. They entered a very small office and Abigail motioned for him to sit down on the other side of her desk.

Abigail opened a drawer and took out the document. Ari asked if he could borrow it and she said she would make a copy for him. "Everyone seems interested in this document," she said quietly. Abigail kept her hands on the desk. Calm hands, unvarnished neat fingernails. No wedding ring. There was a photograph of a young boy on her desk. When she saw Ari looking at it she smiled and said, "My son." That was it.

"Other people interested in Benny's request? Was there already someone else from the police department here?"

Ari was looking at the document as he spoke, but he listened very carefully to her reply.

She was calm. "No. A member of the Knesset called and asked for a copy of Benny Sasson's latest requests."

Did she sound surprised? He couldn't tell. "A Mr. Shai? Mr. Porat?"

"I don't know. One of the students who works here took the call."

"There must be a record of the request. Could you find out and let me know?"

"Sure. I'll call you." Now he looked at her directly. "Was this something that happened frequently? I mean, a person calling about someone else's research request?"

She looked at him and he saw perceptive brown eyes. "Never."

Benny's disappearance was not yet in the news. He had not told the librarian why he was there, and he noticed that she had not asked any questions. She was either discreet, or she already knew about Benny. He was going to wait and see if he needed to talk to her again. She told him to call if he had any other questions. He gave her his card. She did not ask why. She held it firmly in her left hand when she shook hands with him.

When Ari got back to the station, Abigail called. When he hung up, he called the Knesset. He didn't expect to speak to Zev Shai right away, but as soon as he identified himself, a woman who worked for Shai said, "Just a minute, the M.K. would like to speak to you." And there was Zev.

"Glad you called, sergeant. Any news?"

"Not really. We have so few leads. I know that you're personally concerned, and I wanted to assure you that we're doing everything we can to get to the bottom of it. I went to the library this morning to see if anyone saw him there. He was working on a book on Buber."

"A book on Buber? I had no idea."

"The librarian told me that you called to ask for a copy of a document Benny had requested."

There was a brief silence on the other end. Had he surprised Zev?

Zev apparently decided not to deny it. "I didn't know it was a Buber document. He told me on the phone that he was planning to go to library to get a document for the article he was writing on the rights of Arab workers. That's the article for which he was so eager to talk to me. So naturally I wanted to know what was in it."

When Ari said nothing, Zev added, "I'm, of course, not competing with the police. I'm a politician, not a detective. But given Benny's sudden disappearance, I just thought I wanted to see if I could find out some more about his work. Shed some light."

Ari was holding the phone between chin and shoulder and was taking notes. He reassured Zev. "Naturally. Any clues in the document shed light on Benny's sudden disappearance?"

Ari took a sip of tepid coffee from a mug on his desk and resumed his note-taking.

"Sergeant, I don't want to jump to conclusions here. It's too early to talk about a disappearance. But there is the issue of Benny Sasson's extreme views on Arab rights."

Zev paused. Ari made a sound to indicate that he was listening attentively. Zev continued. "The truth is that Benny wanted to revive Buber's ideas about a bi-national state. It's important to examine all leads. Excuse me. My secretary just walked in." He must have covered the phone because Ari could not hear anything. He waited and took another sip of the very bad coffee.

Zev was back. He now spoke in a brisk voice. "Sorry. I apologize. Something important is coming up on the Knesset floor so I must go. By the way, sergeant, you keep his wife Rena informed?"

"Yes, Mr. Shai, as you suggested, the lieutenant and I went to see her."

"Good. Good. I wouldn't mention any theories to her. It'll be premature without the full facts."

"I understand, Mr. Shai."

Was Benny in fact reviving the bi-national idea? Ari made a note to check Shai's whereabouts on Monday.

CHAPTER FIFTEEN

Malka arrived wearing dark pants and a blue cotton blouse, dressed neither for work nor for leisure. Rena thought to herself that if there was a dress code for this kind of unbearable waiting, no one knew what it was.

Sarah had returned to Shomriya. "Mike locked Benny's office," she reported. She had brought a large pot of chicken soup. "My mother used to make this soup for me when I was sick. This is her recipe. I always make it when I'm upset. It comforts me." She put the pot in Rena's kitchen. She greeted Malka and offered again to go with Rena to Benny's office. After a few minutes, she left.

Mendel arrived with bags in both hands. He placed them on the table and turned to Malka.

"Don't say a word. I know you, proud and stubborn. But you all need to eat, and I know how to cook. I, too, am proud. Don't ever think of shaming me by refusing."

Without his famous white apron, but with his usual efficiency, Mendel began to take out containers and with deft and experienced hands arranged the food neatly on the table.

"Mendel, you have prepared this little speech on pride in your kitchen. I wouldn't dream of refusing you. I have no illusions about my cooking. I am grateful for your food and so is my family."

Mendel was still arranging things. His eyes focused stubbornly on the table. "You don't need to say anything. I love your Benny. He was Raphael's best friend. That's all I'm going to say about how upset I am and how my heart goes out to all of you." Mendel looked around. "Where is Zohara?"

"In my backyard with Shoshi. Coping as best she can in my garden." Malka started to cry.

Mendel took one of the napkins he had just put on the table and gave it her. He took another one and quietly blew his nose. "I'll go over and give them one of my drinks and some chocolate cake. Rena, would you like me to get dishes and set the table?"

Rena felt as though Mendel had suddenly adopted her. If he had said *'tayere kind,'* in Yiddish, she could not have been more touched. "Thanks, Mendel, I'll do it. It'll keep me busy. But you go give the girls a soda. How did you find out about Benny?"

"Iris came by this morning to tell me. Everyone in Shomriya has heard about Benny. The news has spread even faster than usual."

There was no handbook for how to act after the disappearance. The Abarbanels were there even before the police arrived, Sarah returned with soup, Mendel came with food. What Rena did not know was how the rest of the town would react.

There were always the curious, the nosy, the gossipmongers.

On Thursday night Sammy came by to report that the police had suggested they run an ad in the Friday newspapers. Sammy handed her the proposed text. Rena had a hard time reading it. Her hands were shaking; she could not focus.

"Take your time, Rena. I'm in no hurry." He did not offer to read it for her. He must have known it would be worse for her to hear these excruciating words. Sammy waited.

"Benny Sasson, age thirty-six, six feet tall, black wavy hair, light brown eyes. Last seen getting off the bus at the central station in Jerusalem. He was wearing a short sleeve white shirt open at the collar, short khakis, and sandals. He carried an army knapsack and a black leather briefcase. If you have any information on his whereabouts, you are requested to get in touch with the police."

How could Benny be reduced to his mere physical appearance? How many times had Rena seen similar ads for missing persons in the paper? She had often thought, how could anyone be missing for a long time in this small country? Mental distress, financial worries, family feuds were all things mentioned by those who knew the missing persons.

Benny was her husband, Zohara's father, Malka's only son, a person. His pillow, his towel, his clothes, his army boots, his books were waiting for him. Everything was where he had left it.

But these facts of Benny's life could not offer a substitute for the terrifying reality that he himself was not there.

"It takes Benny out of the privacy of his life here and places him in every home in Israel. People will read it, shake their heads, and wonder. Speculate." Rena took a deep breath. "Let them put it in the newspapers."

On her porch lay the ad copy for a missing person who was her husband, and over the porch wafted the evening breeze. All around her, life went on. Neighbors called their children to come in, people turned sprinklers on and off, radios blared. Dogs chased the last bus.

Sammy sighed. Rena had never heard him sigh. "I'm so sorry, Rena. I had hoped that it would not come to this." He looked at Rena. "I just think that we have to go along with the formal police investigation and do our own as well. I've already talked to some trusted friends."

Rena went inside to get him a cup of tea and turned on the lights in all the rooms and left them on. She felt chilly and put on a sweater.

The cup shook a bit when she handed it to Sammy, but no tea spilled. Sammy wanted to know how Malka was doing. "Kibbutz Kalaniyot may have resented her leaving, but that was years ago. In their own way they care about Malka. They loved Yair. Benny is their son. Born there, he is a kibbutz child. Nothing can change that. It's obvious that Kalaniyot is still their home. Malka will hear from the kibbutz."

Rena was afraid she would give in and cry. Sammy seemed determined to help her keep her dignity.

"Rena, is there anything you need to do? Your brother in America, does he know?"

"No."

"Do you want to let him know?"

In her anguish she hadn't been thinking about her brother at all. At least not in the way that Sammy was suggesting. "It's complicated, Sammy. He is my brother, but that doesn't mean he is part of my life."

"Family relations are often complicated."

"There are some real issues, anger and resentment, between us that we have never sorted out."

Was she really saying this to Sammy? She had never had a personal conversation with him before. She had always liked him but felt somehow intimidated by his formality. Perhaps it was the harsh words he had used about the police lieutenant that made him seem more human. Still, she couldn't believe that thoughts and feelings she had guarded so carefully for so long had just come out.

"No harm in giving it a thought. If you want to call him, you can come over to our house."

"Call him?"

"Maybe not. But you never know."

Sammy just sat there, not really taking sides. After all, what side could he take? She didn't present her case. And her brother was a lawyer. If he were there, he probably would have made his point of view much more persuasively than she could have.

Rena looked out into the yard and there in the rock garden sat the turtle. Having a turtle in her yard for several days was unusual. She had never seen a turtle just sitting in her garden. There he was sticking his neck out, moving slowly around, scaled short legs and a scrawny wrinkled neck sticking out. He was ugly yet lovable.

Rena would be the first to admit that she could be impulsive, but she had not expected to act irrationally right then. She said to Sammy, "I'll call him. It's now early morning in the United States and I'll try his office. If he isn't there yet, I'll call his home."

Sammy waited. Rena wondered if she should change her mind. What if her brother had the wrong response? But she could not even say what the right one would be. "I would like to go back with you and call from your house. Thank you. I don't want to do it from the Ramot house."

She went inside and combed her hair without looking in the mirror. She took her purse and made sure she had her brother's address. She would ask the operator for the phone number.

When she came out, Sammy was standing looking at her unfinished painting. "I'm working on getting a phone for you."

As they drove to the Abarbanels' house she was relieved to be in the car and not walking. She could not bear to talk to people.

In Sammy's study Rena called the operator and gave her brother's name and city. She heard the operator speak English with a Hebrew accent. "Is this the law firm of Mr. Klein? This is a long-distance call from Israel. Mr. Klein? Just a minute."

All the way from Chicago her only living sibling said in English, "Rena, is that you?" Their first conversation and it was in English. That was fine with her. She had decided after the war never to speak Polish again. She had come to regard it as the language of those who had betrayed her family, Nazi collaborators. Perhaps this was unfair to condemn an entire nation. But the pain she felt overshadowed any consideration of fairness.

When Rena heard her brother's voice she could not speak. All she could think of was how different his voice sounded from the way she remembered it. Perhaps it was the English. There was no question about speaking Yiddish. She finally managed to say in English, "It's Benny. He has been missing. He went to Jerusalem two days ago... did not arrive. He disappeared."

There was first a muffled sound from the other side. Then she heard Joe's voice. "Rena, I'm so sorry. I'm stunned. I can't imagine what you must be going through."

Maybe it was not such a good idea to call him.

"Rena. Are you there?"

"Yes." She was holding the phone so tightly her knuckles hurt.

"Listen. I'm going to come. It'll take me a few days to get things in order, but I should be in Israel on Sunday or Monday. I've wanted to come for a long time. Now is the right time."

"The right time?"

"Yes. That is, if it is okay with you."

She wanted to say that she did not know if it was okay with her. But she said, "Okay."

Joe repeated, "Okay."

"I'm going to give you my friends' phone number. Please call them when you know your arrival date and your flight number."

When she came out of Sammy's study, Pnina took Rena by the hand and said, "Come have a cup of tea with us and then Sammy will take you home." She led Rena to the table and made her sit down. "Did you speak to your brother?"

Rena had thought she was a bit more composed now. But then she heard herself say, in one rapid breath, "My brother Joe is coming. I haven't seen him since he went to America. I don't know how I feel about it. He'll be here next week, Sunday or Monday. I gave him your phone number, so he'll let you know."

Pnina put the tea in front of Rena. "We'll take you to the airport."

Rena said, "I don't know how to thank you and Sammy."

"We are family," Sammy said.

Family. Her parents and sisters murdered in Poland. Her brother, a stranger. Her husband missing.

"Drink some tea, Rena. I'm sure that even with all of Mendel's good food, you've eaten very little. You look awfully thin to me. How would you like a sandwich? It's never too late to eat something nourishing."

The kids in pajamas came in to say hello to Rena. Benjamin sat in her lap. He cupped his little hands over her ear and whispered, "I'm going to make Benny come back. Just don't tell anyone." Rena nodded and hugged him tightly.

When the children went to bed, Pnina asked, "Would you like to have a Sabbath dinner with us Friday night? You can all come. Malka too. We'll extend the table."

"I appreciate it, but I've already told Mendel he can bring food; he, Iris, and Jacob are going to join us. But Zohara may want to go to synagogue with you. I just don't want her walking on Saturday morning on Ben Yehuda Street and the fools of our town talking to her." Rena knew she sounded harsh. "I know that some of them would sincerely believe that they were being kind but would upset her even with their good intentions."

She drank tea and took a bite of Pnina's delicious sandwich of cheese and tomatoes. "Could Zohara come on Friday and sleep over and go with you on Saturday? I haven't talked to her yet about staying over, but I think she'd like it."

Sammy and Pnina nodded. They arranged for Sammy to pick Zohara up on Friday. "I won't let any fool near her when we go to synagogue," Pnina assured her.

By Friday, Rena realized that the police were still at a loss. No clues. No eyewitnesses, no new information. According to Sammy, the lieutenant was extremely optimistic about the ad in the missing persons section because, the lieutenant said, "in our small country, people don't disappear into thin air. Sooner or later, they are found.

Unless of course they have crossed the border into an Arab country, a dangerous move, of course. Or have left the country by air or sea. Which we checked. Unless of course Benny Sasson left under an assumed name."

Rena felt nothing but rage. "Left under an assumed name? Oh, I see what he is doing. If they fail, it's not because they are incompetent. It's because Benny left the country under an assumed name. What should I do, Sammy? I'm just so angry."

"I wish I could tell you that the lieutenant means no harm. Pnina said to remind you to eat. Now I'll get Zohara and we'll prepare for the Sabbath as best we can."

Herzl Street was busy, people coming home from work; a few stopped at the gate and called out a greeting to Rena. She saw Yael's husband, Yitzhak, go by, and realized that he had not stopped at all to ask how they were doing. Odd, she thought.

She looked at her watch; it was three thirty in the afternoon. Until his disappearance, Benny had usually been home by three on Fridays. Three suddenly became far more than a time in the day. It marked a painful divide between before and after the disappearance.

Zohara came out carrying a large canvas bag. She looked nice in her Sabbath clothes – a dark skirt, a white blouse with a lovely satin collar. Her hair was nicely braided. She held two white ribbons, and she asked her mother to tie them in the braids. Rena knew that Zohara could have done it herself. She was grateful to her daughter for this moment.

Rena thought that on any other Friday Zohara would be unlikely to go to the Abarbanels. There was the secular Sabbath of the majority in town. And then there were people like the Abarbanels, part of a small religious community. Shomriya agreed on an uneasy compromise, in which the mostly secular population would not offend the observant.

Watching Zohara get into Sammy's car and waving to her, she hoped her daughter would have a good time.

Rena saw Mendel on his bike. He was actively opposed to those in the synagogue who wanted to impose a ban on traffic from sundown Friday to sunset Saturday. Mendel considered that any move to accommodate the synagogue was equivalent to giving in to blatant religious coercion. He reminded people that birth, marriage, and death took place under religious laws imposed on secular citizens.

Once at a town meeting Mendel had said, "The religious want to control everything, including how I should spend my Sabbath. I always ride my bike on the Sabbath and will continue to do it to the day I die. I didn't come here to build this country to be oppressed by a minority of fanatics. It is we, secular Jews, who built this country."

Rena stood at the gate watching Sammy leave and Mendel arrive. The Sabbath divided friends. On the Sabbath, secular Shomriyans visited each other, but their observant friends were not invited, nor would they come if an invitation were extended.

Her daughter was an exception. Zohara was going to spend the Sabbath with the Abarbanels. Rena hoped that being with her friend and going to synagogue would be helpful to Zohara. She envied Zohara's relationship with God. But she knew that for her daughter it would still be a Sabbath without her father.

CHAPTER SIXTEEN

Rena was waiting for friends to join her for dinner.

It was quiet on the porch with Zohara gone. Rena did not turn on the radio and did not put on any of her favorite music. Mendel was there. He stood at the table unpacking the food he had brought over earlier. Mendel was a wiry, bald man in his sixties, darkly tanned, a man who, without his white apron, looked more an outdoors man than an expert cook.

There were few cars on Ben Yehuda Street and most children on Herzl Street were already inside, washing up, preparing for dinner. Even the dogs were silent.

Yael Ramot came over, walking carefully on high heels, wearing a long black skirt and a black blouse, looking quite elegant. In the evening's stillness Yael's voice was louder than usual.

"I don't know how to put it to you, Rena. Let me first say that we've always liked you and Benny, even though we never agreed with your politics. You know that Yitzhak and I have been good neighbors. We were more than happy to take phone calls for you. I have to say that unlike some people, you were careful not to take advantage of us. I give credit where credit is due."

When Rena asked if she wanted to sit down, Yael raised her right hand. "No, no." Her silver bracelets clicked as she brought her hand down. Yael looked at the table that had been moved to the middle of the porch. On a white linen tablecloth, Mendel had arranged some of his famous dishes and serving utensils. Yael nodded to him as he began setting for five people. He greeted her politely.

Yael kept her eyes on the food. "I see that our chef has prepared a feast for you. It's good in troubled times to make space for the Sabbath and for a nice meal. We're not religious, but we have a special dinner and I even light candles."

Mendel was just about to place napkins next to the forks. Instead, he put them down, and came over and stood close to Rena. She felt her face getting red but looked directly at Yael. "You didn't come to talk to me about the importance of the Sabbath."

Yael touched one of her long earrings. "Well, this is really hard for me. I told you how sorry I was about Benny and that we'd be glad to take messages, especially from the police. Given the circumstances, we were ready to take more than the usual calls. We wanted to continue to be good neighbors. But..."

Rena did not say a word. Mendel was still.

Yael's eyes continued to focus on the table. "Well, Yitzhak didn't want me to come at all. But I said, 'Yitzhak, we need to be honest.' So, I must tell you that you have to make other arrangements. I hate to say it, but I have no choice. It's too much. It's just that I'm no longer comfortable. Yitzhak thought that I should wait. But you know me. I am always honest, and I think it's best to tell the truth."

Rena took a step forward and stood between the table and Yael. "What is the truth, Yael?"

"Well, if Benny left the country..."

Rena went to the screen door, and holding it wide open she said, "Go home, Yael, and light candles."

Yael did not move. "I don't see why you need to be sarcastic. I'll wait until you make other arrangements to get your phone messages. The police of course have a right to call anyway."

Rena refused to stay calm. "I think that you need to tell anyone who calls, including the police, that you'll no longer take messages for me. Since you're an honest person, you can tell them why. Go home now."

"You're overreacting, Rena." Yael turned to leave.

Mendel spoke up. "You should be ashamed of yourself, Yael. You'll regret it one day."

Yael turned around. "Are you threatening me, Mendel?"

Mendel seemed to wipe his hands on an apron he didn't have. "No, I'm just trying to be as honest as you are."

Rena just stood there holding the screen door, her knuckles white against the red paint.

Mendel put an arm around her. "Listen, Rena. All kinds of people came to Palestine. Not all of them were good, or smart. Their children, born on this land, not all of them have good sense or a kind heart. Some unfortunately live in Shomriya and some regrettably happen to be your neighbors." Yael left without another word.

Rena felt bile rising in her throat and a slight headache in her temples. In a hoarse voice she said, "Mendel, this is only the beginning." He got her a glass of water. She had to hold it with both hands.

Rena tried to recover from Yael's words. She sat down, drank some water, and said to Mendel, "I'm glad Zohara wasn't here to witness the first Shomriya betrayal of Benny." The prospect of more people like Yael who would be willing to believe the worst of Benny was hard to take. It dawned on her that even Benny's military credentials had not been as strong a shield as she had wanted to believe.

Mendel finished setting the table. "There are plenty of friends in town as well. But it would be foolish on my part to dismiss your fears. All I can say is, I'll be here."

"My brother Joe is coming."

Before Mendel could say anything, she added, "I don't know if I did the right thing. There is so much unresolved between us since we left Poland. I called and told him about Benny. If he had not offered to come, I would have been even angrier.

But I don't know about his coming. I feel that I have too much to deal with as it is."

Mendel said, "I have always wondered why your brother never came to visit." He added, "I'm no expert in fixing family relations. My own son is angry with me all the time."

Before she could say anything, Malka, Iris, and Jacob arrived. As they sat around the table, Rena told them about Yael's visit. Malka moved in her chair, sat up tall and straight, and said, "I thought she was just an empty-headed bourgeois woman in search of the latest gadget for her kitchen. I've always known she wasn't one of us. I just never thought she had such malice in her."

Malka turned to Iris. "What am I missing here? I'm not exactly naive, but I didn't expect this from Yael."

Iris, eating a rice and mushroom salad, put down her fork. "There can be many reasons why people react with fear or cruelty to the pain of others. We think that people would be empathetic in time of crisis, but some turn on the sufferer."

Iris went on to say that people were scared. If someone as beloved as Benny could disappear, she said, people wondered what might happen next. She looked at Malka. "Sadly, some people will distance themselves from you. Others may be hurtful, either unconsciously or deliberately."

Rena, who barely ate anything, was breaking pieces of challah with her fingers, using the Sabbath bread to make a pattern on her plate. "What am I going to do about Zohara? How will I protect her? What will happen when Yael's malicious words, 'if Benny left the country,' go from her through her kids into the school and on to the street?"

Mendel passed around tomato and eggplant salad, tahini, stuffed grape leaves, roasted chicken, and rice dishes, urging them all to eat. He agreed with Rena. "Zohara is the main concern here. How can we help to protect her from rumors and innuendos?"

Jacob said gruffly, "I can take out my gun."

Malka told him, "You don't have a gun."

Jacob put his hand through his completely white, still-thick hair. He was proud of not going bald in old age. He looked at Malka and smiled. "Well, if I had a gun, I would get it out. If they hurt Zohara's feelings, I can put on my crazy act and warn them. People will think I'm going to lose it, and they'll pay attention."

"You didn't exactly win friends at the last town meeting when you acted out. And you lost the vote," Rena reminded him.

Jacob did not seem deterred by facts. "Yes. I know. I would have lost the vote anyway. But at least, when I got wild, people paid attention. The whole town talked about me the next day. Didn't they?"

Rena laughed. Jacob, she realized, had a purpose when they all assumed that he was just out of control. Mendel said, "You were the talk of the town. For one whole day, customers paid more attention to your story than to my food."

Rena moved pieces of food around on her plate. "I'll have to talk to Zohara, tell her what could happen, and go from there."

Malka urged Rena to eat. Pausing then, she looked closely at her daughter-in-law and said slowly, "You and Zohara could always move to Tel Aviv for a while. You have your studio there, and she can go to school." Malka looked around the table. "I know you're all surprised. It's not like me to even talk of running away. But I'm thinking of Zohara. Maybe it would be better for her."

Rena tried but could not eat. Instead, she was having one of Mendel's fresh juices, a mixture of orange, tangerine, and strawberries in a tall glass. She put it down. "If I believed that it would be good for her, I'd do it in a second. This is a small country. What difference would a move make? The best thing is to stay here with all of you."

It was a balmy April evening and through the open windows a light breeze brought in the fragrance of honeysuckle and sweet peas. Iris and Jacob cleared the table and Mendel brought out an apple strudel and coffee. Rena heard the gate open and sighed, preparing for the worst.

It was Yehuda Manor, the new history teacher. "I don't know if this is a good time. I just wanted to see how Zohara was doing. She wasn't in school the last three days. I thought I'd come by and tell you how sorry I am about her father."

Rena said, "Zohara is at the Abarbanels and we're having coffee. Won't you join us?"

Jacob brought a chair and Mendel got another cup, plate, and fork. Rena asked, "Do you know everyone?"

"I know you, and of course Mendel from the cafe."

Rena introduced the others. When she got to Iris, Yehuda said, "I've heard about you. I'm glad to finally meet you."

He turned to Rena. "I wanted to know what I could do to help Zohara come back to school. I realize how hard it is for her. I'm now the official eighth grade homeroom teacher. I'll try to make it as easy as possible, talk to the kids, keep my ears open, and make myself available to parents and students who want to talk to me."

Rena thought how unlike his sour and bitter predecessor this man was. She replied, "It was very good of you to come. The kids like you. They call you the young teacher and say that you look like Paul Newman."

If Yehuda was self-conscious, he didn't show it. "Well, I'm not as young as they think. I like the kids here and I like your Zohara. She is quiet in class, but when she speaks it's obvious that she is very bright. She writes beautifully and has great insights. She's a very talented girl."

Mendel turned to Yehuda. "My friend Shlomo enjoys having her come to his bookstore. She reads everything, he tells me. As soon as a good book is translated into Hebrew, Shlomo gets it. When Shlomo gets it, Zohara reads it."

Yehuda laughed. "Yes. She reads more than anyone in her class."

Jacob, piling dessert on his plate, spoke in a serious voice. "Zohara reads more than many of the adults in Shomriya. I am sorry to say, Yehuda, that you'll find a lot of ignorant people here."

"You don't want to scare a new teacher," Malka cautioned.

"Malka, there are some smart people in town, but you'll admit that Shomriya has some shallow minds as well."

Yehuda didn't seem to mind Jacob's warning. He told them the news. "It seems that Mr. Eldan won't be coming back, and I have been offered his position. I like it here. I think I'll stay."

Iris put her elbow on the table and her hand under her chin and looked at Yehuda with interest. Rena told Yehuda she was grateful to him for his interest in Zohara.

Yehuda thanked them for the dessert, and he promised Rena to stay in touch.

By ten thirty Mendel and Jacob had left and Iris was in the kitchen putting away the last of the dishes. Malka had said goodnight and gone across the road to her house to try and get some sleep. Rena could see that all the lights in her house were still on.

Rena thought again of Yael's visit. Obviously, Yael was not the source of the rumor that Benny had left the country. But Yael seemed very eager to believe it and would not hesitate to repeat it. Rena wondered who, then, would want to slander Benny. She thought of Iris's psychological explanations. She did not dismiss them. However, Rena thought there could be a political motive behind this outrageous lie. But to what end?

She heard a car and then an engine turning off right at the gate. Rena couldn't imagine who would come over at that late hour. She went to the porch. Sergeant Ari was getting out of his car.

CHAPTER SEVENTEEN

Ari apologized for coming by so late. Rena asked him to come in. "Would you like something, tea, coffee? Some pastry?"

"I really would like some coffee. I had a long day." Ari stood on the porch looking around. He saw Rena's easel standing modestly, almost hiding, in the art corner. He got closer, moved it a bit and looked at what seemed to be an unfinished charcoal sketch of a prickly pear and a turtle, surrounded by scattered rocks.

"I started working on it the day before Benny disappeared."

Ari sat down on one of the comfortable chairs, crossed his legs, and drank his coffee. He was not a handsome man, but his red hair made him conspicuous. Rena sat down facing him. "I was relieved to see you here on Tuesday morning. Do you still paint?"

Ari sighed. "Not as much as I would like."

"You were good in art school. I loved your metal abstract pieces."

"You were the star of our class. I saw your show *Gifts from America*. I thought it was brilliant."

Rena thought how distant her show seemed now. She surprised herself when she told Ari, "I see Benny so clearly standing in front of my work, and I want to go over and just stand there with him."

Ari looked at her. "I'm so sorry. I think I know how you feel. Since Dina died, I have a recurrent dream. I see her at the end of our street, I walk toward her. I'm so happy that she is there, full of life, smiling warmly. I already know how it would feel to have her in my arms. I hurry, but when I get to the end of the street, my arms stretched out, she vanishes."

They sat silently for a while listening to the frogs.

Ari drank the last of his coffee and put the cup down. "I thought it was best to acknowledge that we knew each other on Tuesday, but not to indicate friendship. The lieutenant advocates total detachment. We're not to be influenced by relationships, politics, or anything. We are first and foremost cops, he lectures us. Above all, he warns, he won't tolerate nepotism or favoritism of any kind."

Rena leaned forward. "I was afraid when I saw you arriving so late that you'd come to tell me you had to take yourself off the case."

Ari laughed and asked if he could change his mind and have some dessert. Motioning Rena not to get up, he went to the table and took a piece of Mendel's strudel and a fork. "To answer your question, I have thought about it since Zev Shai called the police station. At first, I thought he didn't know that you and I were students in

Jerusalem together, or that I had a friendship with Benny in those years. Now I'm no longer sure. I've made up my mind. I'll stay on the case for as long as they let me. If they tell me I'm off it, I'll go from there."

Rena went over to her art shelf and from behind the paints and brushes she took out the envelope with the Knesset emblem. "This came in the mail four days before Benny disappeared. I didn't open it right away. It was the day before Zohara's birthday, and I was sewing a dress for her. The letter didn't seem important."

She swallowed hard. "When it arrived, I had no idea that it was from Zev. It was only after Benny disappeared that I even remembered the letter. When I opened it there was just a brief note. It said, 'Dear Rena, I just saw your show, *Gifts from America*. Pretty bold, as usual. But I also know that you have a self-protective side, and you know which lines you should not cross. Zev.'"

Ari looked at the letter. "I don't get it. What's it all about? Is he talking about your art?"

Rena sat down. She gave Ari the envelope as well. "It's hard to know where to start. You know about Rachel's death in kibbutz Oz and the rumors about Zev?"

"Just the gist of it. I understand that there were rumors. But the police ruled her death a suicide. I haven't heard about it in years."

"Rachel and I were roommates. Rachel found out she was pregnant. When she told Zev, she said he went wild. He told her to have an abortion right away and not tell anyone. She told him that she was going to have the baby. He said, 'Never. You're not going to have my baby.'"

Talking about it was as hard as Rena had thought it would be. She continued. "Rachel's body was found at the edge of the vineyard where she had been working. Rachel loved working in the vineyard. When the first tiny grapes appeared, she was so proud. At that stage she worked there alone. People came to help only during the harvest."

Ari watched Rena and waited for her to continue. "I came back to the room at about nine. Only then did I realize that I hadn't seen Rachel in the dining hall and that the clothes she had put on a chair to wear after work were still there. Her after-work sandals were there, but her working boots were not. That's when I knew something had happened."

Rena was still quite composed, but she could feel herself getting upset. She heard the crickets and continued. "When Rachel told me about Zev's reaction to the pregnancy, she also said, 'If he kills me, no one will believe it.'"

"Did she tell anyone on the kibbutz?"

The old agony was gripping her. Rachel did not think that anyone on the kibbutz would believe her. She was just a dumb girl from a small town in Russia, from a poor family.

Rena skipped over her response to Rachel's desolate prediction. She looked out the window and saw Malka's house ablaze with light. "The autopsy said she died of rat poison. It confirmed that she was pregnant. Zev didn't deny paternity. He claimed he knew nothing about the pregnancy, that Rachel never told him."

Ari put his cup down. "Rat poison. Who had access to it?"

"On the kibbutz? Everyone did. It was in the supplies barn. Any adult could ask for the key."

"It could have been anyone on the kibbutz, then, including Rachel."

"That's what Zev said. He claimed that Rachel committed suicide, that she was far more emotionally troubled than we knew. Very few people knew Rachel."

"How well did you know her?"

"When I did go to the police, it was my word against his. He claimed that Rachel and I were not close, which was true, and that she would not have confided in me. When the police asked me if it was true that we were not close friends, I had to be truthful. Zev also said that I disliked him and that my animosity was my motivation for fabricating the story. When the police asked if it was true that I didn't like him, I admitted that as well.

"The police had no evidence against Zev or anyone else. They concluded that it was suicide."

"Do you have any idea what he means in this letter about you having a sense of 'self protection'?"

"I don't know what he means. That happened years ago." Rena was still silent about how she felt about what she had done, or not done.

"If confronted, Zev could say that to read a threat in his letter would be paranoid. He was just talking about your art and saying that you know how to make a political statement without crossing too many lines of the national consensus."

Rena checked the coffee pot. "Would you like more coffee?"

"No, thanks. But I wanted to talk to you about Benny. Do you feel up to it, or would you like me to come back tomorrow? You look exhausted."

Rena picked up a shawl and put it around her shoulders. Facing Ari, she put a pillow behind her head. "Now is good. But I need to know, are you jeopardizing anything by being here tonight?"

Ari laughed. "I have the lieutenant's blessing. I told him I was going to my mother's and that I could easily make a detour to see how you were doing and assure M.K. Shai that we keep in touch with Benny's family. My being here was registered as good public relations."

"Will there be serious consequences for you if Zev Shai suspects that we're friends?"

Ari stretched his legs out and looked comfortable and clearly not alarmed. "If Dina were still alive, I might have reacted differently. Now, I have the immunity of a childless widower, I have no dependents. I can take care of myself. The worst they can do is fire me. I'll survive."

"You can always go back to art."

"Right now, I need to know if it was common knowledge in your circles that Benny was writing a book on Buber."

Rena was surprised. "Benny had been going to Jerusalem once a week for the last two years to work on it. I'd say anyone who knew Benny knew about the Buber book. I don't understand. What does the Buber book have to do with Benny's disappearance?"

Ari seemed to think about what he was going to say. "I don't want to alarm you. But when I mentioned the Buber book to Zev Shai, he claimed he didn't know about it. So, if the book was common knowledge, I have to ask myself why he is denying it."

"I don't understand it, but he is lying. When he lies there is a reason."

"How much of a manuscript did Benny have?"

"Ten chapters. About two hundred and fifty pages, I think."

"Is there more than one copy? One at home?"

"There are his handwritten notes. Some of them are here at home but most of them are in his office. I think that the first two chapters, which Benny considered quite polished and ready to go to press, are here in the house. The rest is in his office in Tel Aviv."

Ari sounded firm. "I don't know what's going on with the book, but I suggest that you go to Tel Aviv and get the copy, all the notes, and take them home."

Rena tried to find a comfortable position. She had been sitting for too long. She planned to take a walk early tomorrow. "You know when Mike first came to tell me about Benny, I asked him to lock Benny's office. He seemed a bit reluctant, but he finally agreed. Under pressure from his wife, he did go and put a lock on Benny's door. I'll call her tomorrow morning and go to his office right away.

It'll be a good Sabbath deed to bring his manuscript home."

Ari got up and she was glad for the opportunity to stand as well. "Sounds good to me. We may have to read the manuscript. See if there is anything there that Shai might find objectionable or disturbing."

Rena put her cup on the table. There was still plenty of dessert there.

"Zev would find everything in it distasteful. He opposes everything that Buber stands for. I still can't figure out why he came to the kibbutz or why he is in our party."

Ari walked to the screen door. Rena followed him. She felt very tired. "Benny wanted equality for Arab workers. Zev wouldn't support it."

Ari's hand was on the door handle. "Where is the manuscript on the rights of Arab workers?"

Rena stopped moving. "I know that there is one copy Benny keeps in his office."

Ari took out a piece of paper and a pen and wrote something. "Here is my mother's number in Tel Aviv. When you get to his office, give me a call and let me know what you've found."

Just as he stepped outside, he asked, "Do you by any chance know a librarian at Hebrew University by the name of Abigail?"

Rena was surprised by the question. "Sure, I know Abigail. Why? What has she done?"

Under the streetlight in the empty Herzl Street, Ari laughed out loud. "Of course. I should have known. I met her and she didn't mention that she knew you." He laughed even harder. "She only answered my questions. It never occurred to me to ask if she knew you."

Now Rena was laughing with him. "Of course. You are the police. She doesn't know if you are Benny's friend or one of us, a leftist." For a moment they stood there laughing. Ari got into his car, started the engine, and rolled down the window. "Don't forget. Call me as soon as you get to Benny's office."

CHAPTER EIGHTEEN

Rena went to Tel Aviv on a balmy Shabbat morning. The world was unchanged by Benny's disappearance. The streets were full of people walking to the beach, strolling, enjoying the sunny day. She found it difficult to watch them without feeling resentful. She had been afraid to make the trip for this very reason. In Shomriya Benny's absence had registered and there was a void where he had been.

In Benny's office at *Kol Hapoel*, Rena held Benny's phone and called the number Ari had given her.

"Rena? Where are you calling from?"

"I am in Benny's office at the newspaper. Can you come over right away?"

"I'll be there in a few minutes."

When Ari arrived at the *Kol Hapoel* building, the guard showed him in. Rena introduced him to Sarah.

Sarah was standing with Rena in Benny's office. The drawers of the filing cabinets were open and empty. Rena spoke quickly. "Sarah and I came in a few minutes ago. We had the key; we unlocked the door and opened the filing cabinet and found nothing. The desk is bare, the desk drawers are empty, all the files are gone. The Buber manuscript is missing. So is Benny's typewriter."

Only the orphaned mug of pencils and the black phone remained. It looked like the office of a recent retiree. It certainly did not seem vandalized or even burglarized.

Rena could tell by looking at Ari that he was shocked. His eyes carefully scanned Benny's office. On the wall, a large black and white photograph of the family in 1947, Benny, Yair, Malka, Rena, and a five-year-old Zohara, a smiling family without a hint of things to come. Whoever took Benny's papers had left everything else in place.

Sarah's demeanor did not match her cheerful red sundress. She was clearly agitated. "I asked Mike to put a lock on the door when we returned from Shomriya and he did. I just didn't think to open the door and see if everything was in order. It was after midnight. It's my fault."

Rena was enraged by the looting of Benny's papers, but she could hear her friend's agony. "No, Sarah. You're not responsible for this. Whoever has done it was just much smarter and faster than any of us." She turned to Ari with some hope in her voice. "What do you make of it, Ari?"

Ari looked around, but he was careful not to touch anything. He checked the lock on the door. "It doesn't mean that someone was in the office before the lock was placed." He went over to Sarah "Rena is right. This is not your fault. The lock is not a very sophisticated one and the person who took the documents, the manuscript, may have come in and decided to lock it again."

Sarah refused to be reassured. She turned to Rena. "I'm so sorry. I feel that I've let you down. I hadn't realized how urgent it was to come to the office."

They heard footsteps in the long corridor and saw the guard at the door. He wanted to know if the sergeant needed anything. Rena was aware of how silent *Kol Hapoel* was on a Sabbath morning. Nothing like the usual commotion.

"No copies of the Buber book, no notes, no article, no typewriter. I know it's all connected to Benny's disappearance, but I don't get it. Why his work? Why rob him of his words?"

Ari still looked around carefully. "I don't know what's going on. But I am going to find out."

Ari was examining Benny's bookshelves. Without turning his head, he asked Rena, "Is it possible that someone other than Zev may be behind it?"

Rena was open to the idea. "It crossed my mind, but I don't know." She was bracing herself to speak. She looked at Benny's chair, touched the seat gently, and decided to sit there. Sarah and Ari remained standing, waiting for her to speak.

The office was silent and warm. They were sweating. The windows were closed. "I have a feeling that Benny is still alive." Sarah came over and put a hand on Rena's shoulder. Ari said, "I'll do whatever I can to help you." They both looked at her with great pity.

What could she say? That her heart would know right away if Benny were dead? Yet that was exactly how she felt. She would have known, and long before she was officially notified, just as she did when her parents and sisters were murdered. She knew it before she got the telegram. On the day of their murder, she was sitting in her art class when everything went black. She did not faint, but she lost consciousness, could not hear what the instructor was saying, could not feel her body. For a moment she felt paralyzed, deaf, mute. It passed. She could not say how long it took, ten seconds or five minutes. Then the telegram came, but she had already known.

Ari was looking at her. He said again that he would do his best. Sarah stood muttering, first one thing, then another – that it was her fault, and that for Rena to be hopeful was a good thing. She herself was unconvinced.

Rena touched Benny's desk and turned to look at the family photograph. "It's been five days. No one has seen Benny since Monday afternoon. All his files are gone. I have to talk to Malka about it."

Sarah seemed to have come to a decision of her own. "Rena, I don't care what position the party or the newspaper takes. You can count on me. I can do more than chicken soup. I have a car, a driver's license, and I don't have a job. My mother will take care of the kids. Let me know what you need." She said to Ari, "My mom lives next door. Sometimes it's a burden. At other times it's a blessing."

A shiver ran down Rena's sweaty back. Getting rid of Benny's life work would allow his opponents to question his character. Without the book manuscript to prove otherwise, Benny could be accused of God-knows-what. Doubts would be expressed by people on the right who opposed his politics and from within the party as well.

Rena and Benny had been involved in political disagreements. But neither she nor Benny had ever believed that it would go from political contention to character assassination or physical harm. They did not think either of them was ever in danger. She had considered Malka's fears exaggerated and misplaced. She said, to no one in particular, "Malka warned me and I refused to listen. She was right and I was wrong."

She turned to Ari. "I would like to take our family photograph and Benny's mug home with me."

"I'm sorry, Rena, it's not a good idea. The best thing would be for me to write a police report and note that nothing this morning was removed from Benny's office. I'll call the lieutenant and the Tel Aviv police."

Rena was upset, but she realized that Ari was right. "My fingerprints and Sarah's are on everything. I guess we shouldn't have opened any drawers. But at this point I don't really care. My trust in the lieutenant is as low as it was when I first met him."

Ari, she knew, was not about to discuss his superior. She did not expect him to agree with her. But he did say, "My guess is that whoever took away all of the stuff didn't leave any fingerprints. This is professional. Let the police come and do their job."

Rena and Sarah followed Ari to Mike's office. The sergeant made the call and they waited for the Tel Aviv police.

CHAPTER NINETEEN

On Saturday Zohara went to synagogue with the Abarbanels. She sat with Pnina and Shoshi in the women's balcony holding the prayer book, but she didn't feel the kind of joy she had experienced before. She waited for some sign of hope from God. All she could feel was fear. She shivered, and Pnina took off her shawl and wrapped it around her shoulders.

She didn't hear a word when Daniel read from the Torah; she couldn't pay attention to the service. She couldn't tell the Abarbanels how angry she was with God.

Back home, on Sunday, she heard that there had been a flood of calls to police stations all over the country. Sergeant Ari told her mother that not a single one had been from a reliable eyewitness.

Most came from what he called 'the regulars,' people who enjoyed calling the police. Zohara was indignant. Her mother tried to explain.

Zohara refused to read *Gulliver's Travels*. She was mad at Lemuel. "I grew weary of the sea, and intended to stay at home with my wife and family." Well, why didn't he? Lemuel was a ridiculous man who should have stayed at home. She was not interested in him anymore and she did not want her mother to read to her anymore. "I'm way too old to be read to anyway."

Her head was full of angry words. 'I'm not going to read this dumb book ever again. Let it just stay there, unopened, on my desk. I just want to forget my birthday. Every bit of it.'

Then, exactly one week after her father had kissed her on the head and said goodbye for the last time, and she had felt embarrassed and now wished that she had not, her American uncle arrived.

Zohara watched her mother and her Uncle Joe at the airport. They looked a bit dazed. Her mother seemed as though she might lose her balance. In the dusty road to the parking lot of the Tel Aviv airport, her uncle in a heavy dark suit kept wiping his face and eyes. He seemed glad to see her. "Zohara, you're exactly the way I imagined you from the photographs. You are just lovely. I have looked forward so much to meeting you and here you are." She had always wanted an uncle.

The Abarbanels walked behind them to give them some privacy. Her uncle walked between her and her mother, who said very little. Zohara told him, "You're exactly the way you look in the photographs."

"How is that?"

"Like from the movies."

Her uncle said, "It's just my clothes, Zohara. I know I look silly in my Chicago suit. But wait until I put on a pair of khakis and sandals. I'll look like an Israeli, like you, a real Sabra." Joe stopped, put his bag down in the middle of road, and gave Zohara a big hug.

Joe then turned to her mother and said something in Yiddish. Zohara didn't understand, but it made her mother cry. Along the sidewalk, a light wind rustled the leaves of the eucalyptus trees. Her father, who loved the way the wind made the trees sway, was gone. Her uncle, the one from the photographs, the one who came all the way from America, noticed the trees. They didn't have eucalyptus trees in Chicago, he told her.

On the porch, with Malka, their sorrow made space for ordinary conversation about the trip and Joe's family in America. They all talked at once. Her uncle spoke antiquated Hebrew, and they all tried their English. Vashti brayed. Uncle Joe had never heard a donkey before, and Zohara promised to take him to see Vashti the next day.

Her uncle looked tired, but he stayed up for Mendel's dinner. He sat on their porch with the jacket of his dark blue suit and blue tie hanging on the back of his chair, the long sleeves of his white shirt rolled up, his cufflinks, the first ones Zohara had ever seen, on the table next to his plate.

By now Joe had met not only the Abarbanels but also some of their other friends, including Iris, whom he had known when they were children in Poland. People came and were introduced. Her uncle spoke a halting, rusty Hebrew, and some, like Mendel, tried their English. Mendel told him, "The British used to come to my café. I always listened to them but pretended not to understand too well." Zohara wondered if Mendel had acted as a spy for the Haganah, but she was too tired to ask. Mendel's son Saul, Ronnie's father, came too.

Zohara was very surprised to hear Saul apologize to Rena. "I came to welcome your brother and to apologize to you for being rude the other day when you came into the café with Iris. I care about Benny and your family. If you need anything, Arza and I are here. We can't cook like

Dad, but maybe there are other things we could do.

"And you too, Malka," he added. "Whatever you need, please let us know. We love Benny. Arza wants you to know it's how she feels too. She is sending her orange marmalade."

All of Ronnie's friends, including Zohara, loved Arza's famous marmalade. When no grown-up was looking, they would attack the jar of the sweet spread and sigh happily.

Zohara's mother took the beautiful jar from Saul and invited him to sit down. He declined. Another time he would come with Arza. "Tonight is a big one for your family. I just wanted to do the right thing." Then he added shyly, "I could also bring some oil for the gate, sounds like it could use some. That is, if you'd let me."

Her grandmother told him, "You are a good man, Saul, and you were a good kid, even when you and your friends took strawberries from my fields at night."

Wow. The things Zohara was finding out. Saul went over to her. "Ronnie says to tell you she'd like you to come over after school, whenever is good for you. I told Ronnie, 'Why don't you also ask Zohara if you can come help her with her chores after school?' She still does farm work. Not like our Lily who can't wait to be a city girl."

Zohara suddenly forgot about Uncle Joe and once again wanted to cry. Saul, unlike his daughter Ronnie, was not very talkative. 'A man of few words,' her father had said about Saul. But Saul had said a lot right now.

That night, Zohara wrote in her journal. "You know, God, how angry I am with you for not bringing my dad back. I'm still angry. But thank you for bringing my uncle. I know you were helpful in the matter even though I didn't ask you directly and my mom doesn't pray, so she didn't either. It doesn't matter, because my only uncle in the whole world is here with us for the first time. I was worried before he came. I didn't know him. But the most important thing is for you to bring my father back. I realize that I have secrets now. I don't want to tell Mom what the kids in school say about my father. I know that she always told me I could tell her anything. Good night."

On Tuesday morning when Zohara woke up, she went out to the porch, and there was Uncle Joe with a cup of coffee, wearing a pair of khakis, a blue short sleeve shirt, and a pair of sandals. She was glad to see him.

He got up, put his cup down, pointed at his clothes, and smiled at her. "Don't I look like a Sabra? You can be honest with me."

She wanted to say, "You are the best thing that happened to me this week." Instead, she said, "Well, you don't look as elegant as you did yesterday."

He laughed. "I see. I can still improve."

"You look fine, Uncle Joe." She liked saying 'uncle.' She had tried it a few times before his arrival. She had never said it to a blood relative before. It was peaceful outside. Herzl Street was sleepy and quiet. Even the sparrows were starting slowly. Through the window she could see that some of the sprinklers in Malka's fields were already on.

As she pulled out a chair and sat down, Uncle Joe looked at her and said, "You're up early. It's only five thirty."

Before she knew it, words came tumbling out. "Yesterday a boy at school, in the cafeteria, said to me, 'How come your dad disappeared on you?' I'm not going to the cafeteria today. I'm going to stay in my homeroom and that's final. I don't need lunch."

She stopped, took a deep breath, and was not sure she should tell him all this. She saw that her words were not wasted. Her uncle was really listening.

She started to cry. "I want my dad to come back."

Her uncle looked at her directly. "Of course you do. I'm so sorry that I've never met your dad. I am sure he loves you and your mom very much and would never leave you. Never."

Zohara told him that a rumor was already circulating, claiming that her father had left the country. Every time Zohara heard it, she thought, 'This is a nightmare and I'll wake up.' But it was real. When pain and rage choked her, she wanted to do something to stop it, but did not know what to do. She had never felt anything like it.

Uncle Joe said, "Your father would never leave you. He loves you."

She let his words fill the porch and wanted the morning breeze to carry them to every corner in Shomriya. She wanted her uncle's words to be in the air so everyone would breathe them in.

They sat there quietly until she stopped crying. "Uncle Joe, I don't want to go to school, but Mom and Grandma and my teacher all say that I have to. My teacher tries to help, I can tell. So do my friends, Ronnie and Shoshi. Kids yell stuff and whisper. Why do they do it? I thought they liked my dad."

Uncle Joe was quiet for a few minutes. "I don't know the kids in your school. But I think that what they are saying about your dad has nothing to do with him, with who he is, or the truth. It has to do with who they are."

Zohara, for some reason, found it easy to tell her uncle what she had not told her mother or her grandmother or even Iris about school. Since her father's disappearance she felt that her world had changed. The adults she loved couldn't stop it.

Zohara told her uncle, "I went with the Abarbanels to synagogue on Saturday. I thought that God would give me hope, a sign that my dad would come back. But he didn't. I said, 'an indication at least that my dad is safe,' but all I felt was a chill. As though I was coming down with a cold. I don't even know how I feel about God."

Ben Yehuda Street was taking on life as buses and cars drove by. Uncle Joe put down the cup he was holding, crossed his legs, and spoke quietly. "I think I know what you mean. When I got the news that my family, your grandparents and aunts, had been killed, I went to synagogue but could not pray. I was mad at God, I blamed God, I questioned God's existence. I stopped going to synagogue. It took me two years to go back."

Zohara pulled her legs up and rested her chin on her knees. "My grandmother says there is no God, we humans invented God. I don't agree with her, but I don't know if I can forgive God."

She held her breath before she asked, "Do you think that my dad will come back?"

"I hope so, but I don't know. What I do know without a doubt is that he loves you and would not leave you."

Zohara sat straight in her chair and looked at her uncle. "If my dad doesn't come back, God can no longer count on me."

CHAPTER TWENTY

Rena was in the kitchen wondering what she would now say to her brother. They had talked late into the night about Benny. She had done most of the talking. Her brother had asked a few questions, mostly listened. When they said goodnight, he hugged her. He came to support her, he said. She was still not sure what they could say that would make sense of their past.

She looked out on the garden. The roses looked unbearably beautiful. Just a week earlier, this sight would have filled her with joy. She held on to the table and closed her eyes. The food on the table waited patiently.

Since Benny's disappearance, they had eaten on the porch. Her brother and her daughter were already on the porch, and she could hear them talking. Zohara seemed to like him. Rena finished making breakfast, put everything on a tray, and wrapped up Zohara's lunch.

After Zohara left for school, Rena served more coffee. She looked at her brother and knew that what she had to say could not wait. "What happened, Joe? Why did you hurt Dad?"

Joe sat there tall and straight, looking so much like their father. She was her young self.

"You hurt him when you stopped going to synagogue. Telling him you were going to America wasn't enough for you?"

"I can't tell you how much I have regretted it. I was wrong."

"But why? You could have gone to America with his blessing. Why the public humiliation?"

"I behaved badly. At the time, I felt stifled. Coerced. A father who expected me to be like him. To study in a yeshiva, become a rabbi, dress in black medieval Hasidic clothes, marry someone I had never met. I didn't want to be like him. I didn't want a life that was insular and closed to the world."

"He would have accepted that."

Joe gave a brief, bitter laugh. For a moment he sounded like the young man he used to be. "Since I was a kid, there were always command performances in the synagogue."

"I had no idea…"

"How would you know? You were a daughter. When I was a child, it was 'read some Torah, Joe,' then as I grew older, 'read Talmud.' In my teens it was 'offer commentary, Joe'… I was supposed to make him proud."

Rena was stunned. "I was so envious. All of us girls, Tova and Sara and I, were jealous of you. You were the only one who could be close to Dad, to make him proud."

Joe looked at her. "I resented you girls because there was no pressure on you."

"You made him happy just by being a son. There was no way any of us could have ever made him proud or happy in the same way."

"You stayed home with Mom where it was safe and accepting and I had to go and perform for him every single day of my life."

"We girls thought that the way to be close to Dad was to go to synagogue with him."

"I don't think I thought of it as close. Suffocation was more like it."

Rena could hear the radio playing at Malka's house. Like most Shomriyans, her mother-in-law listened to the news, every hour on the hour. Rena could hear the voice of the announcer. By the time his deep voice reached her porch, she couldn't make out any words. The morning news, good and bad, had become background noise. It traveled between the Sasson houses and blended with the familiar sounds of chickens, sprinklers, dogs, and donkeys.

With great difficulty, Rena told Joe, "You said terrible things to me, too."

"You took Dad's side. You cursed me. Not yet sixteen and you cursed me."

"What did I say? I don't remember."

"'May the son you have one day break your heart as you have broken our father's heart.'"

Growing up, Rena had heard women in the village utter this curse. She had used a curse that was familiar and available. "I could've chosen a worse curse."

Joe looked at her. "True. But then you took off for Palestine. I don't remember that that made Dad happy."

"I wasn't his son. Besides, how would you know? You were in America by then and Dad refused to communicate with you."

"Mom wrote to me. Mom stood by me throughout that ordeal. She understood."

"Understood what?"

"She understood my burden. She had known all along that I was not like Dad. She didn't approve of what I did, but she understood it."

Rena was shocked by the news that her mother had supported Joe and kept in touch with him.

"She understood your going to Palestine, too. Your wish to escape her fate as a woman in that restrictive world."

"Her fate? What are you talking about? She loved Dad."

"She came to love him over time. She was lucky, she told me. It could have turned out to be a disaster."

"What do you mean disaster? What a terrible word to use."

"It's not my word, it's hers."

"When? Please tell me."

"Mom told me that when her father chose a groom for her, he told her that she could peek through the window and look at the chosen rabbinic student. If she didn't like him, she could refuse."

Joe was clearly having a hard time with his voice. He cleared his throat and went on. "She saw a tall, handsome young man with the bluest eyes. And said yes.

"The night before the wedding, the women cut off her long red hair. There it lay on the floor while the women shaved her head. She never recovered from the shock. She was determined that wouldn't happen to her daughters."

"Why did she tell you and not me?"

"Because when I told her about my desire to break away, I said that she wouldn't understand. So, she told me her story."

Rena was not ready for this. She felt so resentful and angry about the fact that she, a daughter, had not heard this directly from her mother. She felt cheated. "I had not known that about Mom's life. Now I feel even more an orphan."

Joe nodded.

Rena wiped her eyes and blew her nose. Joe gave her a glass of water. His hands were shaking. She needed some time to rearrange her memories of her parents.

Rena drank and put the glass on the floor next to her.

Joe said, "What a beautiful floor. I have never seen anything like it."

"Yes. It is extraordinary. When Benny and I first saw it, we knew we would buy the house."

She and Joe sat there admiring the floor. In the middle of the clean, spare, white tiles, like an oriental rug, was a mosaic display of green vines and red grapes. At the center of the rectangle was a small square repeating the same design but reversing the colors. The vines were deep red, and the grapes were green. On one side of the square in beautiful black Hebrew letters it read, 'The Season of the First Ripe Grapes.' On the other end of the square it read, 'Numbers 13:19.'

Rena thought about how in 1941, when she and Benny had first stepped into the porch, the morning sun had added its gold to the white, black, red, and green. Every color on that floor was more than itself. Magical.

"Art at our feet. I noticed it as soon as I came in. Is the biblical quote from the story of the twelve spies Moses sent to scout the land?"

Rena nodded. "When we decided to buy the house, Benny and I looked it up. The twelve spies, the Bible says, 'reached Wadi Ashcol, and there they cut down a single cluster of grapes — it had to be borne on a carrying frame by two men.' Grapes are part of this land. The people who built this house made wine. We have excellent wine, Rishon and Carmel. We export them."

Rena was embarrassed by her uncharacteristic patriotic burst. "Even I get carried away in our endless weaving of the past and the present to justify everything we do. It's quite ridiculous."

Rena was saying all of it because she did not want to remember how when they first bought the house Benny went down on his knees and traced the quote on the floor with his strong long fingers. She had to avert her eyes from the floor.

A wagtail came to the south window, displaying his striking blue feathers. He stood there for a moment, rapidly wagging his tail, then spread his wings and flew away.

"You have so much sun in Israel. I'm not used to all this light."

Rena got up to close the white curtains.

"No. It's great. I can look out at your garden. It's April and you have so many flowers. What is this plant with red flowers around the gate? It's beautiful."

"A bougainvillea," Rena said, as she re-tied the yellow sash around the curtain. "We rarely draw the curtains. Benny and I like to bring the outside into the house as much as possible."

"It is so idyllic and peaceful here."

Rena could not help herself. "I used to think so. Now it is just quiet."

Rena sat with her back to the easel in the corner. She avoided the drawing. She had not touched it since that day. She looked for a handkerchief. There were none. She picked up a napkin.

Joe looked at her. She saw pain in his eyes. He placed his hands on his knees. His lips trembled. "When I got the news, I wanted to turn the clock back. I wished I had apologized to Dad. I wanted it to be 1935 so I could say to them, 'We need to leave Poland. Not just me, all of us. Let's go together to America.' Dad would say, 'Of course, you're right. The synagogue will find another rabbi; I'll learn English, be a rabbi in a new language. I'm only forty-two, I can do it.' He would turn to Mom and say, 'Miriam, let's start packing, get the girls ready, we're all going with Joe.'"

He closed his eyes. "At the time I just wanted to get away from him. I kept writing to Mom. After

Hitler invaded Poland, I asked Mom to convince Dad to come to America. She said that he wanted to follow you to the Holy Land. I did send papers and tickets. Too late. They never got them."

All these years Rena had thought that her brother was cut off from their family. In all the letters from home, her mother had never mentioned him.

"I wanted them to come to Palestine, too," Rena said. "The documents and tickets I mailed were too late. Now I find out that not one, but two sets of papers were too late to save them." It was agonizing to think that Tova and Sara, who had followed the commandment to honor their father and mother, had been murdered because they stayed at their side. The rebels — Joe, who had shamed his father, and she, who had lied to her parents in order to leave — had survived.

The strong scent of roses came in from the north windows. The curtains billowed above the tied sash. The breeze passed. The scent lingered. Rena and her brother wept.

She told Joe about Bet Hagoel, Yair's synagogue in Jerusalem, and the ten Sephardi men who recited Kaddish for their dead parents and sisters. "Their Kaddish sounded to me like Arabic. It was so melodically unlike our Hebrew. Then I remembered that the Kaddish was in Aramaic, not in Hebrew, so a Middle Eastern chant was closer to the original." Rena chanted the first verse for her brother. Her voice floated on the porch.

"When I listened to the Kaddish in Bet Hagoel synagogue, I closed my eyes and felt the beautiful sound ascend from the synagogue straight to heaven, to the souls of our dear ones. For one whole year, ten old Sephardi men who had never known our family said Kaddish. I wanted to pay them. They refused. They said I could donate it for a mantle for one of their Torah scrolls. The old mantle was frayed. I asked if I could make one. Consultation went on, I went to Jerusalem to talk to the rabbi. Finally, the rabbi said I could design it, but a religious woman, one of the synagogue members, would have to do the embroidery. I went to Jerusalem during that year to learn the art of making Torah mantles and designed one. I became a friend of Bet Hagoel synagogue, of Rabbi Ovadya and of Mrs. Abulafia, who did the sewing and the embroidery."

The sun moved south. The light on the porch became less orange and more yellow. It got warmer. The breeze was gone.

Joe spoke with some urgency. "Rena, I would like to go to Jerusalem to Bet Hagoel and see the Torah mantle." He paused and looked at her and must have detected some dismay. "Maybe this isn't a good time for you to go to Jerusalem. We can do it on my next visit. I will come again."

Rena was not sure at all if she was ready to share Bet Hagoel with Joe. It was one thing to tell him, but to go to Jerusalem was another matter.

She was silent at first. And Joe said, "That's fine. We'll go next time."

She looked at Joe who was sitting there, who was not the young man from memory but a grown man who was reaching out, trying to connect with her, to be with her.

"No. We'll go to Jerusalem together and see the synagogue."

"My therapist told me that I should write to you, but I was reluctant," Joe said. "Then I started sending the packages and the postcards. It was the best I could do. I was afraid that you would blame me for what happened. I was the son, the eldest."

"You went to therapy?"

"Yes. Five years ago. I felt that the murder of our family had affected my marriage, my relations with my boys. I had become a workaholic. I had no time for my family, no time to think or feel. I knew I needed help if I wanted my marriage to survive and my kids to have a father." And then he smiled. "Your curse, remember?"

She should have gone to therapy. Iris had hinted often enough that she should. She had always been critical of Iris for being stuck in the past. But where was she right now?

Joe went on. "When you called and told me about Benny, I knew immediately what to do. No more regrets about what I should have or could have done. This time I wanted to act, to help you if I could. I hope it's not too late. It was good that you told me about Benny. I would like to hear more."

She did not look at Joe. She heard a car and saw the truck go to Malka's yard to get the eggs. She watched Malka and the driver walking over to the shed. Even from a distance she could see Malka's heart and feel her anguish. A late morning breeze brought into the porch a new mixture of honeysuckle and manure.

She got up and poured coffee for Joe and herself. "Benny makes the best coffee in the world. I have watched him make it so many times, yet I can never make it taste the way he does." Talking about Benny opened her heart. "Thank you, Joe, for coming. How long can you stay?"

"I've made arrangements to be away for one week. I have a ticket for next Monday." He looked at Rena. "Tell me some more about your suspicions."

She suspected that Zev Shai was somehow involved. She stayed with the facts when she told Joe about Rachel's death and about the forgotten letter from Zev. She couldn't sit down. "I know the rumors circulating even right here in Shomriya that Benny left the country. Benny didn't leave the country. If he did, it was only because he was forced, or threatened. I know that whatever happened to Benny, he didn't want to leave us."

Rena did not find it easy to confess that she should have opened Zev's letter the day she got it. She might have told Benny about Rachel, warned him of Zev.

Looking at her, Joe said, "I don't think it would have made a difference. Let's assume you had shown him the letter, told him about your suspicion that Zev had murdered Rachel. Benny, you say, is a consummate journalist. It wouldn't have deterred him. He never made it to the interview. If in fact Zev is involved, we need to ask why. Why would he want Benny out of the way? One reason could be that someone has new evidence about Rachel's death. But if Zev were afraid of revelations, you would have been the target. Another motive could be political, the article, or the Buber book."

Before Rena could say anything, a small van with the official emblem of the telephone company stopped at the gate. Two men, one tall and thin, the other short and heavy, emerged. They were holding an official document. The tall one spoke. "We are here to install a phone in your house."

Malka came over with fresh tomatoes, a shiny eggplant, and red peppers and placed them in a bowl on the table. With a smile she said, "For you, Rena. You can paint them or eat them." She turned to Joe and told him again how good it was that he had come.

Joe got up and gave Malka a hug. Malka, to Rena's surprise, hugged him back. Joe said, "I should have come a long time ago. I'm sorry I haven't met Benny and that my coming here is connected to your sorrow. But I am here now, and I'd like to help as much as I can."

Rena looked at her mother-in-law. Malka, who usually believed in doing a full day's work, had changed from her work clothes. It was before noon and there she was in black slacks and a gray shirt, her feet in sandals, her hair braided like a white crown.

"You would like my son. I know all mothers say it, but it doesn't change the fact that Benny is a good man and I'm very proud of him. He would have never left his family. Never."

Malka looked at Rena and asked her if she had had breakfast. "You need to eat."

When the phone was finally installed and working, Rena told Malka, "I want to go to Jerusalem with Joe. I'll call Zev and set up a meeting with him. I want him to look me in the eye and tell me he had nothing to do with Benny's disappearance."

CHAPTER TWENTY-ONE

On Wednesday morning Rena made four calls to the Knesset on her newly-installed phone. Each time she failed to speak directly to Zev Shai.

"Mr. Shai isn't available right now. I'll give him your message."

Finally, an aide who identified herself as Nurit told Rena that Mr. Shai had gotten her messages, but that he was very busy. A meeting the next day was out of the question. Mr. Shai's calendar was completely booked for the next several weeks. As soon as he had an opening, his office would call Rena. In a chastising tone, Nurit said, "M.K. Shai wanted me to tell you that he is in touch with the police and follows the investigation very closely. He is firmly convinced that the police are doing their best."

Listening to the woman's voice, Rena felt her anger rise. She knew better than to turn it on one of Zev's underlings. Nurit hung up without waiting for Rena's response. Rena could hear the smugness. She sat in her living room, facing the fruit trees. She raged against a protected cunning wolf masquerading as an M.K.

She could hear Joe and Mendel talking on the porch. Mendel, speaking in English, said, "The restaurant business, Joe, is good if you love it. It's long days and few vacations. If you don't love it, you shouldn't do it. Me, I hope to work to the day I die. After a long day of feeding people, when the floors shine and the kitchen is gleaming, I take a shower, I go to sleep. That's it."

She heard Joe speak in his rusty Hebrew but could not make out what he was saying. Mendel was laughing. She heard Joe joining him. After so many years, Joe's laughter was different, no longer the tight, tense laugh of his youth. His laughter was now larger, kinder.

Rena noticed how people laughed. She could tell if they were stingy or generous, mean or kind, by the way they laughed. It was one of the first things she had noticed about Benny. She had said to Iris, "I met this man. I could tell right away that I liked him from the way he laughed."

The phone rang. It was Sarah. "Finally. You just got a phone, and your line is already busy. How are you?"

"I have been on the phone all morning trying to get an appointment with Zev. I called four times. His assistant gave me the usual stuff. Busy. Sarah, he is not going to meet with me. Not if he can help it."

Rena could hear Sarah sigh on the other end of the line. But her friend came straight to the point. "You have to be very careful, Rena. Zev can so easily damage your reputation. If you continue to call, he could make you look hysterical, unbalanced. Even accuse you of harassing him. Be careful. I'd say, very careful."

Rena said, "I will." But she also knew that she was going to point an accusing finger at Zev. Yes, he would depict her as a person whose judgment could not be trusted. He had done it to Rachel so skillfully that even people who thought they knew Rachel had begun to doubt their own judgment. They had begun to say, well maybe she did commit suicide. Perhaps there was a dark, depressed side to her, and they just didn't know it.

She heard a siren on Ben Yehuda Street. To Sarah she said, "Joe and I are going to Jerusalem tomorrow." She did not say that she desperately needed to walk along what would have been Benny's usual route. She had no idea what she expected to find.

"How is the visit going?"

"I think he is trying, and I hope I am trying."

"Call me when you get back from Jerusalem."

"I have to get used to the phone."

"I know. I'm worried about you. I'll tell you what. I'll call you tomorrow evening. Bye."

Rena was just about to talk to Joe when the phone rang again. Her heart went wild, jumping in different directions. She hoped for good news. She prayed for Benny's voice. Yet, she dreaded bad news.

The sun flooded the living room. Rena did not even look at the shutters. She turned away from the window and picked up the phone.

"Rena? This is Miriam. Miriam Carmi, the poet baker from *Kol Hapoel*."

"Yes, Miriam. How are you?" Rena had met the tea cart lady a few times at Benny's office.

"I'm fine. The question is, how are you?" Without waiting for Rena's answer, she said in a lowered voice, "I want to come to Shomriya, but Mike said that your brother is there from America. I don't want to intrude. I heard you have a phone, so I thought I'd call and..." Miriam stopped.

How quickly everyone knew that she had a phone. Mike must have spread the news. "I'm glad you called, Miriam." She could hear Miriam breathing. Was Miriam hesitating? Nervous? Rena was not sure.

"Miriam?"

"I want to say how sorry I am about Benny. But...look. I just thought that maybe we could talk. Not on the phone." Silence.

"Miriam?"

"Yes. I could come to Shomriya. If I won't be intruding..."

Rena felt Miriam's fear. "You're always welcome here. I'm going to Jerusalem tomorrow morning. How about tomorrow evening around eight, or Friday evening?"

"Tomorrow. I'll be there." Miriam didn't hang up.

The phone in Rena's hand was heavy with Miriam's unspoken words. "Miriam, is anything wrong? Would you like to come tonight? Or now?"

Miriam was whispering. "It's just that someone who is creepy is acting, I don't know, creepier. I'll explain tomorrow. I'll be in Shomriya tomorrow. Bye."

Rena could have sworn that Miriam, who was a cheerful and confident woman, sounded scared. Who was the creepy person? But before she had time to think about it, Mendel came in to tell her he had brought lunch and put it on the table. He had to go back to his café. He would come back later in the evening if he wasn't too tired.

Jacob joined them for lunch. There were more phone calls. But Miriam's call kept tugging at Rena. She told herself that she was under stress and must have imagined Miriam's fear. Whatever it was, Miriam obviously thought it could wait until tomorrow evening.

Sammy Abarbanel called in late afternoon to see if Rena wanted him to give her a ride on Thursday. "You won't have to talk to people on the bus. I know that most people mean well. But you and Joe will have more peace in my car."

"I appreciate it, Sammy. But I'll have to take the bus sooner or later. Whatever unpleasant or nasty comments are out there, I may as well face them. Any news from your sources?" She held her breath and closed her eyes. She knew that she should not ask, that Sammy would tell her if he had heard anything. But she couldn't resist the urge. She was not surprised to hear that he had no news. No one had seen or heard anything.

As soon as Sammy said it, Rena felt something terribly familiar. A sharp pain, the "no news" pain. A pain like the one that had settled in her heart after the Nazis invaded Poland, when she had not heard from her family. There was the familiar agony of moving between hope and despair. The torment of being in the dark, of not knowing what had happened to her loved ones. When her family in Poland vanished, there was nothing she could do. The question was what she could do now about Benny's disappearance.

Joe went inside to take a nap. He was still asleep when Zohara came back from school. Rena told her about the trip to Jerusalem. She and Joe would go in the morning and be back in the late afternoon.

Zohara looked hot, her face sweaty, cheeks red. Rena touched her daughter's forehead to make sure she was not running a fever. She gave her a cold fruit drink and watched Zohara empty the glass.

"Would you be okay? I'll tell you what. When you come back from school tomorrow, why don't you and Shoshi come home first before you go to Malka's. I'll call you to tell you how we're doing, and what time we'll be home. How does that sound?"

Zohara was carefully refilling her glass.

"Is something the matter?"

Zohara shook her head. She put the glass down. She looked tired.

"Mom, what if whatever happened to Dad happens to you?"

Rena had feared this question would come. She went over and hugged Zohara, who was slumped in an armchair. She sat on the floor and held her daughter's hand. It was limp and unresponsive. "I promise you I'll be back." She had just made an impossible promise, but she had to say it.

"I know how you feel, Zohara. I really do. But I'll be back."

Rena was struggling to say the right thing. Zohara's braids had lost their morning tightness; they looked wild and vulnerable in their loose rubber bands.

"Uncle Joe will be there with me. Sergeant Ari from the police is going to wait for us in Jerusalem and will spend the day with us. We'll be protected. The sergeant and I have known each other for many years. We were in art school together."

Zohara pulled her legs up, pulled her hand away and retreated into the armchair. Rena wondered what she was doing, making the police sound like a protective agency when they could not even tell her what had happened to Benny. She felt justified in trusting Ari. That part was true.

She could see her daughter's worry had not gone away and she mentioned the phone again. "Remember to go inside the house to take my call because if you sit on the porch, you may not hear when the phone rings. I will call at three."

The phone rang. She said to Zohara, "Go ahead. You answer it."

Zohara got out of the chair. It was Shoshi. Rena could hear Shoshi's excited voice. "Wow. Zohara. You have a phone. Listen, if you can't sleep tonight, call me. My room is right next to the study. As soon as it rings, I'll run and get it and we can talk. Zohara, are you there?"

"Yes, I can hear you. I don't know about calling at night. I'll have to wait and see. What are you doing?"

"I'm working on my dance, 'A Fresh Egg.' See? I'm getting into this farming thing. Tell your grandmother how good I'm getting at weeding, in case she is worried about her garden being pulled up by someone like me."

"My grandmother doesn't worry. She knows you are helping."

"Okay, then. I'm coming over tomorrow when your mom and your uncle go to Jerusalem. Joe is handsome, for an older man, I mean. That doesn't sound right. Never mind, I'll see you tomorrow, unless you feel like calling me later. Don't forget to tell Malka."

"I won't. Bye, Shoshi."

It was quiet in the house. Zohara seemed to bounce back. She washed her face, re-braided her hair. "I'm going to tell Grandma how important it is that she says something nice to Shoshi about her helping us on the farm."

Rena joined Joe, now refreshed from his nap and shower and sitting on the porch. After all these years of tension and silence, her brother was here, in her home.

Later, when Zohara had gone to bed, Rena came out. She told Joe she regretted that the Jerusalem trip would not really give him a chance to see the city.

"That's fine. This visit is for you. I am happy just to go to Bet Hagoel synagogue. I'll come back as a tourist. I'll come with Susan and the boys."

Rena heard the gate creak and Jacob entered the yard. He stood at the screen door declining to sit down. He had come to suggest he go with Rena and Joe to Jerusalem to protect them from nasty people on the bus. Rena, thanking him, reminded him that Malka needed him on her farm. There were strawberries to pick. He looked at the floor as he answered in a muffled voice, "Yes. Malka needs me."

He turned to Joe and in a lighter voice said, "Between you, me, and the lamp post, I wouldn't put my hopes in the police." The two men stood there by the door talking. Unexpectedly, Jacob came over to Rena and hugged her briefly. She could not remember Jacob ever doing that. Before she could say anything, he said, "Don't worry about Zohara. Malka and I will take good care of her."

Rena woke up in the middle of the night vividly remembering her dream. On the street, in her dream, she saw Bertha running after a bus. Bertha, who had lost her husband in the Holocaust and had never stopped looking for him in Shomriya, was crying out, "My husband. Has anyone seen my husband?" In real life when Rena had heard Bertha, she pitied her. Poor Bertha. In the dream, however, she went over to Bertha and hugged her. Wide awake now in the silence of her bedroom, Rena buried her face in Benny's pillow and inhaled his smell.

CHAPTER TWENTY-TWO

Rena felt agitated when she woke the next morning. She tried to think of the Jerusalem she had known as a student, but she couldn't see it clearly. She dressed hurriedly in black slacks and a black blouse. She looked like she was going to a funeral. She changed into a pair of green pants, a beige blouse, and sandals. Joe was waiting for her in his new Israeli attire, khaki pants, a short sleeve shirt, brown socks, and sandals. Unlike the young, rebellious Joe, he was trying to fit in. She wondered if it was age or America.

When Rena put on a large hat, Joe said, "I want to buy an Israeli hat in Jerusalem." Rena just couldn't give Joe any of Benny's hats. She touched his arm. "First thing in Jerusalem, we'll get you a hat."

At the Shomriya bus stop, Rena introduced Joe to some townspeople. Joe was a distraction from unsolicited comforting words or hostile remarks. A few people did tell Rena how much they liked Benny and hoped for his safe return.

The bus came. Rena and Joe sat in the middle of the bus. It was already hot and stuffy. Rena asked Joe to open the window. When he managed to lift it, a nice breeze floated in.

When they got off the bus in Jerusalem, Sergeant Ari was waiting. His uniform gave him an official appearance, but his smile was warm. "I am glad that you're here, Joe. It's good that you came." Rena had a hard time focusing. She looked at the throng of people, she heard greetings exchanged loudly, she saw passengers met with a hug or a kiss by relatives, friends, or lovers. She had foolishly hoped that Benny would be there.

Rena suddenly remembered her dream of Bertha. Throughout the years Rena had heard Bertha roam the streets, searching, calling, crying,

Bertha, her eyes wild and feverish, waving a white, lace handkerchief, pleading, "Sigmund, Sigmund, don't leave me here, take me with you." Rena had felt sorry for her but kept her distance.

Now, in the crowded Jerusalem bus station, Rena wanted to push people aside and, like Bertha, scream her husband's name. Where was he? Why couldn't she see him? If only all these people would leave, she could have a better view. But Benny would not be there. She felt dizzy, suffocated by the thick air of disappointment. She couldn't breathe. She missed a step and stumbled. Joe and Ari each took an elbow and helped her out of the swarming station and onto Jaffa Road.

Ari said, "Let's go to Café Vienna and sit down for a moment. It's right around the corner." Inside the café they found a corner table near the window. Café Vienna was unchanged. The regulars were reading the papers, enjoying their coffee and pastry. Ari asked a waitress for some water. Whether because of his uniform or Rena's obvious collapse into a chair, the young waitress brought a jug of water and three glasses right away. Joe handed one to Rena. "You look so pale, I thought you'd faint. Are you feeling better?"

Rena, trying to steady herself, held the glass with both hands. She managed to take a sip. She put the glass down but kept holding it. "I wanted Benny…I hoped that he would be there… When I couldn't see him, I felt like Bertha."

"Who is Bertha?" Joe asked.

Rena told Joe and Ari about Bertha's strange appearance in Shomriya. How Bertha had appeared in Shomriya one day in 1946. How she had sat in the mayor's office all day without speaking, until someone took her home. How the town and Social Services found Bertha a small apartment, and how it turned out that she had some money. A mysterious bank account in Tel Aviv. Someone, who requested anonymity, had opened the account. Bertha had a checkbook that she knew how to use. She was not destitute.

"Can she take care of herself?"

"Bertha, we found out, has some skills as well as serious limitations. She can shop for herself but refuses to turn on the stove. 'No, no,' she shouted when the landlord tried to show her how to use the stove. 'No gas.' People wanted to give her an electric hot plate instead, but she rejected this alternative just as vehemently. When Mendel gave her food to take home, she ate everything cold. When Bertha was sick, Iris went to her apartment to bring her food. She ate it cold. Over the years Mendel learned to give Bertha soup in a thermos and hoped that when she ate it the soup would still be warm. Overall, she manages. It's been nine years since she came to Shomriya."

Rena could hear the noise of morning traffic on Jaffa Road. Inside the café there was a din of conversations about jobs, families, and social events. A woman at the next table talked loudly about arranging her daughter's wedding party. "It's going to cost an arm and a leg. I'd rather give her the money. But the in-laws want a big wedding."

Her companion said, "Tiny country but big weddings." They complained and laughed joyfully.

People came to Café Vienna not despite the noise, but because of it. Most people raised their voices, so one could easily become intimately familiar with the lives of strangers. Unintended but pleasurable eavesdropping was part of the attraction of sitting in cafés. Rena usually enjoyed the experience. Now she felt only resentment.

Rena thought of Bertha and how she had become a familiar, tragic, and exotic presence in Shomriya. In the winter she wore elegant black dresses, a long black coat, and a black beret. Spring, summer, and fall, she dressed in white and wore a white hat. She got books out of the library and returned them on time. She spoke to very few people and only about necessities, in short sentences.

Rena had always liked Bertha. Yet she had also considered Bertha as different and apart. Especially when she heard her over the years crying out for her husband. Dr. Shalev, from Shomriya's health clinic, said there was no reason to hospitalize Bertha. Her condition was simple. Bertha refused to accept her husband's death and her own survival. Bertha was no threat to herself or to others. Shomriya took care of her. Bertha continued to look for her husband on passing buses. Now, for the first time, Rena felt close to Bertha.

"I know how Bertha feels. I wanted to scream in the bus station, just like her, or stand there, grab people by the sleeve, ask them, have you seen my husband? Am I crazy now?"

Joe said, "It's all right to feel a little crazy. When something inexplicable happens to us we all have a Bertha in our heart. She counters craziness with craziness."

Their waitress arrived. She sorted out their order. Joe was quiet, but Rena could tell there was more he wanted to say. "Joe?"

"It is amazing to me that people could come out of the Holocaust without losing their minds."

Rena nodded in agreement. She closed her eyes and listened to the voices in the café, to ordinary requests for coffee, tea, cakes, and sandwiches. Life went on around her without Benny.

Ari, as though reading Rena's mind, spoke in a lowered voice. When his wife Dina died, he was just angry with all the people whose lives were uninterrupted. How could the world go on when Dina was no longer there? When people laughed, he would think how unfair it was. They were happy and Dina's life had been cut short. She was only thirty-five and so talented. She still had many children's books inside her, so much love to give, so many plans. All gone.

Rena was grateful to Ari and Joe. She drank her coffee. When they came out into the sunny street,

Rena put on her sunglasses and they looked for a store to buy Joe a hat. Inside a small souvenir shop, Joe chose a cloth khaki hat that had on it the words 'Shalom' and 'Holy Land.' He put it on his head, looked in the mirror, and said, "I know why Israelis call it a *kova temble*, a silly hat. But I like it."

Rena smiled at her brother. "Joe, you have gone from looking like a movie star to resembling a clown."

The moment of levity was brief. They turned from Jaffa Road onto King George, and from there went to Ramban Street. The sidewalks were filled with people. The familiar route to Hotel Tikva was a painful walk for Rena. She had taken the route whenever she came to Jerusalem with Benny.

"Does Lieutenant Gad know that you're escorting us around?"

"I'm here on police orders. I'm to escort and protect you, but also to report where you go and who you see. Above all, I'm to make sure that you don't go to the Knesset."

Rena stopped walking. The two men stopped as well. A pedestrian bumped into her. She looked at Ari. "I see. Zev already called the lieutenant. He's portraying me as a hysterical woman who is harassing him. In other words, he will make himself look like the victim and I the predator."

Rena was angry but she could tell that Ari felt compassion for her when he spoke. "That's about it." He paused, motioned for them to keep walking, and said, "I have to do my job as I understand it. Which may not always match the lieutenant's perspective. I can't say any more, Rena, at least not yet."

Rena breathed the air she always identified with Jerusalem, a mixture of coolness from the stone buildings, spices, and the warm roasted nuts sold by street vendors. She said to Ari, "My trip to Jerusalem must be so awkward for you, or worse. I'm sorry."

Ari spoke with the same self-confidence she had so much admired in his art years ago. "I have no worries in this regard. I'll do my job the way I understand it. If I get fired or demoted I can, as you said, always go back to art."

Just before they reached Hotel Tikva, Rena said, "Joe, I want to tell you about Hotel Tikva." She motioned to a bench nearby. She needed a moment before she was ready to face Benny's hotel. She told him that Hotel Tikva had always been a small, family-run hotel and that the owners, a Sephardi family, had known Benny's father's family. They had all lived in the Old City before 1948.

Nathan Tovim, a small, elegant man in a beige suit and a brown silk tie, greeted them as soon as they stepped into the lobby. He kissed Rena on both cheeks and told her how sorry he was about Benny. Rena introduced her brother. Nathan welcomed him, found out it was his first time in Jerusalem and made the appropriate blessing.

Nathan ushered them into his large office and invited them to sit in comfortable armchairs. He rang a bell, and a young hotel employee brought a large, round, brass tray with Turkish coffee, water, orange juice, and pastry. Joe took his cues from Rena. She took the tiny coffee cup, a glass of water, and a small piece of almond pastry.

Nathan said to Joe, "In times of crisis, we need our families with us." Nathan paused. He took a sip from his cup and told Joe that Benny always stayed with them when he came to Jerusalem. He passed the pastry plate around. Joe helped himself to more pastry. Rena remembered how much he had loved their mother's almond cakes. She was afraid to talk. Nathan turned his attention to Joe.

"I want to share with you, Joe, that Benny's family and mine have known each other for generations. Together, our families have seen everything. We lived through the Ottoman Empire, the British Mandate, and now, with God's help, our own country." Nathan paused to offer his guests more coffee and urge them to eat.

"This is wonderful pastry. It reminds me of my mother's pastry, but it's also different."

Nathan's face lit up with pride. "We bake our own traditional pastry. We also offer European food to give our guests choices. But our specialty is a Sephardi menu. These almond cookies are a combination of both traditions." Rena was also thinking of their mother, but she could not say so without crying. She was glad to hear Nathan go on.

"I regret, Joe, that we can't take you to see where our families used to live. Our holy city has been divided and our old neighborhood and the Sasson and Tovim houses are now in Jordanian territory. Rena can take you to see where the city has been divided so that you can see for yourself the walls of the Old City."

Rena wanted to sink into the armchair and stay in Nathan's peaceful office and listen to his Sephardi-accented Hebrew as he talked about the past, about the Sassons, Yair, Benny, anything. If she could only just stay there, look at the walls with the photographs of the Tovim family, dignified women, men in colorful clothing with their adored children.

Nathan may have noticed that Rena's eyes were turned to the photographs. He got up and pointed out a group portrait. "These, Joe, are the leaders of the Jewish community in Jerusalem in 1898, welcoming Kaiser Wilhelm II. This is the Triumphal Arch, which the Jewish community built to welcome the Kaiser. And this handsome man here is Benny's grandfather, proudly leading the Jewish delegation."

Ari sat quietly watching Nathan. When Rena told Nathan that they were going to Bet Hagoel to meet Rabbi Ovadya, Nathan said that a police escort was wise. He mentioned that he had met the sergeant when Ari came to talk to the staff after Benny's disappearance. "I have full confidence in you, Sergeant Ari. It's good to have police protection. But it's also good to have God's protection. Since we have no access to the Western Wall, the synagogue is a good place. We used to pray there. Bet Hagoel is now where we have been praying."

He turned to Rena and said, "Dear Rena." He stopped, but she wanted him to go on. He looked at her. "The spirit of the Sasson family will be with you in our synagogue, and since you have donated the Torah mantle, the spirit of your own family will be there to protect you. Our people have prayed for the souls of your parents and your sisters, may they rest in peace. Your family is part of our synagogue."

Rena felt herself sinking further into the chair. She was wishing, irrationally, that Nathan would miraculously bring back Benny. After Yair had been killed in the war, Benny had talked to Nathan about the kinds of serious matters he would have discussed with his own father.

Nathan assured Rena that the Sephardi community would do whatever it could. "If anyone saw or knew something about Benny, sooner or later one of the Tovim family members will hear about it. As soon as we know something, we'll let you know."

Rena prepared herself to leave. She gave Nathan her phone number. "We just got a phone. Sammy helped me get it."

She looked around and said, "Could I have a copy of the photograph of Benny's grandfather greeting the Kaiser? I would love to have it for Zohara."

Outside, as they walked to Bet Hagoel, Rena faced the truth that Benny was not in Hotel Tikva. Benny never stayed anywhere but at this hotel. Even when he didn't stay overnight, he would go to pay his respects to the Tovim family. When Benny's grandparents died, the Tovim had become his extended family. The fact that they didn't know where Benny was meant he wasn't in Jerusalem.

Rena could not bring herself to say the words, 'not alive.' She said instead, "I think I'm getting more and more like Bertha."

Joe held her by the elbow and said, "This is a difficult time."

"Well, if Bertha is my model, I may spend my life not facing the facts."

Ari told her, "I have known you since art school and I doubt very much that you'll become like Bertha."

"This journey is harder than I imagined. I realize now that I needed to feel, in my bones, that Benny isn't in Jerusalem."

Joe wanted to know, "Do you feel that he isn't here?"

But before she could answer, Ari suddenly began to talk, very deliberately, about his impressions of Nathan and the Tovim family. Rena saw that he was alert, carefully examining their surroundings as they walked. She joined him in discussing Nathan, and so did Joe. They kept it up until they entered the synagogue. Rena then asked, "What is it?" Ari said very quietly, "I think someone was following us. I'll report it when I get back to the station. The best we can do now is go into the synagogue."

Inside Bet Hagoel Rena saw two people studying. One of them closed his book, kissed it, put it down, and came over. He said, "Mrs. Sasson, we heard of your plight. We're all praying for your husband. I'll go and tell Rabbi Ovadya that you are here. Nissim here can show your guests the beauty of our synagogue."

Nissim closed his book and joined them. Joe admired the reading platform that stood to the west of the ark, ensconced in a niche in the eastern wall of the synagogue. Four wooden steps led to the platform, its base covered with marble panels framed by carved wood. On the top part of the platform, a delicate design of brass arches matched the brass lamps hanging from the ceiling.

Rabbi Ovadya, a small man with large dark eyes and an energetic step, arrived. In his high, firm voice, he greeted Rena and welcomed Joe. "We are praying for Benny. But we need your help, too. Since you're here, we can read something from Psalms together so that your voices will stay in this place and mingle with our prayers."

Rena nodded and waited. Rabbi Ovadya turned to Joe. "Your sister says she is a secular Jew, and it is possible that it is only a temporary condition. But it doesn't matter what she thinks she believes, because how she acts is more important. We are not commanded by God to believe. We are commanded to follow a Jewish way of life. When Rena came to see me about saying Kaddish for your family and donated the Torah mantle in their memory, she said, 'I don't believe in God.' But she was doing the right thing, and the rest, I believe, will follow. Every mitzvah, every good deed, counts and adds up in God's book."

Rena was too distraught to remember that she liked this man. She burst out, "I don't want to be disrespectful, Rabbi Ovadya. But how can I believe in God? How can God allow so much suffering to happen? The Holocaust, our family, our father and mother who always wanted to do only good in the world, my two innocent sisters, and now Benny." She immediately regretted her words.

Rabbi Ovadya gathered in her words with compassion and added his own. Her words and his would be bound together. "God understands you, Rena. He does. You are in pain. But in this suffering, a reading from our Holy Scripture would be good. A sentence or two could stay here in the synagogue and that would be enough. Your own prayer would carry the special weight of a wife's voice added to our own prayers. A wife's pleading for her husband will go straight to heaven."

Rabbi Ovadya told Joe to open the Holy Ark so that he could see the Torah mantle. Joe examined the blue mantle that Rena could see even with her eyes closed. At the center of the mantle was an embroidered replica of their father's synagogue, surrounded by the words, 'In memory of Rabbi Yitzhak Klein, his beloved wife Miriam, and their daughters Tova and Sara who perished in the Holocaust.'

Joe recited in a clear voice, "May their souls be bound up in the bond of eternal life and in the company of the immortal souls of the righteous who have merited the bliss of immortality. Amen."

Joe closed the ark and came down the steps wiping his tears. "Did you have a photograph of our father's synagogue? It's exactly the way I remember it."

"No, I wish I had. This is from memory. I have several drawings I made for the embroidery. I'll give you one." She turned to Ari who stood quietly in the synagogue, his own official status deferring to Rabbi Ovadya's authority. She told Ari that the Nazis had burned down their father's synagogue.

"It no longer exists except in our hearts, in our memories, and here."

Rabbi Ovadya gave them each a volume of Psalms and said, "Let us begin with Psalm 102, a prayer for anyone beset by any kind of misfortune." Rena heard her voice joining her brother's as they chanted, "God hear my prayer and let my cry reach you."

Rabbi Ovadya guided them out of the synagogue, through a narrow alley, and into a courtyard, 'the Abulafia headquarters,' as Rena called it. Mrs. Abulafia and her married children occupied the apartments around the courtyard. Mrs. Abulafia, in her long dark dress and colorful headscarf, stepped outside and hugged Rena. "Oh, my dear, my dear girl. So much trouble in your life. You know, Rena, that our dear Benny, may God protect him, always paid his respects to his father's people. Our Benny is always thinking of others, even of the Arabs. Who wants to think of them after 1948? Benny does. He follows our holy

Torah that tells us that God commanded us to treat the 'ger' with kindness because we were once strangers in Egypt. Benny is the pride of our community, like his father and his grandfather before him, may they all rest in peace. All leaders."

Mrs. Abulafia wove Benny's ideas not into political 'left' and 'right' but into a religious worldview. For her, Benny was not a political activist but a man walking with God. Rena felt that the trip to Jerusalem had been justified just by hearing those words. She would bring these words and feelings back to Zohara. Her daughter would like it.

Mrs. Abulafia told Joe that his family was now part of her community. "I have made the embroidery on the Torah mantle for your family and now your parents and your sisters are forever in our hearts and in our synagogue."

She looked at Joe. To be sure her words were going in the right direction, she added, "Every time I finished a name I touched it with my hands, traced each gold letter, and told your parents that their Rena was safe with us."

Rena hugged her and Mrs. Abulafia kissed her on the head the same way Rena had kissed Zohara that morning. She invited everyone to a long table covered with food. "You too, Sergeant Ari. You're Benny's and Rena's friend, so you're our friend." Some of Mrs. Abulafia's children and grandchildren came in, were introduced, ate, took part in the conversation, cleared dishes, brought out more food, and urged the guests to eat.

They asked Joe about Chicago and America and wanted to know when he was planning to come back and bring his family. Joe tried to keep their names straight. Never mind, they told him. For a moment Rena forgot why they were there. She liked their noise, their generosity, and their interest in Joe. Mrs. Abulafia said, "You should come back soon. You can stay at Hotel Tikva, but for lunch you come here. When you come back,

God willing, I'll make special food. Rena, you'll bring Zohara and Malka too."

Rena got out of her chair and walked around the crowded table as chairs moved to let her pass. She went into the kitchen where Mrs. Abulafia was supervising washing, drying, and putting dishes away and storing the huge amounts of leftovers. They all circled Rena with offers of tea, a cold drink, fruit. She shook her head, no. "She is looking for the bathroom," said one of the granddaughters. "Hush," said her mother. Mrs. Abulafia asked Rena if she needed anything.

"It's a quarter to three and I need a phone to call Zohara at three." Mrs. Abulafia said not to worry: they too had a phone. She started to laugh and all the women in the kitchen laughed with her.

One of the daughters-in-law dried her hands, re-tied her headscarf, and said, "They just saw all the Abulafia women, and the office manager said, 'Give them a phone.'" They all laughed again.

Mrs. Abulafia told Rena, "The phone is in the dining room. Do you want us to go out?"

"No. I'd like you to stay."

At three in the afternoon, Mrs. Abulafia announced, "Rena needs to make a long-distance call to Zohara." People lowered their voices.

Rena dialed her own new number. At the other end was the miracle of her daughter's lovely voice. Before Rena could say anything, Zohara said, "Hi, Mom. How are you and Uncle Joe?"

Rena told her that they were all fine and getting ready to come home. Before Rena could ask, Zohara volunteered, "I am fine. School was fine. Mike called. He said to call him as soon as possible. He said it several times, as if I were a little kid, or stupid." Her daughter, deepening her voice, imitated Mike. "Don't forget. Tell your mom it's urgent."

Rena laughed and felt almost happy to hear this light mocking that was not typical of Zohara. She must have learned it from Shoshi. "I'll call him right away. I'll see you later."

She dialed Mike's number. He answered immediately.

CHAPTER TWENTY-THREE

Murdered. That was the word Rena heard and it pounded in her ears. She felt nauseous and her knees wobbled. "Murdered," she said when she put the receiver down. The room went silent. Mrs. Abulafia put her hand on her mouth. In a voice she hardly recognized Rena said, "Mike just told me that Miriam has been murdered."

"Who is Miriam?" Rena could not tell who asked the question. She replied in a raspy voice that Miriam worked at *Kol Hapoel* delivering tea and pastries and was a friend of Benny and hers.

Mrs. Abulafia said, "May God have mercy." She put a large shawl over Rena's shoulders and kept her arms around her. Rena wanted to stay there, but the thought of Zohara and the idea that her daughter could hear of Miriam's murder meant she needed to get home as soon as possible. "I have to go home." She was glad when Mrs. Abulafia made a knot on the shawl, "to keep you nice and warm." Rena was afraid she would lose it. Joe held her arm. In a near whisper, she told Ari, "Miriam called me yesterday. She said she would come over this evening. She was frightened. She mentioned something about a creepy man."

Ari asked quietly. "What exactly did she say about him?"

Rena could hardly speak. "I think she said someone who is creepy is acting creepier... Then she said she would tell me more tonight..."

Ari looked concerned and somber. He said that he would take them to a taxi service. Joe and Rena would take a taxi from Jerusalem to Shomriya. Rena did not object. She had never done it before. She had always taken the bus. Under the circumstances, a cab was not extravagant.

She felt sick. Years ago, when she first came to Palestine, she had had malaria attacks and was given chloroquine. Rena knew that what she was experiencing now was not caused by malaria. Why would anyone murder Miriam? Who would do such a thing? She couldn't allow herself to connect Benny's disappearance and Miriam's murder.

Ari dropped them off at the Allenby Taxi Service. Joe helped her into the back seat of a cab and got in next to her. The driver, an older man with gray hair and moustache, seemed to have realized the gravity of her situation and kept quiet as they headed out the winding road from Jerusalem to the coastal plain. Rena, who had braced herself for a talkative driver, was grateful. It was sixty-eight degrees outside, but much warmer in the cab. The driver had all the windows down to let the breeze in. Rena was cold; her teeth chattered. She closed her window in the back and asked Joe to roll up the window on his side.

Rena's heart felt cold. She said to Joe, "I can't believe it. Who would want to kill Miriam?"

"Who is Miriam?"

"She had the food concession at *Kol Hapoel*. She was a poet, a warm and funny woman. It just doesn't make sense."

"I read about homicides in Israel and the numbers are very low."

Rena nodded.

"There are not many murders here. Which is why it makes no sense."

"Crime is often senseless. A person could be at the wrong place at the wrong time."

"Miriam was murdered in her own home. She lived alone on the ground floor of a three-story apartment building in Tel Aviv." Was she shouting? Rena couldn't tell.

"A neighbor had come out to get the bottle of milk and the morning paper when he saw Miriam's cat outside and the apartment door slightly opened. Miriam never let her cat out. Ever. The neighbor wondered what was going on and found

Miriam, shot, unconscious and bleeding. She was taken to the hospital, but they couldn't save her."

Joe looked at Rena as though he was reading her mind. "It could be unrelated," he said.

"It could." But she felt that Miriam's death had cast an ominous shadow on Benny's disappearance. She didn't want to think about it. "Let's look at the facts. Why would anyone want to kill her? Nothing was taken. Her place wasn't burglarized. If Miriam's murder wasn't about money, it could be a crime of passion. But as far as anyone knew she wasn't romantically involved with anyone." Rena was almost afraid to go on. "So, a third motive could be political."

Joe looked at her more closely. "Rena, are you sure you don't want us to stop and get you something to drink?"

"No. I just want to get home. It's been a long day. For you, too."

"I'm fine. Don't worry about me. You have enough on your mind. I just wish that I could do more to help."

She took his hand. "It's good that you are here."

As soon as they got out of the cab, Zohara and Shoshi came running to the gate. Rena hugged her daughter. Pulled her close. Kissed her and would not let go. Holding on tightly to Zohara she said, "Hi, Shoshi. I'm glad you came to keep Zohara company."

Zohara cried out, "Mom, you're shivering. Are you sick?" The three of them walked together to the porch. Rena could barely make it to the armchair. Shoshi grabbed an afghan hanging on one of the chairs, and Zohara ran inside and got the red wool blanket and a pillow from her parents' bedroom. Shoshi brought a footstool from the living room.

Zohara made tea, put two spoons of honey in the cup, and gave it to her. Rena tried to steady her hands. She decided to wait to tell Zohara about Miriam. The tea felt good. When she finished, she put the cup down. She asked Zohara to come sit next to her. When she took her daughter's hand and held it, Zohara whispered, "Is it about Dad?"

"No. No. We have no news about Dad. The police and our friends in Jerusalem are looking for him. The people at Bet Hagoel synagogue are not only praying for Dad, but they are also looking for him. The whole Sephardi community is listening and watching."

Rena stretched the afghan out to cover her daughter's shoulders as well and held her. Zohara put her head on Rena's shoulder and cried. Rena's blouse was getting wet. With her right hand she wiped Zohara's face. She rocked her as she had done when Zohara was a baby. Shoshi came over and sat on the other side of Zohara and held her hand. Rena listened to her daughter's heartbeat.

Joe went into the kitchen and came out with a tray, more tea for Rena, some of Mendel's mandarin soda for Shoshi and Zohara, and coffee for himself.

They sat quietly for a while. They could hear the sprinklers in the flower garden. Rena knew that Zohara had turned them on. She was grateful for the farm routines that kept Zohara busy. She noticed flowers in the vase on the table. Zohara had picked Rena's favorites, a lovely arrangement of flaming red dahlias, bright yellow zinnias, and delicate pink sweet peas. "Thank you, Zohara, for watering the garden and for putting flowers on the table. It looks very nice."

Zohara was holding the glass that Joe had given her. "Mom, I'm so glad you're home. Uncle Joe made you good tea. You look a bit better."

A car stopped near Malka's house. The dogs on the street began their loud barking. Zohara got up, went to the eastern windows, and said, "Grandma has visitors. She told me earlier that she was waiting for friends from the kibbutz."

Moments later, Malka came across the road with Abrasha, Munik, and Sonya, three kibbutz elders and old friends. Malka looked at her daughter-in-law and rushed across the porch. "Rena, what has happened?"

Zohara spoke before Rena could say a word. "It's not about Dad. Mom came home sick. I made tea for her and then Uncle Joe made her tea and Shoshi and I made her comfortable. And Grandma, the whole Sephardi community in Jerusalem is looking for Dad. Shoshi had known all along that they were looking for Dad." Shoshi looked quite pleased and nodded.

Rena saw her mother-in-law studying her face. She said, "I'm okay. It was just a bit too much. It was a long day. I'm feeling much better."

She was glad to see the kibbutz Kalaniyot delegation standing at the screen door. Malka needed her peers and close friends. Two short, muscular, tough men and a taller woman. They all looked alike, dressed in white shirts and khaki pants.

Rena apologized for not getting up. Before she could finish, they had surrounded her. The men took turns, slowly bending arthritic knees to kiss her on both cheeks. Callused hands patted her shoulders. Sonya attempted a hug, then took both of Rena's hands, and finally let go.

Malka said to the three, "I want you to meet Rena's brother, Joe from America, and Shoshi Abarbanel, Sammy's daughter and Zohara's friend."

Rena looked at the tough-looking, no-nonsense trio. Tanned by years of farm work, confident in their competence. Munik nodded his head up and down. "Yes. We know and appreciate Sammy. Tell him kibbutz Kalaniyot will never forget the guns he brought in the dark of night so that we could defend ourselves when the Syrian army attacked us." Sonya turned to Zohara. "We have a gift for you." She gave Zohara a present wrapped in pink paper and tied with a blue ribbon. Zohara opened it carefully and found a slim, typed volume titled *The Words of Children*.

"When Zohara visited last year, we asked her if she would like to participate in our youth poetry book. Here we are. An honorary kibbutz child."

Zohara clutched the book without opening it. Sonya told her to look at it whenever she felt like it.

When Rena went to bed that night, she saw that all the lights were still on at Malka's house.

CHAPTER TWENTY-FOUR

Miriam's funeral took place on Friday morning. There were more people at the funeral than Rena had expected. Co-workers from *Kol Hapoel* were there. Poets, writers, neighbors, and it turned out that Miriam had one relative, a cousin who had survived the Holocaust. She was there with her husband. The husband, a thin man with sad eyes, said the Kaddish in a Yiddish accent. His wife cried loudly at the grave. "Why? Why did God let Miriam die here in the Holy Land? Was it not enough that her parents, her sisters, and her brothers died?" She bent down, took a fistful of earth, and put it on Miriam's shrouded body lying in the open grave.

People were waiting for Miriam's cousin to move away so that they could approach and place some more soil to cover Miriam's body, but the cousin did not move. She looked up and shook a fist at the sky, a fist that was covered with black soil. "You had to allow Miriam to be murdered, too? By our own people?"

There was a sudden stillness in the cemetery. The wind moved in the branches of the eucalyptus trees. Someone made a move toward the grave and people resumed talking in low voices.

When it was her turn, Rena looked down at the open grave. There was Miriam's body wrapped in a white shroud, lying in the moist dark earth, waiting with great dignity for the last touch of her friends. Miriam seemed much smaller than Rena remembered. She took a fistful of earth. It felt as good and familiar as the soil she had used to give life to her plants. Rena bent down and put it gently on Miriam's body. She had a hard time getting up.

She walked toward Miriam's cousin. When Rena shook her hand, she realized how thin the woman was. Ten years in Israel hadn't fattened her up. She looked at Rena. "This is a terrible country. We were told that in the Holy Land our troubles would be over. But no. Not true. First the War in 1948. They took Shimmel right away, told him his Yiddish name was no good for a soldier. They said his name in Hebrew was Shimon, gave him a gun, and told him to shoot Arabs." She cried and looked at Rena. Some people heard her and walked away. Someone muttered angrily something about Holocaust survivors who always live in the past. Enough already. A few people stood nearby in silence.

Shimmel put his arm around his wife. He said, in Yiddish, "Enough, enough, Gittel. You'll just make yourself sick." Miriam's cousin had a name. Gittel. Malka came over and stood next to Rena. Gittel was not finished. They stood there, a small group of mourners, between so many gleaming tombstones adorned with the small stones placed on top of the graves by grieving relatives. The dead should be remembered. Rena and the mourners waited for Gittel to go on.

Shimmel still had an arm around her. Gittel clutched her purse. "It was Miriam who took care of us when we came here. Two survivors from the camps. Miriam helped us. Not the state as they promised. The Jewish Agency sent us to some godforsaken place in the Negev. They didn't tell us it was desert and hot. An apartment building, all concrete. Nobody spoke Yiddish. They were all from Morocco. In the camps we had wanted to live. Now we wanted to die."

The man from the Burial Society approached. He whispered something about another funeral. Gittel paid no attention. "Miriam came and took us back to Tel Aviv, gave us her bedroom. She slept in the living room on the couch. Shimmel and I screamed in our sleep. Nobody in Israel wanted us to speak about the death camps. But they could not stop us from crying. Miriam told us that we would heal, in time. The sun, the warm climate, the land, our land, we would heal. She found us a place to live not too far from her. 'I need you. You are my only family,' she told us. But I think that she wanted to keep an eye on us. Help us. She helped us find work."

As Rena listened to Gittel, she noticed a man in a dark suit looking at her. Rena thought he might be from the Burial Society. But a religious man would not look so directly at a woman as this man did. When he saw that Rena had noticed him, he moved quickly away and before she could approach him, he was gone. Rena knew that the police were there at the burial. She had seen Ari earlier, but they had not spoken. Ari was gone now. She would call Ari and tell him about this strange man, but right then she wanted to say something helpful to Gittel.

Rena turned to her. "Some of Miriam's friends are coming to my studio. We'll have food and talk about Miriam. Please come with us." She wished she had pressed Miriam to say more when she had called shortly after the phone was installed. Find out why she wanted to come, what was it all about, who was the creepy guy and why he had upset her.

Gittel said that she and her husband would come to Rena's studio. "Miriam was my only family. She said to us that this was a good country. We wanted to go to America, but Miriam said to stay here. There are gangsters in Chicago. Is it safe here? There is nothing safe here. This is a land that devours its people. I told this to Miriam when our friend from the concentration camps was killed in the battle for Jerusalem. Miriam told me to be patient, to give this young country time. You tell me, how much time?"

Rena said, "I don't know, Gittel. I don't know."

Shimmel whispered something to Gittel. She looked at Rena and took her hand again. "Please forgive me. I'm a bitter woman. With your husband missing. How awful." It seemed that she wanted to say more but changed her mind. She patted Rena's cheek. "We will come to your studio. Miriam thought so highly of your husband."

Mike was at the graveyard, talking to journalists from other newspapers. One of them asked out loud, "So what's going on at your paper? Disappearances? Murders? Is that where the Left is going?"

Mike had his hand over his heart. Rena thought that he looked worse than usual. She said to Sarah, "Mike seems very upset." Sarah looked at him. "He hasn't slept all night. Didn't even pretend to come to bed. He is still wearing the same clothes he wore yesterday when he heard that Miriam was murdered."

"Did he say anything to you?"

Sarah shook her head and walked towards the parking lot to bring the car around. "I'll meet you outside the gate."

Joe had appointed himself an escort to Malka. Rena was sure that Jacob had cornered Joe earlier with a request to protect Malka. If Malka had known of this, she would have been furious with Jacob. Or would she? Rena was no longer sure.

When they got out of the car in front of Rena's studio, she said very quietly to Sarah, "I saw a man who tried to look like the Burial Society guys, a black suit and a black hat. Only he wasn't one of them. He was looking directly at me."

Sarah was concerned. "Did he seem threatening?"

"There was something sleazy about him. I have a feeling that I saw him in Jerusalem yesterday, too. When Miriam called me, the day before she was murdered, she said something about a 'creepy' man. This guy looked slimy. I wonder who he was. And why would he pretend to be an ultra-orthodox Jew?"

Sarah looked tired and sad. Alarmed. "You have to call Ari and tell him." Rena nodded. The man frightened her.

Later, in her studio, after everyone had left, Rena and Joe stayed on. She was glad that Joe was there. It held despair at a distance. She needed to do things. Just as Malka and Zohara needed the farm. Only the farm also really needed them. Her art was a different matter, but Rabbi Ovadya did not seem to think so. He had called and told her keep up her art. To know that she was painting would help them when they prayed, he said. It was about hope, the rabbi explained, everything they did that was life-affirming was like a spark of hope, and they needed everybody's sparks. Benny, the rabbi said in his rather high-pitched voice, needed them all to affirm life. Rena tried very hard to hold on to the rabbi's words as she took Joe to the gallery, just down the street from her studio, to show him her exhibit *Gifts from America*. It was still on display. He stood there looking at it. "This is quite an indictment of America and of me. How should I say it? Rich, arrogant, and ignorant, out of touch with the very people to whom we offer our material goods. You are a good artist, Rena. I mean it."

Rena, in a moment of compassion, said, "I know you and Susan meant well."

Joe said, "I really wanted to make peace between us. I could have done better."

He took photographs of her art. In her studio, Joe had admired other pieces of Rena's work, and she had given him a watercolor titled *Mendel's Café*. The painting showed four tables under the jacaranda trees. Several people were sitting around in animated conversation holding tall glasses of Mendel's fruit soda.

Benny liked coming to her studio. She could not even say this to Joe. It would take away whatever it was that was still holding her together. She sat down on a chair, hugged her knees, and closed her eyes. When she opened her eyes, Joe was sitting on a chair looking at her. Rena said, "Poor Gittel."

"Was Gittel right when she said that nobody in Israel wants to hear about the Holocaust?"

To talk about anything was helpful. Even though Rena did not want to admit it, she could not avoid seeing the truth of Gittel's accusation. "We have a day every year, Yom HaShoah, in which we pay respect to the Holocaust. But in our daily lives we don't want to hear about it from survivors."

"Why?"

Rena spoke in an almost-whisper in her quiet studio. "We have this moral attitude that it was their fault. They could have left Europe, as we did. They refused. And yes, the Holocaust was a tragedy, but they should get over it and not implicate us by telling us endlessly about their experiences in the camps."

She could tell that Joe was shocked. She remained as honest as she could. "When they came from the ashes of the death camps, they reminded us of our vulnerability, and we didn't want to be reminded." She heard the way that she used the plural, 'we,' 'they.' She felt ashamed.

"It doesn't sound right to me. It sounds heartless."

"I'm not defending it. Just trying to explain. I have refused to think about it for a long time. Gittel's words brought home to me the survivors' torment and suffering."

Rena knew that the words they spoke were also about their own anguish, about their murdered family. Their parents and sisters were victims who had not been given the chance to become survivors.

They sat in her studio on folding chairs and cried for those who had died and those who had survived and for Benny whose fate was unknown. They drank water from the tap above the sink that Rena used to rinse out her brushes and wash her hands. When they dried their tears, there was a mild but pleasant smell of paints in the room. Joe held on to the painting that Rena had given him.

On their way out Joe covered his head with the hat he had bought in Jerusalem and kissed the mezuzah that the previous owner had left on the doorpost. Neither Rena nor any of her friends ever came close to touching the mezuzah. It was there like an art object decorating the door. Her brother treated it like the religious object it was meant to be. He touched it, then put his hand to his lips and said the traditional blessing that Rena had not heard in years, "May God guard our coming and going from now and forever."

"You changed it from 'my coming and going' to 'our.'"

"I have included you. I have also included Benny. I pray for his safety."

Rena cried again and wiped her tears with her hands.

Joe put an arm around her and said, "It took me a long time to come back to God. I left home to get away from Dad and the synagogue. I could never go back to our father's way of life. I joined a Conservative synagogue, which is both familiar and follows a traditional liturgy, but it is also liberal and open-minded."

Walking to the bus stop, Rena told him that she liked being a secular Israeli. In that respect she was more like her mother-in-law. She could not imagine belonging to a synagogue. She added, "I could only relate to something like Bet Hagoel from a distance and as a total outsider. Now Rabbi Ovadya is telling me they need me when they pray." She added, "Mom and Dad would be pleased that you are praying again."

Joe gave her another hug. "Rena. They loved you. Dad too. He did."

They were close to the beach. The afternoon wind brought the smell of the Mediterranean. Rena wanted to tell him about how no one ever called her *tayere kind* anymore. How her parents' precious endearment stayed in her heart.

"I'm glad that Mom wrote to you." She looked at the crowded beach and added, "Thanks for telling me that Mom approved of my going to Palestine. That was a real gift."

On the morning of Joe's departure, Zohara and Rena went along to the airport to see Joe off. Zohara said, "I wish you could stay."

"I'll come back with Aunt Susan and your cousins. I promise. In the meantime, we'll talk on the phone. Whenever you feel like talking to me, just call."

Rena did not regret Joe's visit. They had both done as well as they could. They had had some good moments. Compassionate moments. Zohara seemed to have taken a real liking to Joe. Having a phone meant that Zohara could get to know her cousins' voices. It was not as good as having siblings, but for Zohara, who yearned for a family, they were the only cousins she had.

CHAPTER TWENTY-FIVE

A month after Benny's disappearance, Rena received a phone call from Mayor Agron. "This is not easy for me. It was not my decision. If it were up to me, I would not be making this call."

Rena realized that something unpleasant was about to follow and she was determined not to help him. She was silent and he went on. "I'm really sorry, but the town council has decided to remove your painting *Mrs. Bialik Comes to Town*. I'll be glad to drop it off at your house."

She should not have been surprised, but she was. "When did the council meet? I'm a member of the council."

"Well, it was an unofficial meeting. We took a vote. A majority wanted it removed."

Rena clutched the phone to steady herself. "What is an unofficial meeting?"

Agron spoke as though Rena were an unruly child. "We chose your painting at a time when things were different. People are uneasy now. There are questions around Benny's disappearance that cast doubt... People feel that if he left the country, you must have known about it."

Rena wanted to hit him or call him a bastard. When the rumors started, she had hoped Agron would not betray Benny. It was excruciating to see how foolish she had been. "Agron, do you actually believe that Benny left the country?"

Agron sighed. "Of course not. But the council is democratic." He raised his voice a bit. "I was outvoted. What can I say?" Plenty, Rena thought. You could have fought for us. There was really no point in pursuing the conversation. She hung up.

Agron came by and brought her painting wrapped like a gift. Rena was waiting with a hammer in her hand. For a moment he looked alarmed. She was pleased. She waited a moment, tore the wrapping, and before Agron could say a word, hung the painting on the porch. Everyone who walked on Herzl Street could see it.

Rena looked at Agron and then at the painting, at Mrs. Bialik sitting serenely and smiling like the Mona Lisa. She was going to make Agron as uncomfortable as she could. She said in a loud but steady voice, "Mrs. Bialik, I apologize for my town's ignorance and bad behavior. Under the circumstances, I'm sure that you will be much happier here."

"Rena, you have to believe me..."

"I hold you responsible, Agron. You are a powerful mayor." She went over and held the screen door wide open and waited for him to leave. "Mrs. Bialik and I would like to be alone." She let the screen bang behind him. To Mrs. Bialik she said, "In life you saw us at our best and now you see us at our worst." More quietly she said,

"Just between the two of us, my heart is broken, and I don't know what to do about it." Rena fell asleep in her chair under the watchful eyes of Mrs. Bialik.

The next day Rena went to Tel Aviv to work in her studio. She locked the door, didn't go out for lunch. She painted with her fingers. No brush could do as well as her icy fingers. She worked furiously. She had a hard time getting the paint off her hands. They were still stained when she got on the bus. She put on her sunglasses. She sat in the back of the bus with an open book. Every few minutes she turned a page, but her eyes saw nothing but the painting she had left behind. If anyone approached her, she would scream.

There was a note on the front porch. 'Outraged at the town council's scandalous behavior. I want to hang this charming painting of Mrs. Bialik in my café. Agron is as good as dead in my book.' It was signed, Mendel.

Two days later, on a lovely Shabbat morning, Zohara went to synagogue with the Abarbanels. Rena stayed home and produced sketches of monsters. She wondered what Rabbi Ovadya would say to that, would it still be life-affirming? She had never made such ugly creatures before. Mendel interrupted her, bringing food for lunch. He looked at the drawings and shook his head. "This is scary stuff, Rena."

"This is a scary time."

"All the more reason to have some good, nourishing food." He started unpacking his pots, and the smell of spices filled the porch. Rena went inside to wash her hands, but the monsters were still in her fingers. She stood at the sink with her hands under the running faucet and avoided looking in the mirror.

Jacob, Malka, and Iris came over. Rena could see them watching her. Malka saw the pile of newspapers on the porch and said, "I've stopped reading them."

Iris chimed in. "Rena, you may want to avoid the papers. It's not good for you. How about going to the beach after lunch?"

Rena declined. She said she needed some rest. An afternoon siesta would do her good. In truth, she wanted to go back to her monsters.

Bertha and Gittel had become her soul mates, her secret sisters. Rena was now both the desperate woman looking for her husband and the bitter cousin mourning Miriam.

When her Shabbat guests finally left, Rena read the bourgeois newspaper *Haboker*. There was an article by Shamir attacking the Left and especially the Worker's Party on its position on the rights of Arabs, 'minorities,' as Shamir called them. He mentioned that one of the Left's intellectual journalists was rumored to have been a spy who had defected to the Soviet Union. No names were mentioned. Shamir took care to say that while it was only a rumor, "It is an indication of the degree to which some in the Left would sell our country's secrets to the Soviets. Before it is too late, I call on the extreme Left to repent, to renounce loud and clear its ties with the communists and to support our alliance with the United States."

Rena smashed her fist into the paper. She crumpled the newspaper into a ball and threw it in the wastebasket. Then she retrieved it, smoothed it, and tore out the article. She pinned it on one of her new sketches of monsters. Her missing husband had been turned into a Soviet spy.

Mike called to tell Rena that there would be a strong response to Shamir's article in *Kol Hapoel*. He sounded terrible, breathing hard, coughing, and sneezing.

On Sunday, after Zohara had left for school, Rena opened the newspaper *Haaretz*. There was a paid ad signed by one hundred prominent people. "We are angry at the rumors surrounding the disappearance of Benny Sasson, a talented journalist and decorated soldier. One ugly rumor suggests that Benny was a spy and a defector.

There is no doubt in our mind that something terrible happened to Benny. We are sad that his family has to endure not only the uncertainty of his fate but the indignity of rumors by those on the Right who want to take political advantage of a terrible tragedy." Buber had signed the ad and so had Mike. She traced each name with her fingers. Zev Shai's name was not there.

There was another ad by Bet Hagoel synagogue. Sammy and Pnina's signatures were on that list.

Malka came in holding a bowl of fresh strawberries. Between Mendel and Malka there was more than enough food in her house.

Malka put the bowl down and said, "Rena, there are also good people. Did you see the ads? We still have many friends."

Even though Rena was touched by the support, it did not undo the malice of so many.

She said to Malka, "I'm seriously thinking of joining Bertha on her rounds. 'Has anyone seen my husband?' I think that Bertha and I together would be a powerful team. All by herself Bertha seems mad, but the two of us together would be another story."

Malka hugged her. Rena had always thought of Malka as just her mother-in-law with whom she had a complicated relationship. Now she let herself realize that Malka was a mother whose son had disappeared. She wanted to tell Malka something about her feelings. Instead, she took Malka's hand and led her outside to the rock garden. "I have to tell you where I got this cactus from."

"I know where you got it from. Just because I say nothing doesn't mean I'm a fool."

"Just because I didn't tell you right away doesn't mean I can't tell you now."

"I know that you brought it from the Arab village, Abu Nabil, north of Shomriya."

"From Saleem's land. Saleem was our friend, and we didn't try to talk the town into asking his village to stay."

"You wouldn't have had the town's support."

"We could have tried. We should have tried. We put off coming into conflict with our own people. We should have done it then. We would have found out who was on our side and who wasn't. I was afraid of finding out. Now the truth is staring at me."

She also wanted to tell Malka that Benny's disappearance was not their fault. They were not careless people just because they believed in justice for Arabs. To be silent about what Benny believed in would be to give up on him. She wouldn't do that.

Malka seemed to understand. "Rena, I'm not blaming you, no matter what I said to you. And I'm not blaming Benny or his politics. We fought so hard to have our own democratic state in which people could disagree safely. Now we have come to this."

Rena was not sure what 'this' meant. They stood quietly in the garden looking at the prickly pear seeming so hopeful in the hot sun. Waiting to grow.

Rena said, "I had a dream about Saleem."

"When?"

"The night after I went to Benny's office."

"And?"

Rena was not used to sharing intimate things like dreams with Malka. She was surprised that Malka was interested. Rena was just about to tell her mother-in-law about the dream when the phone rang. It was Yehuda, the teacher. He wanted to talk about letting Zohara go on the class graduation trip. Rena listened to him speak about how important it would be for Zohara to go. In a voice she barely recognized, Rena said into the phone, "I don't know if this is a good idea."

CHAPTER TWENTY-SIX

Zohara returning home was startled. She hadn't seen Yael. Zohara grasped the handle of the gate, hoping she could get inside the garden and avoid Yael. Too late. "Hi, Zohara. I saw you coming. I want you to know that I don't blame you for what happened. I told my children, and everyone in Shomriya, It's not your fault."

Zohara stood there, her hand glued to the warm handle, her feet stuck, her voice gone. She felt paralyzed. She could neither move nor call for help. She did not know how long she just stood there looking at Yael's stupid face, at the carefully plucked eyebrows, the red lipstick. Suddenly her grandmother was beside her.

Malka, a wild look in her eyes, raised her hand as though she might slap Yael. "Don't you ever speak to my granddaughter about her father, or anything else for that matter. Ever. Do you understand me?" Her hand was still raised.

Yael stepped back. She seemed surprised. "Of course you misinterpret my good intentions, Malka. It's just like you not to recognize when someone is trying to help. Just because I'm not a leftist doesn't mean I can't see that Zohara is suffering because of your blindness." Yael seemed calm, but to Zohara, her voice was shrill.

Her grandmother's voice sounded deeper than usual, and not calm at all. "This is not about my character or my family's politics. I can't stop your outrageous vicious lies about my son or undo your unlimited stupidity. But I forbid you to talk to Zohara." Her grandmother brought her hand down and stood tall and straight.

Zohara wanted to look away, but her eyes remained fixed on Yael. Yael stretched her neck, trying to match Malka's height. "I should have known better than to try to be kind to your family,

Malka." Yael looked at Malka in her dirty pants, her tattered hat, her old boots covered with mud. She then looked down at her own perfectly painted toes in black sandals. "Don't think that you can threaten me. I regret that we have to live on the same street."

Malka hugged Zohara and ignored Yael. "Let's get you a cold drink and something nice to eat." In the kitchen she said, "Let me wash my hands. I'll make us a nice snack. I needed to take a break. It's hot today." She looked at Zohara. "Did she frighten you?"

Zohara came out of her stupor. She threw her satchel on the table. "I hate Yael. I could kill her. I swear, Grandma, I want to kill her. I wanted to run, but I couldn't." Malka hugged her. Her grandmother smelled of strawberries and sweat.

They rocked there for a moment as Malka said, "Me, too. I wanted to hurt her." Her grandmother sighed. She washed her hands, put out drinks, brought down the tin can of sugar cookies,

Mendel's special treat for Zohara. Zohara inhaled the sweet smell.

Her grandmother sat down and rested her hands on the kitchen table. She stroked the smooth yellow surface and looked out the window. The fragrance of Rena's garden filled the kitchen. "I love the smell of flowers. Your mother has made a wonderful garden here. Your father loves her passion for beauty. He just loves her."

That was something new. Her grandmother praising her mother's flower garden and talking about love.

"Your mother brought light, brightness, into his life. That's one reason your father wanted to name you Zohara, as a tribute to your mother."

Malka took her hat off and tucked her hair behind her ears. "When you were a week old your father brought you and your mother home from the hospital. He put a chair in this very garden for her. Not a regular chair, an armchair. When he got out of the cab he walked your mother, who was holding you in her arms, slowly to the chair right there." Malka pointed to a place in the garden. "Your mother laughed and said that she wasn't an invalid. She had given birth, she said proudly. But your father helped her sit down as though she were Queen Sheba. She looked quite royal. This place, this garden, this family is your mother's kingdom."

Zohara drank some lemonade and waited.

"Your grandfather and I had come over ready to welcome you. We were all dressed up. We farmers do have occasions when we know how to look our best. This was a very special occasion. I felt so utterly giddy with happiness. You should have seen us running from our yard, like teenagers. We were out of breath when we greeted you."

As though still catching that same breath so many years later, she inhaled deeply, exhaled, and went on. "There was your mom smiling in a new way. So proud. Your father didn't know whether to look at you or at your mom. She started to laugh.

Stretched her arms and said, 'Go on, hold her.' So, he did. He held you. You had a cute little hat on. White, with red dots. You opened your beautiful eyes for a moment and looked around with intense curiosity. Then you closed your eyes and went to sleep. For the next few days everyone came to see you. All our friends came. Sammy and Pnina came. They brought Shoshi. But she was only one year old."

Zohara said, "Grandma, I couldn't have looked curious. A week-old baby doesn't really see. There have been scientific studies. I read it in our biology book."

Her grandmother seemed pleased with herself. "I'm skeptical not only about God but of science as well. All I know is what I saw. The look in your eyes was intelligent. You took in everything. Mendel and Jacob agreed. It's for me to tell you what I saw. It's for you to believe it or not."

Zohara could not help laughing out loud. "Grandma, even I know that those two would back you up on anything. Jacob is in love with you." She wished that Shoshi could hear her now talking like an adult with her grandmother.

Her grandmother blushed. "You see what I mean? You have proved my point. You still see everything."

They both laughed. Zohara rinsed out the glasses, put on her rubber boots, and went across the road to the barn with her grandmother. She took Vashti out for her daily stroll. She cleaned the barn and rinsed her boots in the outdoor sink. When she went into her grandmother's house, the table was set for a nice second snack for the two of them.

Neither of them mentioned Yael. Nor did they speak of Zohara's refusal to go anywhere these days but to school, Shoshi's house, her grandmother's house, and the synagogue.

When her mother suggested taking her and Shoshi to Tel Aviv to her favorite bookstore, Zohara said she would see. She could tell her mother was disappointed. Then it got worse because her mother suggested, "At least let's go to the beach. We could go early in the morning, before it gets crowded." Zohara refused this as well and would not explain herself. The thing was her bargain with God.

Zohara could not tell her mother or her grandmother that she had given God one last chance to do the right thing. She had struck a bargain in which she, Zohara, would give up the things she loved, renounce pleasures, and in exchange God would bring her father back. She was angry with God. The bargain would be the ultimate test for God. Whenever she thought of God, her heart, like the land in a severe drought, was dry, hard. But there was a small part in her heart, a tiny space, which was still open to bargaining with God. She had not told a single person about the deal she had made with God. She would give up things and God would bring back her father.

She had made a list of things that she loved to do. First was reading. But she soon realized that while giving up reading would be the ultimate sacrifice, it would be impossible. She had to go to school and read for most of her classes. But she wouldn't read new books. She would not finish reading *Gulliver's Travels*. She wouldn't read *The Voices of Children,* the book of poems from kibbutz Kalaniyot. On the list she had included biking and swimming, two things her father had taught her.

Zohara was afraid she would forget his voice. Sometimes she had to close her eyes to remember things about him. She didn't have to close her eyes to remember the first time her father let go of her bike. There she was riding on her own. Since that moment, she loved her bike. She loved the wind on her face. Rounding the corner, signaling to make a left, and parking the bike next to other bikes at the front of the store made her feel almost grown-up.

Zohara and her parents used to ride their bikes to the beach. It was five kilometers from their house. Her father rode in front, Zohara would follow, and her mother would be in the rear. They would often stop midway at a kiosk and buy a cold drink. All three bikes leaning on each other, stacked against the kiosk wall. Just thinking about it made her cry.

Zohara had told Shoshi, one day as they were walking home from school, that she had something to share only with her. She was not to tell anyone about her bargain with God to bring back her father. Before she was finished, Shoshi was against it. "God doesn't want us to deprive ourselves. The Bible tells us that an abstainer, a Nazeer, must atone for taking on deprivation. The Torah does not approve self-deprivation."

Shoshi said it in an all-knowing way meant to indicate that she was older and knew everything. Shoshi now carried her satchel. Wearing it on her back was childish.

"My father says Maimonides wrote that those who make vows of abstention have to make amends, pay for it. Because God wants us to live a full life."

It was a hot day and Zohara was sweating. Shoshi was full of herself.

"Once Daniel was going to strike a bargain with God. He said he would give up soccer if God would make our grandfather well again."

"So?"

"My father told him that praying for someone is a good deed. A mitzvah. Abstaining? No. It was wrong. And he said all the things I just told you about Maimonides." Zohara could hear Shoshi's disapproval. She felt a moment of pleasure. She and Daniel were kindred spirits.

Just as they were about to turn onto Herzl Street, she heard a boy's voice. "Traitor's daughter! Why don't you go with your father to the communists? Go to the Soviet Union, traitor." Zohara stopped right there, her heart pounding.

She picked up a large stone and looked around. She could see nothing but the orange grove across the street, dense and green, nothing moving. Shoshi yelled, "Imbecile. Degenerate. Wait until my brothers get their hands on you. I know who you are. You think you can hide there. I recognize your voice. I hope you die in Hitler's dark grave."

Zohara did not let go of the stone. Shoshi took her other hand. "Don't pay attention to them. Whoever it was. One of Yael's bastards, probably." Zohara let Shoshi hold her hand. She was determined not to cry.

Shoshi looked at Zohara's fist that held the stone. "You were actually going to use it?" And without waiting for an answer, she said, "You are so brave. You really are."

As they approached the gate to Zohara's house, Shoshi stopped. She pulled a red flower off the bougainvillea, held it gently in her palm, and said quietly, "Zohara, please, listen to me. God doesn't want us to add to our suffering." Zohara heard her and said nothing.

The house was quiet and cool, protected by the shutters. In the kitchen, they kicked off their sandals, put their satchels on the floor, and headed straight to the refrigerator. Zohara brought out two glasses from the cupboard and Shoshi took out the cold drink. Shoshi took a long gulp, held the glass against her face, closed her eyes, and said nothing more about God, Maimonides, or the boy in the orange grove.

Zohara was grateful to Shoshi for yelling at the boy. She was upset that her friend was not going to be any help in this very most important matter. Why did Shoshi have to enlist the help of Maimonides? She had made Zohara feel that Maimonides himself was against her bargain with God.

Shoshi seemed to read her mind. "I know that I went on and on about Maimonides. Whatever you are thinking of doing, please don't do it." Zohara could not confide in Shoshi that she was already committed to the bargain.

When the weather got hot and humid, her mother wanted them to go to the beach. "Let's take the bikes and go." Zohara missed the sea. Yet a deal was deal. It was very hard to turn her mother down. She was sorry that the only thing she could say was not quite true. "I don't feel like it. I'd rather stay home."

Her mother looked at her with concern.

Zohara wished she could tell her mother about her bargain with God. It was impossible. Her mother did not believe in God and would try to convince Zohara that her decision was not logical. She would tell Zohara that her father did not believe in God and would not approve of her depriving herself.

CHAPTER TWENTY-SEVEN

Zohara planned to tell her mother about the trip. Her mother had put on a Bach record that Zohara liked and the two of them were having breakfast. It seemed a perfect moment to surprise her mother and tell her that she was planning to go on the school trip.

Zohara's decision was not made on impulse, but out of conviction that going on the school trip would be fine with God because she was not really looking forward to it. She felt she needed to go. She couldn't make her body do what it was supposed to do, but she could decide to feel that she was growing up and going to high school. It was a big deal because the graduation trip was a regional event and eighth graders from three other schools would join the Shomriya kids. There would be four buses and about a hundred kids and several parents from each school as chaperones.

Zohara said, "Mom, I've decided to go on the school trip." She waited for her mother to speak. Rena spoke slowly, "This would be a trip away from home and with all kinds of kids... Kids say hurtful things; at least here in Shomriya you can get away and come home. On a trip it'll be different, more difficult. If you decide to go, I should come as a chaperone."

Zohara knew she had to say it straight. "Mom, you would be a great chaperone, but I really need to do this on my own. You'd be the greatest mom to go with a bunch of kids. I must do this without my mother. I really must. Shoshi will be there and some of my other friends. There will be three girls to a room. Shoshi, Ronnie, and I will share one."

Her mother seemed to have decided to tackle the easy question first. "I thought that Ronnie and Shoshi didn't like each other."

"They didn't in the past. But now they seem to like each other much better." Since her mother was silent, she added, "Mom, you're not trying to discourage me, are you?"

"If you really want to go, you should."

There had been moments in the last few weeks when Zohara felt not only her own pain, but her mother's as well. She had woken up early one morning and seen Rena sitting at the kitchen table in what used to be her father's chair.

Zohara had watched her mother holding one of her father's shirts against her chest. She was rocking slightly, her eyes closed. Her mother had been crying. She wanted to go over and comfort her, but instead she went quietly back to her room. When she heard her mother moving around, she came out and hugged her.

On the day of the trip, her mother came along to see her off. As Zohara was about to get on the bus her mother said, "Remember, we have a phone. You can call me if you want." Zohara said,

"Mom, it's just three days." Her mother said, "You're right." She stood and waved.

On the bus Zohara set next to Shoshi and Ronnie sat next to Abe. The bus went along the shoreline to Haifa. They toured the city; saw the Technion, the Bahai Temple and the Haifa Museum. At the end of the day, they traveled to kibbutz Teva and slept there. The next day early in the morning they went to the beach in Nahariya.

Zohara knew that Nahariya had a beautiful beach. No swimming for her, which felt like a big sacrifice, but she could wade. She would stay close to the beach and let her feet have a taste of the water. A few kids did not wear bathing suits, and like her had on shorts and tee shirts and were playing games on the beach. That she was not swimming did not seem odd. When one of the teachers announced they would leave the beach in about thirty minutes, she was walking slowly in shallow water. It was nice and warm, and she thought that she would go back when the water reached her knees. Suddenly she was no longer walking. She felt herself plunged into what felt like a hole with a powerful current and when she tried to start swimming she failed. She began to struggle but felt gripped by a force she had never experienced. Frightened, she tried to kick her legs, stick her hand out, breathe so that she would float. "It'll be hard for you to drown," her father had told her when he taught her how to swim. "You are a natural floater." She remembered it, and then a hand was grabbing her hand and she held it. She was on the beach coughing water and Shoshi was crying. "It's all my fault. It's all my fault." Yehuda Manor shouted, "She is fine, she is okay."

She felt very sick in her stomach, her throat hurt. But when she heard the words *ambulance* and *hospital*, she gathered her strength. She had a hard time talking, but with Yehuda's help she managed to prop herself to a sitting position and say in a hoarse voice, "No hospital. I'm fine. My grandmother will have a heart attack."

Shoshi yelled, "She is fine. She is an athlete. A strong swimmer. Her grandmother has a heart condition and when she hears the word hospital there is no telling what can happen." Even in this difficult moment Zohara wanted to laugh and say, "You don't have to embellish, Shoshi." But her throat hurt, and she was grateful for Shoshi's loyalty.

Rivka, the school nurse, was running toward them. Shoshi pleaded, "Rivka, Rivka. Tell them that Zohara doesn't need to go to the hospital." Yehuda and Shoshi helped Zohara get up and at the same time whispered something in Rivka's ear. She checked Zohara. Zohara would be fine in the kibbutz, at the nurse's station. Zohara was standing up trying not to vomit. She made every effort to seem fine. The idea of a hospital terrified her, and she knew it would terrify her mother and her grandmother.

The lifeguard who saved her was a young guy with an athletic body and deep tan. He said, "It happened so quickly. I keep my eye on the water all the time. You can see, there is a white flag, the water is calm, but she walked a bit too far to the left where there are sometimes undertows. Sometimes an undertow can get instantly ferocious."

Suddenly, a voice from the crowd of kids shouted, "Maybe she just wanted to disappear like her father." A hush fell over the group.

The lifeguard said, "She did everything she could do. It's not her fault and this is not the first time we have had forceful undertows here." Then he looked at the huddled kids and said, "I don't know who among you is the moron who said the most idiotic thing I have heard lately. This is a beautiful girl who got caught by a strong current. She grabbed my hand right away. Whoever you are who made the comment, I think you are a moron."

Shoshi seized the moment. She looked at the huddle of boys and yelled, "You are an idiot and a coward. Wait till I tell my brothers about you. They will teach you a lesson." Despite the bitter taste in her mouth, Zohara wanted to laugh at the idea of the Abarbanel boys attacking anyone.

Yehuda said to the lifeguard, "I'll deal with the boy. Thank you for saving Zohara."

The lifeguard looked at Zohara. "I deal with idiots every day. You take care now." He gave his surfboat a push, jumped on it, and rowed away.

Yehuda spoke with Rivka about taking care of Zohara. The bus would drop them off at the kibbutz and continue the tour. He asked Zohara, "How are you doing?"

Zohara was surprised that she had a voice. "I'm okay. I have to call my mother."

"Of course. It's a good idea. You can call from the kibbutz. Rivka will take care of it. We'll see you later when we come for supper. You can join us tomorrow for the last part of the trip." Yehuda urged everyone to get on the bus quickly so that they could be on their way.

When they got to the kibbutz, Zohara and Rivka got off and so did her two friends, Shoshi and Ronnie. Zohara looked at them. "Why aren't you going? Don't you want to go see the rest of the Galilee? Shoshi, you said you wanted to see Safed in particular."

"Oh, Safed. The city of the Kabbalists will have to wait."

"I'm glad the two of you are here. But this is our graduation trip. You'll miss so much. A whole afternoon in Safed."

"It's eighty-five degrees already. Why do we have school trips in such heat? Look at me." Ronnie stretched her arms and legs. "Red. Unlike you two, look at you, good tans and all. Me, I just get red like a tomato. If I'm lucky I'll have no blisters, just more freckles."

"You're like my mom."

"Exactly," Ronnie agreed, and seemed pleased. She, like Shoshi, adored Rena, and was an aspiring artist. Ronnie wanted to be a fashion designer and talked about going to Paris.

At the health clinic, the kibbutz nurse checked Zohara. She heard the whole story and didn't seem alarmed. She seemed more concerned about Ronnie's red skin. She went to a small refrigerator and took out a cup of yogurt and a jug of iced tea while also chatting with Rivka about the differences between being a school nurse in Shomriya and a kibbutz nurse.

The nurse poured iced tea into four glasses and told them all, including Rivka, to drink. She then took the yogurt and told Ronnie to extend her right arm. She put her hand in the yogurt and spread it gently. "Do you think you could do it for the other hand, legs, and your face?" Before Ronnie could say anything, Shoshi jumped up. "Let me do your face. I have never seen anyone use yogurt for sunburn. Wait until I tell my mother."

She stopped herself. "I'll just watch how you do it, Ronnie."

Ronnie, who had first looked annoyed, said, "Okay. You can put it on my face. Just don't get it in my eyes."

"How does it feel?" Zohara wanted to know.

"It feels good and cool. I can feel it sucking the heat out of my body."

"You look funny, like a mummy. All white. Only your eyes make you look like yourself," Zohara said.

There was a ceiling fan in the nurse's station and another fan standing in the doorway. Every time Ronnie felt the fan she said, "It feels good. I should have been more careful on the beach. I'm the real patient here."

Rivka said, "I should have noticed your sunburn, but I was focused on Zohara. You're right; you're better off here. Let's stay here until noon. Then we'll go to the dining room and have lunch and take it from there."

"Joining you meant avoiding a possible ugly fight with that moron who insulted Zohara."

They all looked at Shoshi. The kibbutz nurse said, "A fight?"

"A moron said something awful to my friend Zohara. I was going to punch him. Moron, by the way, is not my word. It's what the lifeguard said. Just in case you wonder if I tend to exaggerate. Which I sometimes do."

Rivka, looking uncomfortable, said, "Our teacher is looking into it. The boy will probably be sent back home with one of the chaperones. I'm glad he was not a Shomriya boy."

She seemed to want to close the conversation on what the boy had said. She turned to Zohara. "Would you like to call your mother? Could we use your phone, Miki?"

"Yes. Just tell our operator that you're at the nurse's station." She took Zohara to the front office and left.

Zohara heard her mother's voice and tried hard not to cry. She did not want to frighten her. "Mom."

"Zohara? Where are calling from? Is anything the matter?"

"Mom. I'm fine. Really. But I'm going to cry first. Then I'll tell you."

"Sure. Of course, first cry a bit. Then tell me."

Zohara cried and said, "Mom. I was so scared. I almost drowned. I was wading, in shallow water. And suddenly something pulled me in. I tried to float. The lifeguard came and got me out. It's not that I forgot how to swim. There was an undertow, and I was unprepared."

"Oh, my God, of course you were frightened. How awful. How are doing now? Where are you? Would you like me to come and get you?"

She could tell that her mother really wanted to come and get her. "No, Mom. I really want to stay here and be on the last day of the trip. We are coming home tomorrow evening. I just need to stay here. We're in the kibbutz, at the nurse's station. You want to talk to the nurse? Which one? Rivka? Both? Okay. I'll get them."

Rivka went first. "Rena? Hi. She is fine. Really. Yes, I would tell you. It was very brief. She didn't lose consciousness and didn't swallow much water. She was sitting up right away. Yes. I know that she is brave. I'm here, keeping an eye. No need to thank me. Just doing my job. Zohara is a great kid. If she says she wants to stay, then this is the right thing. No. We have a whole crowd here. Shoshi and Ronnie are here. Ronnie has quite a sunburn. Yes, I can give you the number here. But we'll be here only until lunch. The nurse is going to give us a fan. Yes, it's hot here too. Don't worry, Rena. Yes. I know it's easy to say. I have kids too. You want to talk to Miki, the local nurse? Sure. Hold on."

When Miki had finished talking to Rena she said, "Your mom wants to say goodbye."

"Zohara. Do you want to talk some more? Anything else you want to say?"

"No, Mom. I really feel better now that I talked to you. Please tell Grandma it was no big deal."

Zohara tried not to cry again. "I'll see you tomorrow, Mom. Tell Grandma not to worry."

"I'll tell her. I love you."

Zohara put the receiver down. She was glad that no one had said a word to her mother about the moron. She did not think of herself as vindictive, but she hoped with all her heart that the boy had been sent home in humiliation. She hated him.

***

As soon as Zohara hung up, Rena ran to Malka's house and saw her mother-in-law in the strawberry field. Rena must have said something because Malka, who was on her knees weeding, turned around. Rena just fell right there on the gleaming strawberries and cried. Between sobs she managed to tell a frightened Malka what had happened. She managed to repeat that Zohara was fine.

Rena could smell the strawberries but could not stop crying. Malka lifted her, held her in her arms, rocked her, and then helped her up. They walked back to the house, their arms around each other. Rena could not tell which one of them supported the other. But it was Malka who went inside and made tea and brought it out; they sat on the porch drinking tea.

"I wish I could go right now and bring Zohara back. I wish I hadn't let her go on the trip."

Malka shook her head. "No, Rena. You did the right thing. It was important to her. You can't keep her in this house forever. As it is, she stays home way too much. It's not healthy. Benny wouldn't want it either."

Malka looked down at her hands as though seeking guidance from her years of farming. Apparently reassured, she looked directly into

Rena's eyes. Rena saw Malka looking at her with great pity.

"I wanted to say it to you many times over the years, but I used to think that I shouldn't interfere, afraid that you'd think that I'm overstepping boundaries. I was wrong, I should have brought it up a long time ago."

Rena waited.

Malka's eyes did not change their expression. "I know that you blame yourself for what happened to your parents and your sisters, but you're wrong. It was not your fault. You tried everything you could. You sent the right papers, and it was just too late. Your parents and sisters were among the first to be killed. You are not to be blamed for what happened. It is the murderers who are guilty. I should have said it to you a long time ago and I'm sorry I did not. There is nothing, my dear Rena, that you could have done to save them. Nothing. There are things in life that are beyond our control."

A breeze swept the porch, but it did not take away Malka's pity or Rena's heartbreak. When Rena stopped crying, she took Malka's hand and held on to it. She felt so grateful that her daughter was alive.

Iris arrived. She heard about Zohara and took out the prayer for the traveler. She held it carefully in her hand and gave it to Malka. "This is the prayer in my father's handwriting."

"I'm glad you remembered. What beautiful handwriting." Malka touched it lightly, gave it back to Iris. "Tonight will be a good time to say this prayer for Zohara." She looked at Iris and said in a voice full of compassion, "You said that according to your father we should make it personal and specific."

Her mother-in-law, the atheist, who always declared that needy humans had created God, now offered to pray for Zohara. Three unbelieving women huddled around a prayer written years ago in Poland. They read it together.

CHAPTER TWENTY-EIGHT

It was the end of the school year. Zohara went to her graduation ceremony. She got two awards, in history and in literature. Her mother, Malka, and her friends congratulated her. Shoshi performed a dance for her classmates for the last time. The town's photographer took pictures of beaming parents and exhilarated students who could not wait for summer to begin.

For Zohara, smiling for the camera was difficult. Her father was not there. There were rumors that he had left the country. His destination changed depending on the story. In one version, her father had gone to Russia because he was a leftist, in another he had run away to America to make money. According to yet another version her father was an adventurer, a gold digger just pretending to be a leftist, who went to South Africa or Australia. She heard an uglier rumor, too: "Benny was a Soviet spy."

Zohara was not looking forward to the summer. Shoshi was now going to Tel Aviv to a summer dance class for gifted students. Zohara missed her company. Shoshi did suggest, more than once, that Zohara meet her in Tel Aviv. Zohara refused. She held on to her bargain with God. She looked at her friend and thought how Shoshi was fourteen but looked sixteen. Zohara hadn't yet had her first period. Her breasts had just begun to show. That was encouraging.

Zohara was in the barn when she saw Mendel coming to get the eggs from Malka. She was just going to say 'hi' when she heard them talking. Mendel had given Malka a bag of food. He said, "You need to eat. You look too thin. Starving yourself won't help. Believe me, I know. When Raphael died, I didn't want to eat, and I didn't care if I died. I was wrong. I still have a family and so do you. You have a granddaughter who needs you."

Then her grandmother cried, like Zohara had never heard her before. "There are mornings, Mendel, when I'm sorry I woke up. I have to talk myself into going on. I have to wiggle my toes to remind myself that I'm alive. I put one foot on the floor, then the other. I talk myself into going on. 'Malka, put on the kettle, make some coffee, turn on the radio.' I stand in the kitchen and look out the window. I see my son's house. I tell myself that I have to go on without him."

Mendel said something that Zohara could not hear. Then more clearly, "I know how you feel. It's exactly what I had to do at the beginning. I'm not saying that it gets much better." Then muffled sounds, then sobs, her grandmother's and Mendel's.

A few minutes later, Zohara stepped out of the barn. Their eyes and noses were red. They smiled at her. She wanted to run and hug her grandmother. Instead, she said, "What did you bring today, Mendel?"

When Daniel showed up unexpectedly, she was walking Vashti. Zohara was glad to see him. Daniel was handsome. His dark curly hair falling over his forehead just above his eyes. Unlike Shoshi's, Daniel's eyes were blue with dark lashes. He had begun to shave, and Zohara wondered what it would feel like if she touched his face. She was happy that she had begun to have breasts. She wondered if Daniel noticed her the way she noticed him.

Walking Vashti together, Daniel told her that he had come because he wanted to see her. He missed her, now that she was not visiting Shoshi so often. Zohara was pleased and didn't worry about blushing. Daniel came along when she took Vashti back to the barn and asked if he could put the food in her trough. Zohara filled up the bucket and handed it to him. Their hands touched briefly.

The barn smelled only faintly pungent because she had just cleaned it. Vashti let out one of her famous brays and they both laughed and patted the donkey. Daniel said, "She looks quite old, but her bray is strong and musical."

"This is exactly how I see her."

She liked Daniel's voice. It was deep and almost grown-up. In the days that followed she remembered Daniel's visit and the way their laughter mingled in the barn.

CHAPTER TWENTY-NINE

Rena tried desperately to hang on to Rabbi Ovadya's idea to join her sparks of hope with Bet Hagoal prayers. How could she hold on to hope when there had been no word? At what point should she give up?

A disappearance was not like death. Death had a clear tradition of moving from intense to reduced mourning. Seven strict days of shiva, followed by thirty days of lesser restrictions, and finally, at year's end, mourning was complete. Was there a pattern of diminished hope? Was the period of hope ever officially over? She had not asked Rabbi Ovadya about any of this.

At five thirty in the morning the phone rang. Rena's heart was at the phone before her hand picked up the receiver. "I'm sorry to call you so early, Rena. I know that you are waiting for news, but I really need you. Mike is in the hospital."

Sarah's voice was paper-thin. It bore no resemblance to the strong voice of the woman who had driven trucks with the Hebrew Brigade in World War II. Rena sat down. "What happened?"

"I woke up last night, and Mike was not in bed. I thought he couldn't sleep, which is not unusual. Since I was awake, I thought I could make him a cup of tea." She started crying. "I went to the kitchen and there he was, on the floor, gasping for air. He pointed to his heart. He couldn't get up. I called an ambulance. He looked bad. I thought he was going to die… He'll be fine. At least that's what the doctors tell me. Without test results they don't really know."

Rena looked outside and saw gentle mist settling on the garden. The flowers were covered in dew, like a bride under a veil, shy and soft.

"You know when I first saw him on the floor, I thought the worst. With Benny gone, and Miriam murdered, I don't know... I just don't know what I'm thinking any more."

Rena did not want to wake Zohara and spoke quietly. "I could come to Tel Aviv. Would you like me to come to the hospital?"

"Mike is resting now. At least that's what they tell me. I'm at home. My mother is here, but I'll have to tell the kids and hold my mother's hand. You know how she is. Please come. Come, if you can. That would be helpful."

Rena could still mobilize herself into action. It felt good to be needed. For the first time in months, she cut some roses, clipped the thorns, and wrapped a bouquet of yellow roses in a wet towel. Sarah could take it to Mike.

When she arrived in Tel Aviv she went straight to their house. Ruth, Sarah's mother, opened the door. "The newspaper is cursed." When Rena was inside Ruth seemed mortified. "I should not be saying it to you of all people. With your husband missing." Ruth took the roses and placed them in a vase. Rena said, "Sarah can take them to the hospital later."

Ruth opened the French doors, and they stepped out onto the terrace. Rena looked at the sea shimmering in the morning sun. It seemed lovely and remote. Rena let Ruth make her tea. Ruth said, "The terrace and the view of the sea are the best part of this house." She anxiously watched the sun's progress. She got up and rolled down the awning to shade the table and sighed deeply, shaking her head.

Sarah came home a bit later to report that Mike was resting, but she could not find a doctor who would talk to her. She thanked Rena for the flowers. "It will mean a lot to Mike. He thinks you blame him for Benny's disappearance." Rena was no longer sure who to blame. Sarah didn't look well. Her face was drawn, she had dark circles under her eyes. Sarah then looked more closely at her and said, "Are you eating, Rena? Are you taking care of yourself?" The two of them eyed each other, sitting in Sarah's gleaming kitchen cradling cups of tea. Sarah tried to figure out if there was a cardiologist she knew who would give her an honest opinion.

Rena was standing at the door. Sarah said, "I don't know if you heard that Yigal the accountant went to Paris with some money stolen from the paper."

"No wonder Mike is sick. How much money did he take?"

"It's not clear yet. No one knows yet if it has anything to do with…" Rena nodded. She vaguely knew Yigal. Now he had become another disaster. She could have asked for more details. She didn't. She went back to Shomriya without stopping at her studio. If the paper was falling apart, she refused to let the information into her heart. On the bus she closed her eyes and pretended to sleep, just in case any Shomriyans were tempted to talk to her.

Sarah called later to say that a cardiologist had examined Mike and said he had had a mild heart attack, what he called a warning. Mike would recover nicely, but he would need to drastically change his habits. Mike had to lose weight. Sarah paused and then told her that Mike had appreciated the flowers. He wanted Rena to know that he had been doing all he could. As soon as he could get back on his feet, he would resume his efforts.

On Sunday Rena was glad to be home and grateful for the evening routine. Malka came by but did not stay for dinner. She was going to eat with Jacob. "Jacob likes my cooking. I suppose it's better than his own cooking." Rena and Zohara ate a simple dinner of bread, salad, and cheese and spent the rest of the evening reading. The ritual of reading aloud to Zohara was gone. She was rereading the same books, seemingly stuck, not moving forward. Rena kept herself from asking yet again, "Don't you want to go to the library and get some new books?" She was glad that the bodily changes that Zohara had waited for were finally happened; she was becoming an adolescent.

There was a knock on the door. On the porch Rena saw Sammy Abarbanel. Rena could tell that something had happened. She was afraid. When she finally opened the door Sammy said, "Why don't we step inside?" He spoke in a near whisper.

In the living room the shutters were already closed for the night. Rena saw that Sammy looked at the windows.

Hardly breathing, she asked, "What's going on?"

Sammy asked, quietly, "Where is Zohara?"

"In the kitchen, reading."

Rena could hear her heart beating. She and Sammy remained standing near the radio. Rena wanted to speak but couldn't. Sammy said, "Tell Zohara we have news that Benny is alive, but we can't talk about it."

"Alive? Are you sure?"

"Yes."

She raised her voice to call Zohara. She could barely say the sentence. "Zohara, come here. Sammy has something to tell you."

"Mom, are you crying?"

"I'm crying, but it is good news," she whispered. In the living room, with the radio blaring, Sammy said, in the same low voice, "We have news that your father is alive."

Zohara began to sob. Rena held her.

She cried, "Does Grandma know about Dad?"

"Pnina went over to tell her."

Rena could hardly breathe. She heard her own voice but didn't recognize it. "Sammy, tell me I'm not dreaming. Tell me this is really happening."

"It is. Benny is alive."

"I don't understand. Why all this secrecy? The whispering? Where is Benny?"

Sammy said that Nathan Tovim had called. Benny is alive. We should not talk to anyone until we have Benny back. Security concerns.

"Is he hurt?"

"He was injured. He is recovering. We hope for his return."

"Is it certain? That he will come back?"

"We hope. What we do know is that he is alive."

Benny was alive. She did not want to think about anything else. But her mind was filled with questions. "What danger? Where has he been? How did he get hurt?"

"The person in touch with Nathan was brief but reliable."

Rena's mind was flooded with questions. If Benny was still alive, why didn't he get in touch with her? Who was holding him? Why? Why three months without a sign of life?

"Do you know what Benny's physical condition is?"

"I don't know more than I have told you."

Rena hugged Zohara tightly. She let herself cry. Malka arrived and embraced them both. Rena put her hand up and touched Malka's face.

CHAPTER THIRTY

Benny woke up in a dark room. He tried to turn and felt a sharp pain. He couldn't raise his head or move. He heard himself moan. He saw a person, male or female, he couldn't tell. The figure moved quickly across the room and left. A few minutes, hours, or even days later, he wasn't sure, someone sat near his bed. "How are you feeling?"

Benny wanted to say, "In great pain," but only another groan came out.

"You are in pain, I know. I'll give you some medication."

Benny thought that the man said, "You are among friends, have no fear." He was not sure whether these were the words of the man now holding his hand, taking his pulse, or his imagination. As he drifted back into delirium, he thought that the voice sounded familiar.

When Benny woke again, he was still in pain. He opened his eyes. His vision was blurred, as though he were wearing foggy glasses. He wondered if he was going blind. He still couldn't lift his head. He could hear cars honking, children shouting. He thought he must be dreaming because the shouts were in Arabic. He could hear a woman yelling in Arabic, "Go play somewhere else. Why are you always under my windows?" For a moment it was quiet. He heard doors open and close. Music was blaring from a radio. He recognized Umm Khulthum, the Egyptian singer. He wondered where he was, but he couldn't stay awake.

Benny heard the muezzin calling the faithful to pray and opened his eyes. His vision was clearer. A man was sitting in a chair looking at him intently. He looked like one of the people from Bet Hagoel, the same dark hair, a trim dark beard, and large dark eyes.

"My name is Abu Ali. I'm a physician, and you're in my house."

The man spoke accented but perfect Hebrew. Benny tried to speak. Even though his voice was raspy and barely audible, he heard himself ask, "Where am I? How did I get here?" The muezzin ended his call. Benny could tell it was daylight, though the drapes were heavy and drawn tight.

"You are in Jerusalem. In what you call the Old City. Officially, you are in Jordan."

The pain came back. "Why am I in Jordan? How did I get to East Jerusalem?"

The doctor shook his head from side to side. "You're here because you were beaten up so badly that you probably would have died if you hadn't been found."

Benny tried to think clearly. He wanted to drift into sleep again and had to fight to stay awake. "Who beat me? Who found me?"

"Don't you remember?"

Benny's head began to throb. He had to struggle to keep up his end of the conversation. "Who brought me here?"

"I can't tell you that. It's too dangerous for the person."

Benny was exhausted. He wanted to ask, "How come you speak Hebrew?" He couldn't get the words out.

"We'll talk when you feel a bit stronger. I just want you to know that as long as you're in my house, you are safe."

The words danced in Benny's hazy mind. It was important information, but he couldn't stay with it. His body hurt. He touched his head and realized that it had been shaved.

When he woke up again the room was dark. He was not alone. From the breathing and the slight snore, he could not tell whether the other was a man or a woman. He tried to remember why he was there. Instead, he remembered his dream. He wanted to stay in the dream. Things were familiar, the terrain, Hayim from his unit, and himself. In the dream he was in the army traveling with Hayim, a Holocaust survivor. They were in an army jeep. Away from their unit on some mission.

Benny had met Hayim in 1949. He befriended him and invited him often to Shomriya. Hayim had no family in Israel. He spoke Yiddish to Rena for hours. He followed her around and couldn't stop talking. Rena listened and gave him tea, which he drank from a glass with a piece of sugar on his tongue. Hayim needed, Rena told Benny, to speak in full sentences to someone. Rena, who refrained from speaking Yiddish, had made an exception for Hayim. His Hebrew was limited. He struggled for words. When Hebrew words would not come, he would use an Arabic curse that he had picked up from the Israeli soldiers. Benny told him that it meant 'a curse on your father.' Hayim didn't care. "I will speak Hebrew. With no accent. I will be a writer. A Hebrew poet."

"Good," Benny said. "The country needs poets."

"Like hell. This country needs soldiers."

In the army Hayim's gun always had grains of sand, and in his spare time he wrote poems in Yiddish. He didn't show them to anyone. He wrote in tiny letters, in a small notebook, with a small pencil that he constantly sharpened with his pocketknife.

The person in the room sighed, then snored louder. A male snore. Benny remembered more of his dream; it was clear and detailed. He and Hayim were driving in what looked like the Negev desert. Hayim said, "It's so beautiful here. So peaceful." He paused, looked at Benny, and asked, "How come you never asked me where I got the name Hayim?"

"Your parents must have given it to you."

Hayim laughed. "Spoken like a Sabra."

Benny waited.

In the dream, Hayim laughed again. Even when he laughed it was more with bitterness than joy.

"I gave myself the name Hayim, 'Life,' when I realized that I had survived. The only one in my family. I took my Polish name, I dug a grave, I took my name, I buried it, I covered it. 'You're dead,' I said."

"What was your Polish name?"

"Are you crazy? Didn't I just tell you, it's dead? Have you Sabras no respect?" Hayim was suddenly screaming. His face was red, his eyes bulging. Benny was afraid he would explode. He slowed the jeep and stopped in what seemed the middle of nowhere. He sat there and waited for Hayim to calm down.

"My father had a large textile factory. More than a hundred employees. The best employer in town. He was fair and generous. He was good to his employees, and they were loyal to him. Loyalty was a key word in the factory. City officials came to our house; my father was their friend. When the Nazis invaded Poland, my father went from city officials to his own employees, asking them to take in me and my younger brother. To hide us. He offered a reward. Half of the money he would give right away and the other half when the war was over. Not one of them, not a single one of his so-called friends or loyal employees, would agree to hide two Jewish boys. My father pleaded, 'They are blond. No one would know.'

"I'll tell you who saved me. The janitor. I was walking on the street when he grabbed me. 'Your parents and your brother were just taken by the Germans. Be quiet and come with me.' The one person my father did not think to ask. My father had no sense of who you could trust. Who was safe. None whatsoever. When the war was over, that's all I could think about. How come my father didn't know who was safe? They all betrayed him, except the janitor. There was no monetary reward. One of my father's so-called Polish friends took over the factory. He claimed my father had sold it to him."

Benny saw a hawk in the distance. A light desert wind moved dry twigs around. A lizard disappeared into the ground.

"I guess you Sabras never had to ask yourselves which of your neighbors you could trust if something terrible happened and you needed to hide."

The hawk took off with his prey. Benny said to Hayim, "You're right. The question never crossed my mind."

Benny was grateful for this dream because it was so vivid and detailed. He could not think of when he had ever had such a vivid dream. Did Hayim ever say something like that in real life? Did he tell Rena about his father and how the janitor saved his life?

Benny felt thirsty. His lips were dry. He must have said something or made a sound because the man on the chair got up, gave him a glass with a straw, and left the room noiselessly.

CHAPTER THIRTY-ONE

When Benny woke up again, he found Dr. Abu Ali looking at him intently.

"How long have I been here?"

"Almost three months."

Benny felt a new sense of panic and fear that he hoped he was not showing. "Three months? Why don't I remember it?"

"Because of your condition and the pain killers."

"Why am I here?"

"You keep asking me that question."

Benny was puzzled. "I don't remember asking you."

"It could be the drugs." The doctor paused. Benny could see that he was debating what to say next. "You may have a memory problem. I'm not an expert on head trauma. Memory loss is possible."

Benny knew the meaning of memory loss. He could clearly remember his family. He knew who he was.

"Before you were brought here, you were in another location. Do you remember that?"

Benny thought he detected alarm in the doctor's eyes.

"No, I don't. Where was the other location?"

The doctor spoke quietly. "Perhaps it would be best to forget it."

"Why am I here?"

"You are here because a mutual friend brought you here. Because I am a doctor, he knew he could trust me."

"You told me that I am in the Old City of Jerusalem. But I have no friends here. Why would I be here? From our side of Jerusalem, I can see your Jordanian soldiers stationed along the wall if I look closely enough. It looks like a border to me."

"Jordanians are not 'my' soldiers. I'm not Jordanian. The border is not tight. Easy to cross if you know how."

"I mean, Jerusalem is divided, and the Old City is Jordanian territory, and we are at war. I don't know who my friend could be here."

"Are you sure? Is your name not Benny Sasson? What about childhood friends?" Benny was ashamed. How the war had divided them! Of course, in his childhood his father had taken him to the Old City to visit his grandparents. He had had Arab friends, but that was a long time ago.

"The friend who brought me here. Who is he?"

"I'm sorry, I can't tell you that, either."

"Why?" As soon as he said it, he began to understand the gravity of his situation.

"I can't tell you who your friend is. It's too risky for him."

"You must be taking a risk for me."

"I took the Hippocratic oath."

"But not an oath to take care of an Israeli, an enemy. This is your house."

"My house is also where my clinic is. I see patients here. It's the best place for you to be right now. People come and go. The best hiding place is where it seems improbable to hide.

"That's why the drapes are drawn tight all the time, day and night."

Benny repeated, "You are taking a risk. Why?"

"I have my reasons. You need to heal more before you can leave."

"Why can't I leave today?"

"How do you think you'll do it?"

"How did I get here? I mean to Jordan?"

"You don't remember how you got here?"

Benny was not sure whether the doctor believed him. He tried very hard to remember and all he could feel was a void followed by panic. There was a blank space in his life.

"I have a daughter, Zohara. She turned thirteen just before I…" He stopped. He could not tell before what. He decided to hold on to the facts of his life he did remember. "I have a wife, Rena. And a mother." And he went on, telling this total stranger, "The last time I saw my mother she didn't approve of me."

The doctor nodded. "That's good."

"That my mother disapproved of me?

"That you remember it all."

Well, that was a good sign. "I feel as though something is there, I mean about what happened, but it's locked up. I know it's there, but I have no access to it."

"I don't know much about amnesia. But this sounds like amnesia to me. I think that one day you may be able to remember."

"Is it a psychological amnesia?"

"It may be both. The trauma to your head from the beating and the trauma to your psyche. Time will tell."

"Who attacked me?"

"I truly have no idea."

"And my friend. The friend who brought me here, can I see him?"

"I don't think so. As I said, it would not be safe for him."

"Did he tell you why I'm here?"

"He said he didn't know."

"Did I come here to see him?"

"You didn't." Benny was trying to keep the conversation going. "How come you speak such good Hebrew?"

The doctor looked somber and suddenly angry. "I grew up in Haifa. When the war broke out in 1948, I was in England doing my residency. I couldn't return to my house in Haifa. When the war was over, I was considered a refugee without the right to return. I came to East Jerusalem where I had family. I wanted to do something for our refugees, make their lives more bearable."

Benny wished his head was clearer. That he could say something meaningful. He wanted to say that he could speak Arabic, but he was afraid it would sound condescending. He wanted to find words that would say more than that he was sorry. But all that came to his mind was a question. "Do you dream of your house in Haifa?" He regretted his question. Abu Ali did not take it in the wrong way.

"Yes, I do, I dream of it all the time. When I close my eyes, I can still smell the salty breeze from the Mediterranean coming through the windows of our house."

There was a very soft knock on the door. The doctor got up. "Get some rest."

CHAPTER THIRTY-TWO

Benny could distinguish day from night even with the drapes and the shutters fastened. It was the sounds outside that told him when it was morning. He heard people talking, occasional shouting, radios turned up and the noise of impatient cars. When the doctor left, Benny tried to assess if he could wait a bit longer before he had to make the difficult journey to the bathroom.

In the last few days, slowly and with great effort, he had been able to get out of bed. He now knew that the room he occupied was in a self-contained unit with a large, cheerful bathroom. Blue tiles on the walls and a blue ceramic floor. With immense exertion he reached the blue bathroom.

He was shocked when he saw himself in the mirror for the first time. He shuddered. His hair was gone; short stubble on his head couldn't hide the scars on his skull. Huge black circles surrounded his eyes. He had a wild beard and sunken cheeks.

The shower was both bliss and torture. When he finally made it back to the bed, he could hardly breathe.

Benny was gasping for air, waiting for the trembling to subside, when the doctor knocked lightly and came in. Benny hoped he had not heard him cry and curse. Benny spoke instead about the blue of the tiles and the floor of the bathroom.

"The house was renovated by a high English official during the British Mandate. He brought his family to Jerusalem and put in a bathroom for each of the bedrooms. He was obsessed with cleanliness. He liked the blue so often used in Palestine. You should see the kitchen."

Making fun of the British. They both laughed. The sense of camaraderie was short-lived. Abu Ali said, "Maybe one day when we have peace, you could come back, and I could show you the kitchen." They stopped laughing. Bitterness crept into the doctor's voice and chased the lightness away.

Benny could not find a way to rearrange the simple fact. Someone was living in Abu Ali's house in Haifa. It was hard for Benny to say something meaningful to the doctor. Abu Ali had not been in Haifa in 1948, so he had become an absentee and could not return to Israel.

Even if Abu Ali were allowed to return, he would not have full or equal rights in the state. The doctor might blame Benny for his exile from Haifa.

Now he was in the doctor's house, helpless, in hiding, unable to remember the last few months of his life or comprehend why he was on the Jordanian side of Jerusalem. "What is wrong with me?" He did not mention how shocked he had been by his own appearance in the bathroom mirror.

"You suffered trauma to your head and your body. You had fractured vertebrae, which is why you were immobilized. The good news is that you are healing much faster than I expected, and none of your internal organs have been damaged, which is a miracle."

"How long will I have to stay here?"

"I would say not too much longer."

"And then what will happen to me?"

"I don't know yet. Our mutual friend has to contact me."

Outside, early morning chased away the night's silence. Children were yelling and drivers honked as obsessively as drivers on the other side of Jerusalem. Benny needed the anonymous mutual friend. "What will happen if he doesn't appear?"

"I don't know. Let's hope that he does." The doctor sounded irritated and unhappy.

Seeing the doctor's worry at the prospect of being saddled with him, Benny thought again of Hayim. He yearned to have other dreams. He longed to have a dream in which he was back home. He remembered Zohara's birthday. Zohara had graduated from eighth grade, and he had not been there.

He had a wild idea that if his family were in his dream, he could let them know that he was alive. It was agonizing to imagine them searching for him. Wondering what had happened to him. He thought that his friends, the people of Shomriya, his army buddies were looking all over the country for him.

All he had was his dream of Hayim. His father would probably suggest that rather than thinking of the Hayim dream as the wrong dream, he should think of it as useful. Benny's father had grown up steeped in Jewish mysticism. A dream was a sign. An omen. A message. Benny had grown up in a secular world with a father who was no longer a practicing mystic and a mother who thought that God was created by needy men. Yet, he was thinking about his Hayim dream. Was there a hidden message?

In his dream, Hayim had assumed that having to think of who to trust was a question that Benny, a Sabra, would never have to ask himself. Benny wished that Hayim would tell him if the unknown friend was going to come. Benny closed his eyes and saw not Hayim but Rena smiling at him in the gallery on the day of the opening of *Gifts from America*.

CHAPTER THIRTY-THREE

Sammy called Rena on Sunday evening.

"I am on my way to pick you up to drive to Jerusalem. We have good news."

Rena's legs were shaking, her arms hugging sobbing Malka and Zohara.

In the car Sammy said that Nathan had called. Benny was at Hotel Tikva. No other details.

Rena wanted to see Benny. Touch him. Smell him. Hold him. Ask him what had happened. Why hadn't he gotten in touch with her? She was gripping her purse for support. Sammy kept his eyes on the road. "On the coming Sabbath we'll say Birkat Hagomel, the blessing for those who have survived danger." Rena let herself cry.

It was after midnight when they got to the hotel. The street was sleepy, the windows of the surrounding buildings dark. The hotel's neon sign shone in large horizontal letters and the front walk was well lit. Rena wanted to fly into the hotel, but she noticed Sammy's measured steps. She walked next to Sammy trying to look normal. They rang the bell and there was Nathan Tovim. He took Rena's hand, held it for a moment, and motioned toward the corridor that led to his apartment. Rena could hardly breathe.

Nathan pointed to a closed door and let her approach it alone. The room was dimly lit, just a night light and a bed. She let out a sob as she ran to the bed and fell to her knees. She flung her arms around Benny and would not let go. Benny whispered her name over and over in a hoarse voice.

He put his arms around her, but he did not raise himself much.

"Are you in pain?"

"I'm in some pain, but I don't mind. Just to hold you."

Rena shook her head and cried. She had not allowed herself to imagine this moment.

He was very thin. He had grown a beard. His hair was short. She traced visible scars with her fingers. "I can't believe that I'm with you. I was so afraid that I'd never see you again."

She could feel his ribs. She wanted to count them. She could tell her touch was painful.

"My ribs were broken. They are mending, but they are still tender."

On the drive from Shomriya she had imagined he would be as she remembered him the day he left. He would come back the same, in the same clothes, frozen in time. He was back, but he was not the same. He wore pants and a shirt she didn't recognize. He had a beard and scars.

Benny wanted to know about Zohara and Malka. Rena wanted to tell him everything and nothing. She wanted to be silently grateful and to yell, 'Where have you been?'

He must have heard her unspoken question. "There was nothing I wanted more than to let you know that I was alive. There was just no way to do it."

Rena knew that her gratitude was justified and her anger misdirected. She put her head carefully on the pillow next to her husband's head. Reunions were about the simple miracle of breathing the same air. Breathing together the breath of life.

Rena heard a light knock followed by Nathan's voice. She got up and opened the door. Nathan and Sammy came in. They put chairs close to Benny's bed. Sammy touched Benny's shoulder and said, "It's good to see you, Benny."

As he sat down, Sammy said, "Your father, may he rest in peace, came to me in a dream. We were standing in my parents' house in Jerusalem, looking in the direction of the Western Wall. I told him that I was distraught because you were missing. Yair told me, 'Don't underestimate the power of a father's love.' Before I could say anything, he was gone. And here you are." Sammy was crying.

In all the years that Rena had known Sammy, she had never seen him cry. Not even at Yair's funeral. Sammy wiped his tears. "Since I heard the news I kept thinking, why didn't Yair come to me in a dream earlier? It would have helped me to know that he was watching over you. But what could I have done? Your father was very wise."

For the first time, Benny laughed. "Zohara is going to like this story about your dream, Sammy. She is going to tell it to her children and grandchildren."

Benny knew Zohara in a way that Rena did not. There had been times when she felt left out of things they shared. Even though Benny was a secular man, he had his own relationship with mysticism. She knew just holding his hand that he was right there in the dream with Sammy and felt his father's presence. If Sammy had told her, she would have dismissed it as a mere dream. The dream belonged to Benny.

Benny said to Sammy, "You can't imagine how close to reality your dream was. All these months I was in the Old City. I'm here today because people risked their lives to take care of me."

She was right about reunions. They all breathed the breath of surprise, amazement, and gratitude. They waited for Benny.

"So far, you are the only ones to know that I was in Jordan. Nathan suggested to call Sergeant Ari. He is on his way."

Benny was in East Jerusalem, and she had looked for him in West Jerusalem. Same city, wrong side. So close and yet out of reach.

Nathan went outside to wait for Ari.

A ceiling fan turned quietly. Rena sat on the floor holding Benny's hand. His hand felt familiar and so thin. The wedding ring was missing. She touched his ring finger. "Your ring is gone."

"It's in my shirt pocket." She felt it.

"Everything else is gone. I guess they didn't care about a wedding band." They? Who were 'they'? Rena was angry. She felt her hand clench into an angry fist. She wanted revenge, but she was so profoundly grateful.

Nathan returned with Ari. "Benny. I'm so glad you're here." He hugged Rena. He shook hands with Sammy. He picked up another chair. They surrounded Benny.

Benny tried to lift himself up. "I was in East Jerusalem. Someone found me unconscious in no-man's-land, badly beaten. He brought me to a doctor's house. He and the doctor in East Jerusalem saved my life."

Benny managed to take the glass of water Rena handed him.

Rena looked at him drinking, and her eyes saw him in that desolate spot, a mangled body tossed between two borders, hovering between life and death. She let out a cry. It did not sound like her voice, but like Bertha's.

Benny put the glass down and took her hand. "It looks worse than it is. I'm just very tired."

Nathan said to Rena, "A cup of tea would be good. Let me go get us some tea." He went out and came back with tea, coffee, juice, and cookies. He put the tray on a small round table and sat down.

No one moved. They all sat there waiting.

CHAPTER THIRTY-FOUR

In the dim light, sitting on the floor, Rena wanted to crawl onto the bed and hold him. Benny moved closer to her. He spoke to everyone in the room, but his eyes were on Rena. "It's going to be difficult. I promised not to reveal where I have been. I don't want to endanger the lives of those who saved me. They did not turn me over to the Jordanian authorities. The man who found me came back to see me. He called Nathan to let you know I was alive. He was the one who brought me here. It was dark. He knew his way. He left me not far from the hotel. I can't tell people where I've been all these months."

Rena put her hand on his arm, thin and warm. "For how long?"

"I don't know. Possibly until there is peace between us and Jordan." It was like saying he would be free to speak in the days of the Messiah. Who in Israel had faith in peace?

"I can't endanger the people who saved my life," he said to the room.

Rena wanted every moment of those months. Who were the people who took a risk?

Ari said quietly, "Yes. People will want to know."

"I gave them my word."

They all looked at Rena. "They saved his life." She wept in gratitude and anguish. Benny touched her face. He wiped her tears with his thumb.

"The doctor who treated and sheltered me said that after the disappearance my life would never be the same again. People would want to know where I had been all that time. Rumors would put pressure…"

"Who? Who did this to you?" Rena's anguish filled the air.

Nathan offered Rena some orange juice. She used both hands to take a sip. She gave Benny the rest.

"Are you tired?" Ari wanted to know. "Would you like to rest a bit?"

"I'm tired, but I need to ask you something."

"I'll try to do my best."

"How much do the police know about who abducted me, beat me up, and left me to die?"

"The police know very little, I'm afraid. Despite months of searches, investigations, and numerous calls from people who claimed they actually saw you before you disappeared, the police could never establish a single fact that would support any of these claims. We are now waiting anxiously to hear from you what happened. Your account would shed light on the whole thing."

"I had hoped that the police would have some leads or clues. This is difficult to say. I don't remember anything of the assault. No one, except the doctor, knows about my memory loss. Amnesia."

Rena felt dizzy. "How did it happen?"

The room was tense.

Ari spoke. "I don't want to sound any alarms, but I think the sooner we know the facts, the better we'll be able to help you. Since you have been in Jordan, we have to think of how to deal with it."

Benny looked at Rena. "I think right now I need to talk to Ari alone."

Rena wanted to stay. "Do you think that you're still in danger?"

"I don't know. I need to talk to Ari and then to Security Services."

CHAPTER THIRTY-FIVE

When Rena left the room, she saw several men standing in the corridor. She watched them go into the room and shut the door. She stood outside, feeling excluded. Her husband had become a security issue, a state matter. She could hear low voices from inside the room. Nathan came over and invited her to his office. "Sammy will be with us in a minute."

She felt shabby in her old blue pants with spots of paint, her faded green shirt, and the ratty black sweater she had grabbed as she left the house. She pulled at the sweater.

Nathan said, "Benny is alive, thank God. We hoped and prayed for his safe return. All of this must be so hard on you. Yet, God who brought him back will continue to shine his light on Benny as he finds his way back into life."

Rena sat in the same comfortable armchair that she had sat in months ago when she first arrived there with Joe. "I am thinking about the people in East Jerusalem. Our enemies, who saved Benny's life. I have always wondered how I would act if I could save someone's life at a risk to myself."

"I have asked myself the same question. How would I respond! I don't know the answer."

Rena looked at Nathan. Dressed in suit pants, a long sleeve white shirt, a gray wool sweater. Dignified.

"I am thinking about my family. Did they ask their Polish neighbors for help? How did their neighbors act when they were taken away?" Haunting anguish wove itself into Benny's near-death and rescue.

Rena heard more steps in the corridor. A toilet flushed. Doors closed. "I have so many feelings right now, Nathan. It's hard to sort them out. I can't believe that Benny is here. Alive."

She was sobbing when she thought she had no more tears. The handkerchief she had taken out of the pocket of her pants was uselessly drenched. Nathan gave her a large, beautifully folded handkerchief. She buried her face in it. She breathed the scent of sun-dried laundry.

"Benny is alive. I'm so grateful. I feel angry at those who wanted to kill him. I'm angry at the people in Shomriya who turned against Benny. I'm furious at the kids who bullied and frightened Zohara. Shomriya will not be the same place."

Nathan leaned forward. "You're right. It won't be the same. Benny is a strong man. He has you and many others who love him. With God's help you will both get through it."

The big clock chimed. It was one in the morning.

"We have come to know and love you and I thank God that you're in the Sasson family." As though he had just remembered something good, Nathan sounded animated, almost cheerful. "Rena. You can design another Torah mantle for our synagogue. You know that we have more than one Torah scroll and some of them could use new mantles. You could design a new one for a scroll that we brought from our synagogue in the Old City. It's rather frayed. You can honor that Torah and design a new mantle. It would be a good way to celebrate Benny's return."

A wave of happiness suddenly came to her. In vivid colors of orange, brown, and yellow. Joy came to her in a design for a mantle for the Torah scroll that had made the journey from the Old City to West Jerusalem. She could see the design clearly, as though she had already made it. She knew that the Torah mantle she was about to make would be her very best work.

CHAPTER THIRTY-SIX

On Tuesday morning, Benny was on the porch of their home. He was lying on the bed Rena had had Jacob place beneath the painting of Mrs. Bialik.

Rena brought out breakfast. The radio was on. "Benny Sasson, the well-known journalist who disappeared three months ago, was found alive yesterday. A police spokesman confirmed that Benny Sasson had been abducted and seriously injured. The motive for the attack is under investigation. The police declined to give any details." News about the coming elections followed. Rena turned the radio down.

Benny's voice was still raspy. "It's unsettling to be the news."

Just to hear his voice.

"There is more in the papers."

"Let's hear it."

Benny praised her coffee. Rena smiled. She opened the paper and read. "The police confirmed that Mr. Sasson was happy to be back in his home in Shomriya. At their request, he declined to give any interviews. All those who have known Benny Sasson over the years know his enormous integrity. There must be compelling reasons for a journalist of his caliber to remain silent."

Rena said, "The mayor added his own official statement. Would you like me to read it?"

Benny was laughing. "I can't wait."

Rena refused to join in his laughter. She had not forgiven the mayor. "The police, whose excellent investigation brought back our beloved citizen Benny Sasson, had imposed silence on Shomriya, a community that has stood with the Sasson family throughout this terrible ordeal. We ask the public to respect the police request."

Benny had issued a brief statement to his fellow journalists. "Naturally, you want to know about my ordeal. I understand. I am a journalist. But since the attack is under police investigation, I will follow my late father's custom and invoke Ecclesiastes: 'A season is set for everything, a time for every experience under heaven, a time for silence and a time for speaking.' Now is the time for silence."

Rena could tell that Zohara was pleased with her father's statement. "What do you like about it?"

"I like that Dad quoted from the Bible."

Zohara looked more grown-up. "I am off to take care of Vashti. When I'm done collecting the eggs I'll come back and see if you need anything."

There was a knock. When Rena opened the door the woman introduced herself: Hagar, the physical therapist. She had had a call from Hadassah Hospital in Jerusalem. They recommended physical therapy for Benny.

Rena went over to her drawing for the Torah mantle. She was not leaving the porch. Hagar warned her. "He is going to complain. You may not like it."

A small, delicate-looking woman started manipulating Benny's legs. Whenever he could manage to catch his breath, Benny told her how much it hurt. Rena felt her own muscles squeeze tight.

"Atrophy is bad, pain is good," Hagar told Benny. Rena wanted to hold him. Her fingers were on her painting, drawing and erasing.

Hagar brought a walker and a cane. "We'll start with the walker." She showed Benny some exercises and encouraged him to walk as much as he could. Watching him, she said, "Really, all you need is exercise. Both your legs are fine." The medical report from Hadassah Hospital was extremely encouraging. Hagar looked at Benny. "If ever you aren't using the walker or the cane, don't hesitate to lean on others when you need it. The important thing for you is to move and use your muscles. You should redefine pain and think of it as good. I'll see you tomorrow."

Rena held on to the idea of redefining pain. Hagar was out the door.

Malka must have seen her leave. She came over to the porch, and Rena went inside.

Malka looked at the walker and the cane, touched them, tried not to cry. She kissed Benny on his scarred head.

Malka poured lemonade for Benny. She sat down on a chair facing the bed. She had already worked a few hours in the fields. "All the time you were gone I kept thinking that the best thing I could do for you was to support Rena and Zohara. They probably thought the same thing, because they did everything to help me. The farm helped us; it needed us, the animals, the fields."

She told him that people from kibbutz Kalaniot had come. "No matter what happened years ago, they are our family. You're their son. They helped look for you."

Malka laughed. "Not that we came up with anything useful. Every morning, I got myself out of bed for Rena and Zohara. They needed me and I was not going to let them down." She was silent for a moment and then added, "This time the kibbutz didn't let me down."

Benny said that he remembered a morning in the kibbutz. There had been a big argument that had to do with him. He must have been five years old.

"How is it that I can remember a forgotten event in childhood, but I can't remember the attack?"

Malka waited.

"I remember. We left the kibbutz because I wanted to sleep in your apartment, not in the children's house... I used to run away at night to your place. And you let me sleep and in early morning when it was still dark, you'd sneak me back to the children's house. People saw us and made a fuss. I remember it. I remember someone shouting. Am I right?"

Malka's old pain returned. Some hurts never vanish.

"Yes. It happened. Bella shouted that I had broken all the rules. I shouted back: 'My son is miserable. He is just a little boy. He is frightened. He needs his parents. If you don't let us be his parents, we'll leave.'"

"This shouting match was when we got caught?"

"Yes. There was a big meeting after that incident and your father and I decided to leave."

"Why does everyone say that you left because you insisted on women's rights?"

"That too was an issue. The kibbutz felt more comfortable with this explanation than that we had challenged its children's sleeping arrangements. Women's rights were not as controversial as children's houses. That threatened core kibbutz beliefs."

"Weren't you angry?"

"Yes. I was angry. Your father was too. We were disappointed and sad. You had a right to feel safe. We had a responsibility to make you feel safe."

Benny sounded tired. "Mom, I don't get it. Why can't we ever tell a straight story? We always have a story to cover up another one so that some national entity, like the kibbutz, could feel better about itself."

Malka looked at her son. She could not make him safe after all. Instead, she talked about history. "When my generation came to Palestine, we needed to cover up one story in order to tell another. You were right about the Arab question. I have thought about it since the day you were gone. We were so desperately anxious to have a homeland. We refused to see there were Arabs here. At the time I didn't understand your father's position, or Buber's about a bi-national state. The Arabs didn't agree with them either."

She paused, looked at her son. She had decided that now was as good a time as any. "The Holocaust, and then the 1948 war, just strengthened my feeling that we had exclusive rights here. Our land. I could not see anything else."

She began to sing the famous Zionist poem:

Here in the land of our ancestors

All our hopes will come true

Here we will live and here will create

A glowing life of freedom.

"You have a lovely voice, Mom."

"I used to sing it to you. It just never occurred to me that the Arabs could feel the same way."

Malka looked out the window at the rock garden, then turned and looked at Benny. "I thought about all of this before you came back." She didn't mention the fact that he had been sheltered and saved by an Arab doctor. They had agreed that no one would talk about it for the time being. But now it was a part of their lives and their silence couldn't change that. The doctor was now a presence. The man who walked Benny safely from the Old City to West Jerusalem would forever be part of their life.

A car stopped at the gate. By the time Malka had stood up, Shifra was at the screen door. Shifra came over and gently touched Benny's shoulder. She told him that Mike and Ari would be there shortly, that they needed to talk to him together. She looked at him. "You know, religious people have a blessing that they say when they see someone who survived an ordeal. There is nothing comparable in Marx or in any socialist text. It's so good to have you back."

"I'm glad to see you, Shifra. How are you? Do you still go to that little Yemenite restaurant?"

Shifra laughed. "I've never had much time. I ate my meals at my desk most of the time. After

Mike's heart attack, I filled in for him. Now he thinks I want his position."

"You'd make an excellent chief editor."

"Probably. But I'm not after his job."

"I just need to ask you about Miriam. You must have seen her the day before she was murdered. Was she worried? Did she say anything?"

Shifra suddenly lost her composure and began to cry. "I still can't believe it. You know Miriam and I were friends. We met when I stayed in Tel Aviv. We sometimes went to dinner or the theater or just took walks on the beach."

Malka saw a bee circling Shifra's head. She got up and opened the screen door and let the bee out. She moved to the bench and let Shifra sit closer to Benny.

"Miriam looked upset, but we were all worried about you then, so at the time everyone at the paper seemed tense. In hindsight I think she was frightened. I'm not sure. Maybe I'm reading the events backwards."

Shifra looked out the window.

"There is something I have told the police. You should know about it. Mike and Ari should be here, though, so let's wait. It's part of why we are all here."

Malka gave her a cup of coffee. Across the street a radio blared. "This is the Voice of Israel. It is eleven o'clock and here is the news." Then a more muffled sound. Someone must have turned the radio down.

Rena came out and hugged Shifra. "I missed you." She went to sit next to Malka on the bench.

Mike arrived. He moved surprisingly quickly, a new, thinner, more agile Mike, and went over to Benny. "I care about you."

In the silence Mike spoke again.

"My heart attack was not just about my health and my clogged arteries. It was also about your disappearance and Miriam's murder and the slander directed at our party and our newspaper. Suddenly the Right turned us from Zionist socialists to Stalinist traitors. You should have seen Shamir's article; the man is shameless."

Malka looked at Mike. Was he even the same person who had come over that terrible night? Mike went on. "There was something I have told the Tel Aviv police and no one else at their request. Something important. But I'll wait until Ari is here to tell you."

Then he touched his hand to his forehead to indicate he had just remembered something. "I have food in the car from Sarah." He almost ran back to his car and returned with a pot. "You always praised her couscous and she made some for you. She wanted to come, but I told her this was a work meeting. She'll probably come over tomorrow."

Mike put the dish on the table and looked at Benny. "Your mother also likes Sarah. Do all of you think a nice woman like Sarah would stay with me if I were the fool your mother believes me to be?"

Malka was not worried by the idea of a 'work' meeting.

"Mike, take a deep breath. Look at my son. Take a good look, see the walker and the cane. This is not about you."

Before Mike could say a word, Ari was at the door. "Benny, you look so much better without the beard." He helped himself to a glass of water and sat down. He was wearing his uniform and seemed hot in it. He put his hat on the bench and wiped his face and head.

Shifra said, "You had a beard?"

Ari smiled. "If you had put a black hat on him, he would have looked like a Hasid."

"I shaved it yesterday."

Ari helped himself to another glass of water. "Why don't we get started?"

Shifra turned to Ari. "Benny asked me a few minutes ago about Miriam. I want to tell him what you and Mike already know, that Yigal Adir, our bookkeeper, is gone. His going is related to Miriam."

Malka looked at Shifra and heard Gittel's heartbreak. She took Rena's hand.

Shifra was not her usual calm self. The day after Miriam's funeral, Yigal called in sick. He said he would be out for a few days. He sounded sick. Something was wrong, she could hardly understand him. His voice was muffled.

"In hindsight, I think he wanted me to believe that he was sick. He coughed dramatically. I was concerned. I knew he lived alone. I asked him if he needed anything. No, he said. A neighbor had brought a pot of chicken soup. He would be fine. All he needed was rest."

Malka knew that this was not a story about illness.

Shifra went on. "At first, I didn't think it had anything to do with Miriam. I knew Miriam didn't like him, and I don't think he liked her. But I saw no connection between his illness and Miriam's murder."

She stopped for a moment and went on. "Now I know that his 'illness' was connected to Miriam's death."

Benny shook his head. "Yigal Adir, our bookkeeper? He was in my army unit. He acted the same way he did at work. Remote. He was a loner. He did his duty, but no more. Where is he?"

"That's the big question. We got a letter saying he was tired, his aunt in Paris had sent him a ticket, and he was going to France for a few weeks. He was sorry to inconvenience us. Two days after he left, I had a letter from him. A short note. He wrote that he had needed money, so he took some from the newspaper's bank account.

"How much?" Benny wanted to know.

"We don't how much; our new accountant is working on it."

Ari sat there quietly. Mike shifted in his chair as though he was still a heavy man. Malka was still holding Rena's hand.

"The books were in order a few months earlier. It was not a long-term embezzlement."

Shifra looked at Ari. "If the police know something about Yigal, they haven't told me. But I think his departure is connected to Miriam's death. He could have wiped us out and he didn't."

Mike looked at the floor. "Yigal never took a sick day in all his years with the paper. His story didn't make sense. Yigal's story didn't sound right. Not even the missing money made sense."

Benny tried to sit up. He looked in pain. Malka asked if he needed a pill or wanted another pillow behind his back. Was this all too much for him?

"I am fine, Mom. I want to hear it. Sitting up a bit helps."

Ari said, "I'm going to let Mike speak first."

Mike had lost not only weight but some of his overbearing confidence as well. He spoke with new humility. "The day you disappeared, you left me a letter marked CONFIDENTIAL. It was on my desk, but I got a phone call, went to the bathroom, talked to a couple of people. When I returned to my office your letter was gone. Just like that." Mike snapped his fingers.

He drank some water and continued. "You know how messy my office is. I started looking frantically on my desk, making a bigger mess. I became frustrated. How could it just disappear from my desk? By now my desk, every chair, the floor, everything was littered with stuff." Mike got up, poured himself some more water, and asked Benny, "Can I get you something?"

"No thanks, Mike."

"Your letter just disappeared, Benny. I swear. Miriam kept saying that she had seen it. She wanted to help find the letter. The more she tried, the more irritated I got. As she was leaving my office, she said, 'It was right there on top of the pile. I was with Benny in your office when he put it there. He thought it was very important.' And she left."

Benny closed his eyes. Malka thought about the amnesia and the questions her son must have in his head.

Mike stood up and sat down again. "The letter was gone. I was mad at you, Benny. I know I don't make any sense. I told the Tel Aviv police about it the next day, but they said not to tell anyone. Just as they have told you now not to talk about your abduction." Mike choked up trying to go on talking.

"I didn't tell anyone, not even Sarah. For months she has been mad at me. She thought that I was hiding something incriminating."

A breeze swept the porch. No one interrupted.

Mike was upset. "If I had opened your letter right away, Miriam might still be alive. We could have looked for you in the right places. I should have opened the letter." He was holding his face in both his hands, hunched forward, and pleading. "What was in that letter, Benny?"

Malka felt her son's agony over his loss of memory. He had told her and Rena that he could not remember his last day in the office. Now a note was added to a blank in his mind.

"I understand, Mike, not opening the letter right away. I don't understand why you didn't mention it to Rena or my mother. I think at that point you were concealing important information from my family."

Malka was hurting for her son. He had told her he had tried very hard to remember the last day in the office, but all he could recall was going to Tel Aviv. A whole day and subsequent days and weeks were locked away somewhere. What a torture it must be to wonder what was in the letter. All Malka could think of was the strangers, Arabs in East Jerusalem, who had saved his life. But was he safe now?

Mike suddenly seemed not only thinner, but smaller. "I'm sorry. I can't tell you how much I regret it. If I could turn the clock back, I'd do it. Losing the letter was my fault. I'm going to resign from my position."

He turned to Shifra, "You can have it."

Shifra looked at him and said, "I don't want it. The letter was missing. It's not your fault."

Mike ignored Shifra and spoke to Benny. "I told the police about the letter. I did everything I could to find you."

"I hear you."

Ari picked up his hat, put it on his head, made sure it was sitting properly, and said, "I think that Benny looks exhausted, and we have told him as much as we can for the time being. I'll be in touch."

Mike asked, "What was in the letter, Benny?"

And before Benny could speak, Ari said, "The content of the letter is part of the investigation, Benny can't talk about it."

Mike said, in a pained voice, "You still don't trust me." Shifra was the last to leave. Rena walked out with her. Malka could see them talking in the rock garden.

CHAPTER THIRTY-SEVEN

"You look so pale, Benny. Should I get the doctor?" Malka put her hand to his forehead just as she had done when he was a child. "You feel cold. Are you cold? Would you like a blanket?" When she covered him, she tucked his hands under the blanket. "Are you sure that you don't want me to call the doctor?"

"I'm fine, Mom. I promise you. You could make me a cup of tea. That would be nice."

"It's Mike. I knew there was something about Mike. I have never really trusted him. When you worked on your article on the rights of Arab workers, I felt that if things got nasty, Mike would abandon you. He would leave you out there, all alone in the eye of a political storm."

"You didn't want me to write the article. You were angry with me."

"I was worried. I was frightened that something might happen."

Malka brought some fresh tea. "Now I lie awake at night because my heart is full of gratitude. I could almost go with Zohara to synagogue." She was laughing now.

Zohara came in. "Dad, you're really, really here. Grandma, Dad is here."

"Of course, I'm here."

Vashti brayed and Zohara cried at the top of her lungs, "Vashti, I still love you. But you're second now. My dad comes first." Vashti let out a short snort. "She sends her love, Dad."

"Thank you for taking such good care of her. How was school and graduation?"

Zohara didn't look at him. "It was fine. No, it wasn't. You weren't there."

Before Benny could say anything, Zohara went on. "One day after you disappeared, kids were yelling that you were a traitor. Suddenly, Bertha was there. Walking right into the orchard where they were hiding."

"What did she say to them?"

"Nothing. But the kids were afraid of her."

Malka looked at her granddaughter. "Where was Jacob?"

Zohara laughed. "Dad, you know I had this whole brigade of people protecting me. Shoshi called them Malka's Brigade. At first it was just Jacob. Then Mendel. Then the brigade grew to include all the Abarbanel kids and Shoshi. And then there was Bertha. I think that Bertha is much smarter than people think. Some kids are afraid her."

"Are you?"

"I like Bertha. The only time I was afraid was when I almost drowned. When it happened, I forgot what you told me about what to do if I was ever caught in an undertow."

Malka thought of how they had given Benny details of their lives in his months of absence.

"Is there anything more that you want to tell me about the drowning?" She seemed to think about it. "Maybe, but not right now. I'm going to wash and change and if you don't need anything I'll go to the library and get a book."

Benny closed his eyes. Malka watched him fall asleep.

CHAPTER THIRTY-EIGHT

Rena was talking quietly to Zohara. It was night. The lamp bathed the porch in soft colorful light. Zohara was sitting close to her on the bench. Benny opened his eyes. They both spoke at once. "You're awake."

Benny smiled and said, "When I was away, I kept thinking of you. I looked at the clock and wondered what you were doing. Not knowing what happened to me."

"Dad, what was the worst thing for you?"

Rena put her left hand on her mouth and her right hand held tight around Zohara's shoulder.

"That I could not let you know I was alive."

"What was the best thing?"

"Hmm. The thought that I would go home."

"Were you afraid that you wouldn't?"

"I was alive and knew that I would get better. But there were moments I was afraid."

"When did you really feel that you'd be okay? Was it right away when you opened your eyes the first time?"

"I can't remember when it was, because at first I was in and out of consciousness."

Zohara went to sit next to him. "Don't worry about it. If it comes back to you, let me know."

"I promise."

A light wind brought the fragrance of flowers and the smell of wet soil after the evening watering.

Rena asked, "Benny, would you like to eat something?"

"In a little while. A cup of tea would be nice."

Rena looked at Zohara. "Would you like some tea? Or hot chocolate?"

"No, Mom. Thanks. I'll just sit with Dad until you come back and then I'll go to sleep. I'm really tired."

Rena went inside and when she came back with tea and sandwiches, Zohara was saying goodnight. Rena put the tray down next to Benny. Zohara yelled, "Good night, Vashti." She waited. After a moment the donkey gave a long bray, sounding like the last note of the shofar on Rosh Hashanah.

Rena poured tea. "Hayim called when you were gone. I don't know how he knew we had a phone. Then he called me 'sister' in Yiddish. Your husband, he told me, still in Yiddish, will be back. I wanted to get angry and tell him I didn't need calls from clairvoyants and crazies, but instead I heard myself thanking him, in Yiddish. It was the magic of Yiddish. You can say anything in Yiddish and make it sound plausible."

Benny told her about his dreams. About Hayim telling him his father had not known who could be trusted.

A breeze filled the porch.

"I don't often remember my dreams..." Rena paused. "When you were missing, I had a dream about Saleem. 'I have a letter for you from Benny.' And he began to hand me this letter and my name was on the envelope in beautiful Arabic letters. I reached for the letter, but Saleem pulled it away and as hard as I ran, I could not reach his outstretched hand. I woke up heartbroken because there was no letter."

A car stopped at the gate. "It's Ari in a police car. It must be official."

Ari was in uniform, but his eyes looked unofficial.

Ari apologized for coming late. He had some news. Rena offered him a sandwich. For a moment they seemed like an ordinary gathering of friends sharing a late snack.

"I won't keep you long. I wanted you to hear it from me first. It'll be in the news tomorrow."

Rena held Benny's hand.

"Yigal Adir was a Soviet spy. He is now in the Soviet Union. There was no aunt in Paris. The only 'aunt' is the Kremlin."

"Yigal was a spy?"

"Benny, how well did you know Yigal?"

"I would have never thought that Yigal could be a spy for anyone. He was just too detached and uninvolved. I didn't pay much attention to him."

Rena looked at the porch floor with its beautiful mosaic. Was there a lesson in the image of the spies' story? Twelve spies had been sent by Moses, twelve had returned. Ten spies said that the Promised Land was a terrible place. Only two called it a fine place and said that the people should go on. The biblical spy story was different from the Yigal spy story, but there was an ominous lesson here, because the Israelites in the biblical story had gone with the majority of the spies and asked Moses to take them back to Egypt. Into bondage. Yigal Adir had chosen a new pharaoh, the brutal Soviet Union. He had chosen to betray his country.

Ari had more to tell them. Miriam had been murdered by the spy network.

Rena's heart was pounding. She held Benny's hand tightly to steady herself. "It's one thing to be a Russian spy, it's another to murder Miriam. Why? Why?" She could hear Gittel crying at the cemetery.

"We think that she saw the letter Benny left on Mike's desk."

"If only I could remember. What could I have written? It's heartbreaking to think that Miriam is dead."

Ari turned to Benny. "Do you remember Mike telling you about a rumor he wanted you to check out, about someone high up spying for the Soviets?" Benny said he didn't remember.

"You made several calls before you left for Jerusalem. You must have learned something significant. Yigal probably got news that you were onto something. What I think could have happened is that you said something to Miriam about the content of your letter, even a casual comment. Yigal saw the two of you talking and was afraid she knew something."

"Yigal could have been standing there, but I probably paid no attention to him."

Ari put his empty plate on the table. "We don't know that Yigal killed Miriam. It's quite likely he alerted his superiors. Someone decided to eliminate Miriam... We don't know who."

"If that is all true, Mike was lucky he didn't read my letter; but it also means that I'm still in some danger because they don't know I have amnesia."

Rena was sitting upright. She looked at Ari. "That's scary stuff. Benny is caught up in something he doesn't remember."

"But the spies don't know that. We are putting out the news that the police interviewed Benny, and there is an ongoing investigation. People in the Security Services think that by now those involved in the spying believe Benny told the police everything." He turned to Benny. "There is no longer any sense in killing you. Whoever is involved will go underground."

Rena said fiercely, "We're dealing with brutal killers."

Ari looked tired. "I agree. We're already keeping a close watch on you and your family. We're checking everything."

"When my brother was here, and we walked from Hotel Tikva to Bet Hagoel, someone followed us. Was it one of the spies? And the guy in the black suit at the cemetery at Miriam's funeral?"

"They could have been."

"And the creepy man that Miriam mentioned on the phone?"

"It could have been any one of them. Perhaps she was thinking of Yigal. We'll never know."

Benny tried to lift himself. Lying in bed, he had to look up all the time. Rena offered some pillows to support his head and shoulders. She sat on the floor by the bed. She thought of her family. What she did not know about their last journey. Her sisters' laughter now stitched in the Torah cover.

Benny looked at Rena crying. "The spies don't know about my condition. As far as they're concerned, I have told the police everything. With the story out, there is no reason to eliminate me."

"I don't know… it's still terrifying…"

"Rena, we'll keep a close watch on you. I chose the men myself. They are all from the Jerusalem police, all with impeccable records. I'm also sure that the Security Services are keeping an eye on you, although they have not shared the information with me. Your mother, Benny, will have a new farmhand for a while. The word will be that she has been feeling a bit weak from all the stress, and needs extra help."

Rena wanted to know why the Buber manuscript had been taken from Benny's office.

"Probably to make it all appear connected to Benny's political views on Arab workers and

Buber's ideas on a bi-national state. The manuscript was taken to make the police look in the wrong direction."

"What about Zev? Is he involved? Wasn't he the one to suggest that Benny disappeared because of what Zev called his 'pro-Arab' position?"

"We don't know yet. The investigation is in the hands of the Security Services. I understand that in the press conference tomorrow only Yigal Adir will be mentioned by name."

"What will happen to him?

"I think the government will try to bring him back. Negotiate some kind of a deal with the Soviets."

Rena thought of the best-case scenario, bringing Yigal back to Israel. She hoped that it would happen. She felt that punishment for Yigal was important; but it would not bring Miriam back. It would not change Benny's ordeal.

Ari turned to her. "There is a new investigation into Rachel's death. A member of kibbutz Oz had gone to the police after Zev became an M.K. It's not clear whether much would come of it. It must have rattled Zev enough to send you a letter warning you."

The blood rushed to Rena's head. Finally, Rachel would have justice. And Rachel had thought that no one would stand up for her.

Ari got up. "I'm going to go over to tell your mother how tomorrow she'll have 'hired help.' He is a kibbutz member so he knows something about farming. He will look authentic."

After Ari left, Rena told Benny about Rachel. How Rachel had said that if Zev killed her, no one would fight for her. Zev, her main suspect, she told Benny, had had the temerity to call to congratulate them on Benny's return. Rena had said 'You bastard' before she hung up.

Rena brought out her notes in which she had written down what Zev had said. It was pointless.

All those months taking notes had kept her hope up. She had felt she was collecting evidence. As it turned out, the police were not interested in her notes. The Security Services told her to keep them.

Benny was interested. He wanted to read her notes. "I don't remember the months that I was in the doctor's house. At least I would know what you were doing and thinking."

"Life has not been the same since your disappearance."

"Some things will never be the same again for any of us. Hayim's life was never the same after the Germans invaded Poland, even though he survived. Dr. Abu Ali's life was not the same after 1948, even though he has a thriving practice in East Jerusalem. But we can speak up for what's right. I will write my book on Buber. I will publish my article on the rights of Arab workers…"

"And I am not going to forget Rachel. With the police reopening a new investigation, I will testify."

Late at night, Rena put her head on Benny's chest. She listened to his heart. "Were you afraid in East Jerusalem?"

"I was in pain. Not knowing what had happened to me, remembering most of my life so clearly and yet in the middle, a white blank amnesia...not knowing about coming back home..."

Benny stroked her head and whispered into her hair. "The man who found me and saved my life that night was Saleem."

CHAPTER THIRTY-NINE

Friends came to visit Benny from far and near. Mendel brought food. Rena told Benny how Mendel had brought food the first few weeks after his disappearance. At some point she had told Mendel to stop. Now, with so many visitors, Mendel argued that they could again use his food and his fruit drinks. Rena agreed, but she wanted to make an early breakfast for her family before Hagar arrived to do physical therapy.

Hagar came at seven thirty every morning. She left Benny sweaty and shaking with exhaustion. He worked hard at getting his strength back. He used everything, the exercises, the walker, the cane.

Rena put flowers again in the house. In their bedroom Rena placed roses in a green glass vase.

Zohara joined her parents for the daily sunrise breakfast, as she called it. She wanted to talk to both of her parents "together," she said.

She said the coffee was good but not as good as her father's. Rena agreed. But she knew this was not just a conversation about the quality of coffee.

"Dad, when you were gone, I missed your whistling in the morning." Zohara had tears in her eyes. Her parents waited.

"After you disappeared, I made a bargain with God. I asked God to bring you back and in return I would abstain from certain things. Kind of like the Nazeer in the Torah. When I made the bargain with God, I asked God to bring you back."

"I'm a lucky father."

She turned to Rena. "Mom, I need to tell you that part of my deal with God was that I would renounce pleasures such as swimming, biking, or just going to have fun. When you wanted me to go with you, I wanted to but I couldn't. And I couldn't tell you either."

Rena was crying and talking at the same time. "What a bargainer you are, Zohara. You gave up so much."

Birds descended on the garden looking for food and water, chatty and noisy as always. Rena had already turned on the sprinklers.

Benny said, "Bargaining with God…your grandfather Yair would have loved it."

When Zohara had gone, Rena looked at the rock garden. It now absorbed the knowledge that Saleem had saved Benny. What were the odds that Saleem would be the person to save Benny? Zero. Unless you were a mystic. Saleem, Benny told her, had ended up in East Jerusalem. Not in a refugee camp. He had family who had taken him in. The doctor was one of his relatives. When it seemed that Benny was well enough, Saleem organized a phone call to Nathan Tovim. He had offered no details.

"Was he angry with us?

"He didn't say much. Just that he thought he recognized me. Was certain when he saw my identity card. When he brought me back to our side of the city, he knew where it was safe to cross over. He held on to my arm. We walked slowly together. I concentrated on walking. Silence was our friend."

"Did he ask about his home here?"

"He did know that the village was gone."

Hagar knocked on the screen door and said, "Let's get going, Benny."

CHAPTER FORTY

Friday morning, Pnina called. The Abarbanel family wanted to do a Havdalah blessing to mark the end of the Sabbath at the Sassons' house, if she and Benny would like it. Yes, Rena said. The Arbanels would bring the various ritual objects, the cup, the special candle, and the spices on Friday and leave them at the Sassons' house.

In all the years that Rena had known the Abarbanels, they had always had the Sabbath at their own house. To come to a secular house on the Sabbath was out of the ordinary.

She thought of all the months when she had resented Friday, felt outside of life, frustrated. She did not feel that way today. It would be a Friday alive with Benny.

She thought of Saleem saving Benny. In Yiddish she would know what to say to Saleem. She would have to figure out the Arabic word for *Tayere*. She would keep that word in her heart. She took out her parents' letters and pressed them to her lips. She whispered, "Dad, Joe looks so much like you."

Joe telephoned to see how Benny was doing. Rena heard Zohara say, "Uncle Joe, God redeemed himself. From now on I'll be God's defender to all the atheists you met here." What her brother said on the other side Rena could not hear. She saw her daughter nodding her head as though her uncle could see her.

Rena prepared a gratitude Sabbath dinner. She put a white, antique lace tablecloth on the wooden table on the porch. Flowers in the middle of the table. Iris brought two beautiful silver candlesticks. She placed them on either side of the flowers.

Malka brought over a silver wine cup that Rena had never seen before. It had belonged to Yair, she said. Zohara said, "Grandma, you don't believe in God." Malka just hugged her.

Mendel brought challah, the special braided Sabbath bread with poppy seeds on top. Rena covered two challot with a white-lace napkin.

Jacob brought wine. He was wearing his newest hat and a red bandanna. For the Sabbath, he said. He recited the blessing for the wine. "The heavens and the earth, and all they contained, were completed. On the seventh day God finished the work he had been doing," it began, and ended, "Praised are you God who sanctifies the Sabbath."

Rena looked around as they all sat down. Benny watched from his bed. She put his favorite food on a plate for him. Someone outside yelled, "Traitor."

The plate just left her hands. Mendel collected the pieces from the floor. Jacob made a fist. Zohara went to the screen door and yelled back, "Moron. May you die in Hitler's dark grave." She turned around and said, "I learned it from Shoshi. It's a great curse." Zohara looked fearless.

There at the screen door was Bertha. Rena's soulmate. She stood there in her white suit, white hat, and red purse, holding a wrapped gift. When Zohara opened the door, Bertha handed it to her. "For you. Your father is back. It's like a birthday. You like books. I've seen you in the library."

"I've seen you in the library, too. Thank you for the book." She touched Bertha on the arm. Bertha did not flinch.

Benny by now had pushed himself to his feet. Holding on to his walker he said, "Please, Bertha, come in and sit next to Zohara." Rena wiped her tears, held Benny's arm. "Please, Bertha, come and sit with us." And for the first time, Bertha stepped onto the porch and sat down at the table.

Zohara opened the gift. Inside was a special edition of all the writings of Bialik, beautifully bound and decorated with gold letters. Zohara told Bertha how she had admired that edition. Bertha sat looking at her plate, clutching her purse, but she did not run out. Rena felt that Mrs.

Bialik was more than pleased to see this lovely edition of her husband's book.

Rena held on to Benny with his walker and his scarred head and his amnesia. He was alive. And it was a Friday unlike any other Friday.

CHAPTER FORTY-ONE

Just before dusk Zohara saw the Abarbanels turning onto Herzl Street. Pnina and Sammy looked as they always did on the Sabbath, Sammy in a suit even though it was July and hot, Pnina in an elegant turquoise dress and a matching hat. They had walked from their house, one and half kilometers away. The boys, Daniel, Jonathan, Micah, Yehuda, and little Benjamin, also wore suits; Shoshi wore a long red skirt and a white blouse with embroidery on the sleeves.

Her grandmother hugged them all. Benjamin ran to Rena. He wanted to know if the turtle was still in the garden under the Sabra cactus. The twins wanted to go see Vashti.

Iris came and brought Yehuda the teacher. The town's most self-proclaimed atheists, Jacob and

Mendel, wanted to be there, too. Mendel said, "I didn't ride my bike, I walked, out of respect for the event, but just this time. This is not a religious conversion." He laughed. Jacob said, "This is not about God. I'm not changing my mind. This is for our friends the Abarbanels and the Sassons." Zohara could tell he wanted to mention Malka's name but did not. He wore a blue bandana for the Sabbath.

All the atheists were making statements about not believing in God. Zohara didn't care. God deserved this ritual in their house. It was the first one and possibly the last, but she was happy.

More and more people kept coming, Saul and his family, Ronnie who no longer insulted Shoshi, Albert the new farm help, and, big surprise, all of Malka's friends from kibbutz Kalaniyot. Sonya, too, and her father's friends from *Kol Hapoel,* and her mother's artist friends from Tel Aviv. Hayim kissed her father on his head. He spoke Yiddish to her mother. Ari came, bringing Abigail the librarian.

Abigail handed her father an envelope and Zohara could read the words written on it: "The Buber document you requested." Her father gave her one of his big smiles. "Thank you, Abigail. I have been waiting for it."

There were so many people that her mother opened the door to the house so that people could stand in the living room. She left the screen door open so that people could stand in the garden. No one worried about the bees.

When they could see three stars in the sky it was time for Havdalah. Shoshi's father stood at the table with the white tablecloth where her mother had placed the cup, the wine, the special braided candle, and the fragrant spices in a beautiful silver box shaped like the Tower of David in the Old City.

Iris said, "Sammy, before you say the blessing, could you explain what all these things mean?" Iris had a strong voice and people listened. All the people standing in the garden and on the porch and in the house were listening. No one spoke.

Zohara loved to hear Sammy explain things. She was glad that Iris had asked. Yehuda the teacher took Iris's hand. Sammy looked at her father, who stood up for the blessing. Benny was holding on to the walker. "Please, Sammy. Go ahead." There was a real hush.

"Havdalah, as you all know, signifies the distinction we make between the holy Sabbath and the ordinary days of the week. The full cup of wine is like the cup of wine that we blessed last night to welcome the Sabbath." He looked at Benny. "The candle is to thank God for giving us the gift of light, and the spices are to revive the soul. After I say the blessing for the spices, we'll pass the box around so that everybody here can inhale the fragrance and rejuvenate their soul."

Sammy began to chant the traditional Havdalah the same way he would do in his own house. "Behold, God is my deliverance; I am confident and unafraid. God is my strength, my might, my deliverance." When he finished the prayer he said,

"I lift the cup of deliverance and call upon God." He lifted the cup and said, "Praised are you our God who rules the universe, creating the fruit of the vine." He picked up the box of spices. "Praised are you our God who rules the universe, creating fragrant spices." He took the lid off the box, smelled the spices, and passed them around.

Pnina inhaled and gave the box to Zohara's grandmother, who smelled the fragrance and gave the spices to her father, who had to use only one hand to hold on to the walker and then passed the spices to her mother, who gave them to her, and she gave them to Iris, and everyone inhaled the fragrance that revived the soul. The box went around. It took some time. Nobody seemed to mind.

They ended the Havdalah by singing the joyous song of Elijah the prophet. Zohara noticed that some people did sing the words, but others just wordlessly hummed along. They exchanged greetings. "May you have a good week." Hayim said it in Yiddish and hugged her father.

Her father looked exhausted and was lying down. She heard him say to Sammy, "The last time I heard a Havdalah was at my grandparents' house in the Old City." Iris and Rena were crying, others were wiping their eyes. Shoshi held Zohara's hand when Sammy recited, "God is my deliverance, I am confident and unafraid." And when Shoshi squeezed her hand, Zohara was glad she had told Shoshi that she would miss her in history class next year. The truth was she would miss her in all her classes. She would miss the way Shoshi was unafraid to challenge teachers and undaunted by kids' ridicule.

Daniel came over and smiled at Zohara. "You know, Zohara, you are amazing. Really, I mean it." He paused and looked directly at her. Zohara was wearing the white dress with the Yemenite embroidery that her mother had made for her thirteenth birthday. She had never worn it since and was glad she had it on now because it was the right kind of dress to wear when Daniel said quietly, but clearly, "You're also very beautiful."

Zohara took each of his words and carefully stored them where she would recall them just as she could recall the way they had laughed together in the barn. She would forever remember the sound of Daniel's voice and the fragrance of the Havdalah spices that revived the soul.

Made in United States
North Haven, CT
29 July 2023